Rod of Justice

Ronnie Knight and Peter Pitts first met in the mid sixties in London's West End, though their paths were to cross many times during the next thirty years, as they both mixed with the wealthy, the famous and the infamous. Ronnie Knight was previously married to Barbara Windsor. The outcome of the two men's close friendship, *Rod of Justice*, is their second thriller, following *Signed Confession*.

Also by Ronnie Knight and Peter Pitts

SIGNED CONFESSION

Rod of Justice

Ronnie Knight
and
Peter Pitts

POCKET
BOOKS

LONDON · SYDNEY · NEW YORK · TOKYO · SINGAPORE · TORONTO

First published in Great Britain by Pocket Books, 1997
An imprint of Simon & Schuster Ltd
A Viacom Company

The right of Ronnie Knight and Peter Pitts to be identified
as authors of this work has been asserted in accordance
with sections 77 and 78 of the Copyright, Designs and
Patents Act 1988

Simon & Schuster Ltd
West Garden Place
Kendal Street
London W2 2AQ

Simon & Schuster Australia
Sydney

A CIP catalogue record for this book is available
from the British Library

ISBN 0-671-00525-1

Typeset in Melior 11/12pt by
Palimpsest Book Production Limited, Polmont, Stirlingshire
Printed and bound in Great Britain by
Caledonian International Book Manufacturing, Glasgow

Chapter One

The two men in the Jaguar looked relaxed and casual in their business suits, briefcases on the back seat. Passers-by gave them no more than a cursory glance as they hurried on their way. Midday in Croydon was always busy as office workers and businessmen rushed to the shops, pubs and restaurants.

Jimmy North checked his wristwatch, picked up his mobile phone and looked at the man in the driving seat. Mike Lambert stopped drumming his fingers on the steering wheel. A nerve in the corner of his left eye began to twitch as he stared expectantly at the phone, willing it to ring. It would do so at any moment, and then they would know if the job was on or off.

North gave an involuntary start as the phone whistled shrilly. He cursed under his breath, pressed the SPEAK button and pressed the instrument to his ear.

He listened to the short message, then replied sharply, 'Right, we're all in position, and we're on our way now.'

He stabbed at the phone with a forefinger and grinned at Lambert, who was turning the key in the ignition and firing up the engine. 'It's party time. Let's do it. And stay cool, Mike. Try to look like a detective chief inspector.'

Lambert laughed shortly, and concentrated on sliding the Jag through a narrow gap in the traffic.

North squinted through the sunshine reflected on the windscreen as he studied the road ahead, the traffic, the pedestrians. 'Nice day for it, Mike.'

Lambert grunted and lit a cigarette. He passed it to North, then lit one for himself.

The Jaguar turned into the High Street and cruised towards the bank. North took a long drag on his cigarette, inhaled deeply and flicked the half-smoked butt out of the window as he studied the pavement outside the bank. His eyes searched for Delta One. Only North knew who to look for in the throng of pedestrians. For the sake of total security, he kept the Delta One's identity a secret, even from those he trusted most.

Yes, it's OK, he thought with relief, when he saw a leather-clad motorbike messenger leaning against a wall and making notes on a clipboard pad. And the helmet visor – up or down? Up meant there was a problem and they should drive straight on by. Down meant all was well. The visor was down. They were on.

'Eyeball Harry and Billy. They're crossing to the bank,' said Lambert.

'Yeah, and I've got Roger,' answered North as

he spotted the third member of the team walking towards the bank doors.

The Jaguar pulled up outside the bank. Collecting his briefcase, North climbed out. He slammed the door and without so much as a glance at the three men who followed him in, strode through the door, reaching into his briefcase as he went.

Jon Bowers read the note and smiled uncertainly as he looked up. It's a joke, he thought.

But the gunman held a shrapnel grenade in one hand and a sawn-off shotgun in the other, and his distorted features under the stocking mask convinced Jon it was definitely no joke.

'Keep both hands where I can see them. If the alarm sounds off, I'm gonna chuck this grenade over the glass and kill the fucking lot of yer.'

Jon nodded his understanding. He felt sick and started to shake. He slowly placed both hands flat on the counter and glanced nervously around. A dozen or so customers were still conducting their business, unaware of their danger. Jon knew he must do nothing to put them at risk. The bank's policy was customer safety first. Give the robbers the money and let the police take care of the matter.

'Write the airlock door code on the back of that paper and hand it back to me. If it's wrong, all hell breaks loose.'

Jon turned over the piece of paper the robber had passed him with the words 'Do as you are told or you are dead' written in bold print, and quickly scribbled the numbers that would open the inner door to the airlock chamber. He dropped the paper into the security drawer and slid it under the glass screen.

Another man stepped forward, pulling his nylon mask further down over his face as he snatched the paper and walked quickly to the staff airlock door.

'Make sure you press the right button.' The robber pointed to Jon's right where the button was situated that would open the security door, and brandished the hand grenade menacingly. Jon pressed the button and held it down until the second thug pushed the door open and stepped inside, wedging the door open.

'Who's that, Jon?' Maureen Harper was puzzled and alarmed. Her attention had been drawn to the security door as the buzzer sounded. She didn't recognize the man who entered, and her left hand strayed towards the switches that operated the alarm and security cameras.

A thunderous explosion tore at everyone's eardrums and shattered their senses as Jimmy North fired the twelve-bore shotgun at the security camera, which exploded, leaping from its bracket to swing limply on its cord. Harry Turner was now on the staff side of the counter, brandishing a shotgun. He took careful aim and blew the second camera from its mounting.

Three terrified customers ran towards the exit. Billy Kincaid whipped an automatic pistol from under his coat and stepped in front of the door to block their escape. He fired into the ceiling. The boom of the big-bore pistol stopped the fleeing customers in their tracks.

*   *   *

Delta One had been in place for what seemed like hours, watching the bank to ensure there was no unusual activity that might indicate a police trap or anything else that would jeopardize the raid. Everything had been normal up till now: customers coming and going, no sign of extra security, no sign of an unscheduled early cash collection by the security van – Jimmy North would go ballistic if he hit the bank only to find that he and his gang had missed the cash by five minutes.

If, in the few minutes between the arrival of the Jaguar and that of the security van, anything happened to compromise the gang's plan – if the police came or the security van turned up early – the plan was for Delta One to go, helmetless, into the bank, to be held at gunpoint with the customers. That would warn North in time for the gang to get away.

So far, so good, thought Delta One.

The muffled double boom of the shotguns, followed by the flat crack of the pistol, signalled that the raid had begun. Startled passers-by looked round but, seeing nothing unusual, continued on their way. Traffic was heavy: probably a car backfiring.

The minutes ticked slowly by. No alarm bells. They wouldn't sound until later if the gang had done their job right.

The security van turned into the street and headed towards the bank.

Roger Jennings was directly behind Harry Turner

and was covering the petrified staff with his pistol. 'Everybody on the fucking floor. Now!' he screamed. North and Kincaid bellowed the same order at the customers: 'Get down! On the fucking floor, all of you! And don't fucking move!'

Staff and customers scrambled to the floor, except for Maureen Harper, who, paralysed by shock, sat shaking in her chair. Jennings stepped forward, grabbed her by the hair and flung her to the floor, snarling, 'Keep quiet and you won't get hurt.'

Jimmy North appeared behind the counter. He bent over Jon Bowers and pressed the barrels of his shotgun against the young man's temple. 'Where's the fucking money?' he demanded.

Bowers pointed at his cash drawer. 'It . . . it's open,' he stammered.

North grinned and looked up. He noted that Jennings and Turner were busy emptying the drawers. 'Not that cash, sonny.' The gun pressed harder. 'The cash you got ready for the security boys. They're due here in' – he checked his watch – 'three minutes to collect. If you don't show me it, you won't live to see 'em.'

Bowers pointed to steel cabinet doors in the counter next to the security hatch through which the canvas bags were passed to the security guards. 'It's in there.'

North threw the doors open to expose eleven blue canvas bags, neatly stacked awaiting collection. Jennings was beside him now, holding open a big nylon holdall. North scooped up the bags of cash and threw them into the holdall.

'Right, go,' he told Jennings, and he waved Turner out of the door as he backed towards the exit shouting, 'Nobody fucking move! Stay put or get shot.'

Kincaid held the door open while the three villains ran out to the waiting Jaguar, waited until they were all in the car, then followed them out. The alarm sounded.

The security van drew up behind the Jaguar and a guard jumped out. Within seconds he realized what was up. He turned towards Kincaid, shouting, 'Hold it!'

Kincaid looked at the guard for an instant, then raised his gun and fired. The guard fell with a scream of pain as the blast hit him in the legs. Kincaid swung the shotgun to the windscreen of the security van. The driver dived down for his life as the screen cracked and crazed under the impact. Pedestrians fled screaming for safety as they realized the danger.

As the door slammed shut, the Jaguar lurched into motion, rubber burning as Mike Lambert slammed his foot down on the accelerator. The big car leapt forward into the traffic. A Rover police car, blue light flashing and siren wailing, sped towards them from the opposite direction, forcing motorists to swerve out of its path.

North saw it and screamed, 'Do a left!'

Lambert threw the Jag into a broadside skid as he yanked at the wheel, flinging the car out into the busy High Street. A hundred yards ahead, the traffic lights at a pedestrian crossing changed, and the waiting pedestrians surged forward.

Lambert flicked on his headlights and held his hand on the horn as he accelerated towards them. The police car screeched into the street behind the Jag.

Panic-stricken pedestrians tried in vain to escape as the Jaguar ploughed into them, crushing anyone in its way and leaving a trail of blood and broken limbs. A gap appeared, and the car swerved towards it. A young woman pushing a baby carriage, her long fair hair streaming out behind her as she pushed for all she was worth, filled the gap. A dark-haired man ran towards her. The Jaguar surged relentlessly forward.

Phillip Ross looked up from the spreadsheets on his desk and checked the time by the wall clock above the window that looked out over the showroom. He noted with satisfaction that his staff were busy selling and demonstrating the electrical and white goods that the store of which he was the manager specialized in.

Julie and their baby son, Gary, would be arriving any moment, and they were all going to do a bit of shopping and then have lunch. Gary was a happy, gurgling two months old, and this would be his first trip to Croydon. Phillip smiled to himself at the prospect of seeing how the baby reacted to the colour and bustle of the crowds. It was only a few hours since he'd kissed Julie and Gary goodbye when he'd left for work that morning, but his heart lifted at the thought of seeing them again. He could never get over how much they meant to him, how happy they all were. To cap it all, he'd found a good job (OK, it was boring, but it would do until he could find something to suit him better) and so, unlike all too many people, he and his family were free of financial worries. To celebrate his happiness and good fortune, he decided to buy Julie an extra-good lunch, and then take them to Debenhams and buy them both surprise presents, a cuddly toy for Gary and for Julie . . . ? A silk blouse, perhaps, if he could find one in sea-green to match her eyes, or maybe a gold bracelet or a bottle of her favourite Anais Anais perfume – she'd run out only the other day.

He made his way through the showroom, pausing only to tell his assistant manager he'd be gone for a couple of hours and she should look after things until he got back. Then, smiling happily, he hurried out.

He saw Julie the other side of the busy street, pushing the baby carriage towards the pedestrian crossing. She didn't see him, but bent down to talk to Gary as she waited with the other pedestrians for the traffic lights to change.

The lights changed to red. The pedestrians crowded forward. Then all hell broke loose – a living nightmare. Its horn blaring, headlights blazing, a Jaguar with five men inside appeared from nowhere and streaked towards them.

Screams of fear filled the air as pedestrians fled. They pushed and jostled frantically to get out of the path of the speeding car. There were several thumps as the big car connected with flesh and bone. It slowed for a second, as a gap appeared briefly in the crowd, then accelerated again.

In the gap Phillip saw Julie, fighting to get the baby carriage clear. The Jag smashed into her, tossing her high in the air. The baby carriage spun wildly, then tipped over and crashed into the gutter. Within moments, the car had rounded a corner and was out of sight.

In its wake, people reacted with shock, some screaming hysterically, some sobbing and crying, others standing in numbed silence as they gazed at the scene of carnage and horror, the blood, the broken bodies sprawled in the road.

Frantic with fear, Phillip hurled himself across the road to his wife and child. He knew as soon as he reached Julie that she was dead. There was no trace of a pulse, and her green eyes were half open, unblinking. He caught her up in his arms, and held her tightly, his face buried in her hair.

A middle-aged woman came to him, cradling Gary, who was kicking and screaming in fear. 'He's OK. He's frightened, but he's not hurt,' she said gently. 'He's going to be just fine.'

Phillip hardly heard her. All he was aware of was Julie, Julie his love, Julie his life, Julie dead . . .

A police car screeched to a halt within inches of one of the victims. The driver jumped out and ran forward to assist. His passenger remained in the vehicle and shouted into his radio mike for ambulances and back-up.

A tall grey-haired man carrying a black medical bag shoved urgently through the crowd.

'I'm a doctor,' he called out. He bent over a young man whose legs had been smashed and who had gone into deep shock, his skin grey and cold.

A young woman stepped forward. 'I'm a nurse. What shall I do?'

The doctor wrenched open his bag. 'This man has an open fracture. He needs morphine and a tourniquet. I'll see to it. You start checking the others and call me for the most urgent.'

The Suzuki turned into the High Street in time to see the Jag smash into the pedestrians. A fair-haired young woman was flung high into the air, and a baby carriage spun into the gutter.

Delta One braked to a halt behind the police car, gazing in sick horror at the injured people sprawled in the road. Blood trickled in the gutters. There were screams and moans of agony. A dark-haired man was cradling the young blonde woman in his arms, his agonized face half hidden in her hair. Oh Christ! It had all gone horribly wrong. First the security guard, now this. People had been killed and seriously injured. This wasn't meant to happen. Jimmy North was meant to have planned things so that, as usual, the *menace* of the guns would be the only violence. Until now the gang's raids had been exciting, nerve-stretching stuff, and no one had got hurt. But now . . .

An elderly woman nearby was trying in vain to staunch the blood oozing from a wound in her leg. Leaning the bike against a bollard, Delta One pulled out a handkerchief, went to her and bound the handkerchief tightly round her leg, waving away her thanks.

The police were starting to gather witnesses together, asking them what they'd seen, whether they'd got the Jaguar's number. Time to go. Delta One hastily retrieved the Suzuki, turned it and sped away.

Lambert gunned the Jaguar at speed as he threw it into left- and right-hand turns through back streets, to put distance between the gang and the carnage behind them and get back on to the planned getaway route. He slowed to a respectable speed as he approached a major road, and slotted neatly into the traffic.

North was fuming as he struggled out of his jacket and removed his tie. It was all he could do to keep silent, but this was not the time to start recriminations and mouthing off. He had to keep his men calm and positive. It had all gone to rat shit. The police would be stirred up to a frenzy by the shooting and the injured pedestrians.

As the car approached his dropping-off point, he turned to speak to his men. 'Right, it's gone a little bit wrong, but we're on our toes now, so keep calm, stick to the plan and we'll all be home free. I'll see you all in Spain.'

The Jaguar turned off the main road and stopped in a side street. North climbed out carrying the big holdall containing the cash. Turner jumped out of the back of the car, passed him a light-grey leather jacket, and he dived into the front seat.

'Good luck, lads. See you,' said North. He slammed the door and the Jag lurched off. North stepped into a doorway and waited.

Two streets later the car stopped again. Kincaid and Jennings climbed out and walked through an alley to the next street, where they climbed into a Ford Sierra and headed for Gatwick airport.

Lambert and Turner drove to the next street and parked. They checked that nothing had been dropped in the car, locked it and casually walked away. The men went their separate ways. Lambert was clean. He carried nothing to connect him to the robbery. He walked into a mini-cab office, and asked for a car to take him to Heathrow Airport. He was booked on a flight to Barcelona.

Turner carried a holdall, which contained the firearms used in the robbery. He had a friend who lived nearby and asked no questions. For a generous sum of cash, he would look after the bag until Turner returned and asked for it back. Turner was booked on a flight to Gerona Airport.

Delta One turned off the main road and braked to a halt. Jimmy North stepped out of a doorway. Unclipping the spare crash helmet from the rear of the Suzuki, and jamming it on, he climbed on to the pillion seat. He hefted the holdall on to his lap and tapped the driver on the shoulder. Delta One let out the clutch and pulled away.

Keeping to the speed limit, they drove through Sanderstead and Warlingham, dropped down to pick up the Caterham by-pass, then swept on

to the M25 at junction six. They cruised at
seventy miles an hour for several minutes, the
Delta One signalled left and turned into Clacket
Lane service area.

The Suzuki came to a halt in the car park and
North leapt off. He scanned the adjacent lorry
parking area, until he spotted the white Daf
juggernaut that was to take him to Spain, via
Dover and France. It was parked in a line of
heavy lorries. The driver sat at the wheel smoking
a roll-up and reading the *Sun*.

North turned back to Delta One, whose helmet
visor was raised and who screamed at him,
'There's a woman dead back there.'

North was taken back for a moment, then he
shrugged. 'So what? She's nothing to us.' He was
about to say more, but Delta One cut across him.
'And a fucking security guard shot down. You
swore nothing like this would ever happen.'

North's own anger rose and he looked hastily
round to see that no one had heard the outburst.
'Shut the fuck up,' he snarled. 'Keep to the plan,
and none of it will matter. None of them meant
fuck all to us. In a few hours we'll all be out the
country, and the Old Bill will be running round in
circles and disappearing up their own arseholes.
They ain't going to get us, understand?'

Delta One glared at him and then snapped,
'That's the last job I ever go on with you lot. I'm
not having any more of that.'

Realizing this was not exactly the best time to
discuss the situation, North merely nodded. 'OK,
OK. Just get yourself back home. I'll talk to you

later.' He watched as Delta One slammed down the visor without replying, dropped the clutch and sped towards the exit.

North shook his head and walked over to the truck.

Chapter Two

Phillip Ross stared sightlessly down at his wife's grave. 'If only I'd . . . If only . . .' churned again and again through his grief-numbed mind.

He recalled the oath he had sworn at Julie's funeral as he'd stood by the open grave: to search out and destroy the five men in the Jaguar. Then his composure had cracked and he'd broken down. He'd felt as though his very soul had died.

Victor and Mary Thompson were inconsolable over the loss of their daughter, so soon after the death of their son. At the funeral, Mary had barely been able to walk and had had to be supported by the vicar and the family doctor.

Victor, tears streaming down his face, had straightened his shoulders and, with all the dignity he could muster, had taken their grandson, Gary, in his arms and declared, 'Our daughter lives on in her son.' He passed the baby to Mary, who took him with trembling hands and summoned all her willpower to pull herself together as she held Gary close and listened to

her husband's words. 'We have to be strong for
our grandson. He needs us more now than he
ever did.'

Phillip saw again the polished black coffin with
the shiny brass handles being lowered into the
ground. His anguish and sorrow were as raw
today as they had been that day. 'It's too cold.
She'll be so cold,' he said aloud, and shivered as
he pulled his leather jacket tighter round him to
ward off the chill wind. He turned away from the
grave and stared out over the roofs of Dover, far
below him. Smoke rose lazily from a high, lone
chimney stack to be shredded by the wind.

He closed his eyes tightly and buried his face in
his hands. Memories ambushed him: Julie telling
him with a mixture of shyness and pride and
delight that she was expecting their baby; Julie
helping him and her brother paint the ceiling
of the nightclub they were about to open, a
ridiculous smudge of paint on her nose; Julie
on their wedding day; the fresh, gentle scent
she always wore; Julie laughing with happiness
and desire as they made love, her slender body
lithe and eager in his arms; Julie breastfeeding
their son, her face heart-wrenchingly tender as
she kissed the top of the baby's downy head;
Julie clinging to him, sobbing helplessly in grief
for her murdered brother, Gary – at least, Phillip
thought, he'd avenged Gary's death, at least he'd
done that for her, and perhaps, somehow, in the
baby named for Gary, they both lived on. He could
see her now in his mind's eye as clearly as though
she were standing beside him, hear her voice as

she teased him about the boring job he'd taken, or encouraged him as he gingerly held his newborn son in his arms. Tears blurred his vision, and she faded, faded . . .

A hand touched him gently on the shoulder. Phillip jumped, startled, back into reality. He turned and saw Peter Russel, his long-time friend and former colleague in the 22nd Regiment, Special Air Services.

Phillip managed a travesty of a smile. 'I think I'm going mad. I keep seeing Julie, hearing her voice. Sorry, Peter.'

Russel studied his friend. Phillip's face was pale and drawn, his dark-blue eyes sunken and darkly ringed from lack of sleep. His black curls, usually clean and neatly combed, were dirty, unkempt. Two days' growth of stubble darkened his chin. His lean body was slumped and lethargic.

'It's good to get it out of your system, mate,' said Russel, and squeezed Phillip's shoulder sympathetically. 'I know how much you loved Julie. But don't forget you now have little Gary to think of. Life has to go on for him, even if you feel it's over for you.' He looked hard at his friend. 'Now it's time to get angry. Time to get even. The bell's rung, so come out fighting. Find out who the bastards are who killed Julie, and make sure they pay. In full measure. I'll supply any equipment you need. The lads and I will do anything and everything we can to help you, you know that.'

Phillip said wearily, 'There were five of them in the car. They got clean away.' He shook his head, an edge of bitterness entering his voice. 'That prat Richards from the robbery squad won't tell me anything. Just fobs me off with the usual garbage. "We are continuing our enquiries,"' he mimicked.

'Why not go and talk to Chief Inspector Hill? After Gary's murder he fed you information on the Chalmers gang. He knows that you dealt with them all and he didn't even blink. I'm sure that if he knows anything he'll help you. It's worth a try, Phil.'

Phillip nodded. 'I've had the same thought, but I just haven't had the energy to do anything about it.' He took a deep, shuddering breath, and straightened his shoulders. 'I'll phone him today and make an appointment. I'm going to get even, Peter. I'm going to make sure that the men who killed Julie and injured all those others pay in full for the suffering they've caused.' He looked hard at Russel for a brief moment, then continued. 'Hill hasn't openly admitted providing information on the Chalmers gang. So I'm going to force his hand. I'm going to provide him with a signed confession to the killing of the whole gang.'

Russel opened his mouth to protest, but Phillip cut him short. 'We know he helped me, albeit tacitly. We know he wanted me to kill Chalmers and his boys. The last thing that Hill wants or expects is for me to go marching in with a signed confession to the killings.'

Russel looked aghast. 'What if he arrests you?'

'He won't. It might come out in court that he provided the information that helped me get the bastards. Besides, I think he will also want me to go after the gang that killed Julie.' He grinned twistedly. 'I think he hates these bastards nearly as much as I do.'

'I still think you're taking a bit of a chance.'

Phillip nodded. 'Yes, but it's a chance I'm willing to take. It'll make Hill come out into the open. I need more direct help than having files left behind "by accident" when Hill visits my home.'

Russel shrugged. 'I see you've made up your mind.'

Phillip nodded. 'Yes. The first thing I'm going to do, when I've got Hill on his own, is hand him my signed confession.'

A week later, Phillip Ross was sitting in Hill's office at New Scotland Yard. The two men locked eyes across Hill's desk for a moment, then Phillip's gaze dropped to the folder on the big desk between them. He leant forward and reached out for it. Hill pushed it nearer to him, then relaxed back into his chair to watch and wait while Phillip took in the descriptions of the men responsible for his wife's death, poring over their photographs and memorizing the details of their criminal records.

Hill had met some tough characters in his years in the Metropolitan Police, but he doubted that any of them would match up to the man in front of him. A smile of grim satisfaction tightened his lips. Ross was the only man whom the policeman, in his whole career, had not arrested for a serious

crime once he had the evidence against him.
Just minutes before, the DCI had held in his
hand a signed confession to the unlawful killing
of twelve men. He knew in his heart that the
confession was genuine, but had dismissed it as
total nonsense. George Hill had his own plans for
the man in front of him, and seeing him locked
away in Parkhurst for the next twenty years was
not part of them.

Like many good coppers, Hill had for many
years felt a mixture of frustration and fury as
he saw the robbers-with-violence, the murderers,
drug barons and child-porn merchants plying
their trades with impunity because his hands
were tied by rules and red tape. He knew who
they were and what they were up to. He arrested
and charged them. Then they laughed at him as
they walked from court, freed on a technicality
or because a witness refused to cooperate – or in
some cases because a vital witness disappeared
completely. They laughed at him . . . the bastards
laughed in his face! 'Not guilty.' 'Case dismissed.'
His guts twisted as the words echoed round
the courtrooms. The whoops of joy. The happy,
smiling faces of ruthless, violent, bloody *guilty*
men who should have been locked away for the
rest of their lives.

Frank Chalmers and his gang had been a case
in point. Hill had tried hard for years to put them
behind bars, knowing them to be responsible for
extortion, arson, even murder. But their security
was tight, they left alive no witness who might
have been prepared to testify against them, and

he'd never been able to build a case that would
stand up in court. And then they'd made the
mistake – the fatal mistake – of burning down
a nightclub when the owners refused to pay
protection money, and murdering one of the
owners. Those owners were just a couple of
soldier boys fresh out of the army, the gang
reckoned, and the owner left alive would soon
fall into line. What did he know about London's
gangland? He'd be easy meat.

Easy meat? An ex-SAS man, decorated for
bravery in the Falklands, a war hero: easy meat?
Hill looked at the man in front of him. Ross was
alive, and the gang were all dead. Rough justice,
maybe, but at least it was *some* kind of justice, and
Hill doubted that any of the people whose lives
the gang had ruined would care who'd meted it
out – or how.

Phillip ran his fingers through his black curls,
now clean and neatly trimmed again. There was
icy rage in his heart as he read about the men
who'd killed his adored Julie. In the wake of the
anger came a calm determination, displacing the
grief that had overwhelmed him, mind and body,
since her death.

He closed the folder. 'You're absolutely sure
that these are the men?'

George Hill said, 'I'm sure, Mr Ross, or I
wouldn't have shown you that file. It's North's
MO to a T. He and his bunch have lived it up
in Spain for several years now. They only come
over to do a blag, then they piss off home again.'
He grunted in disgust. 'We don't get any feedback

from the normal channels because they're not here to boast or confide in any of our informants. We can't raid their homes, gain access to their bank accounts or building societies. We can't pull them in for questioning or put surveillance on them.'

Hill climbed angrily out of his chair and crossed to the window. He stood staring out across London for a few moments, then turned and looked directly at Phillip. 'We always know when it's North and his gang: the hand grenade, the sawn-off shotguns. They've never actually fired a gun at anyone before, but it had to come – it was only a matter of time. There are always four of them in the bank and one in the car. The wheel-man is a well-known criminal, Mike Lambert. He used to be a racing driver, always insists on a Jaguar as the getaway car or he won't accept the job.' He smiled sardonically as he crossed back to his desk. 'They might just as well leave a calling card on every job. I'm not just sure that it was them, Mr Ross, I *know* it was them.'

Phillip raised the folder. 'May I keep this, Mr Hill?'

George Hill said, straightfaced, 'I'm sorry, Mr Ross, but that is an official file. However, this one' – from the middle drawer of his desk he took another, thinner folder, which he tossed on to the desk – 'is my own personal file of photocopies. I don't look at it all that often, and if it should go missing while I was out of the room, I doubt that I'd notice. Now, if you'll excuse me, nature calls.'

He took the official file from Phillip's hand, smiled blandly and said, 'I'd better return this one to the investigating officer's desk before he returns and finds it missing.' He went to the door, turned and asked, 'Coffee, Mr Ross?'

'Yes, please, Mr Hill,' Phillip replied, not raising his eyes from the file on the chief inspector's desk. As the door clicked closed, Phillip snatched up the file and flicked through it. More than satisfied with the information it contained, he folded it in half, shoved it into the waistband of his trousers at the small of his back and smoothed his jacket over it before sitting back, relaxed and calm, to await Hill's return with the promised coffee.

A plan was beginning to form in his mind. His face was grim as he thought of the blood the gang had spilt: not only Julie's but that of the pedestrians injured as the Jag smashed into them; of the security guard they'd gunned down, who was crippled for life and wondering despairingly how he, his wife and three young children would survive without a breadwinner in the family.

'No mercy,' Phillip said aloud. 'No mercy for any of you bastards.' He remembered what Hill had said: that the men lived in Spain and weren't available for questioning. Oh yes they are, he thought coldly. To me they are. I shall question them and they will answer.

George Hill returned, carrying two mugs of steaming coffee, handed one to Phillip and went back to his seat. The two men sipped in silence. Hill looked measuringly at Phillip, trying to gauge his mood. Phillip studied him right back, seeing a heavily built man a little under six feet tall, with a horseshoe of grey hair framing a shiny bald pate, and piercing blue eyes set in a strong, fleshy face. His mouth was wide and firm, and when he smiled he showed very even white teeth.

At last Phillip broke the silence. 'I'd like to thank you for your cooperation, Mr Hill. Without that cooperation in the last . . . er . . . situation, my job would have been a lot harder.'

The DCI grinned. He had never admitted to 'deliberately forgetting' the file on the Chalmers gang, on a visit to Phillip's flat while investigating the murder of Phillip's closest friend, Gary Thompson.

Phillip continued, 'And this North and his gang – I wouldn't have had a clue where to start.'

'I need no thanks, Mr Ross. The fact that Chalmers and his gang got their just deserts was thanks enough. I can't begin to tell you how satisfying it was to hear that Frank Chalmers and several of his gang had been killed.' Hill chuckled. 'And you wouldn't believe the stir it caused. Special Branch took over the case. Apparently they found some weapons and grenades that had been part of a consignment stolen by the IRA. Plus the fact that two of the bodies discovered at the scene of crime were known mercenaries, paid killers who'd been involved in certain unsavoury activities abroad, in countries involved in terrorism.' He laughed again. 'That caused a right little stir in the ant hill. You have no idea the theories bandied about. MI Five and Six came

into the affair. Even the CIA stuck their oar in
– not that they had the first clue about anything,
useless bastards.' Hill propped his elbows on the
desk and said, more seriously, 'As for us coppers,
we were bloody glad to get shot of the case. No one
here gave a toss. Chalmers and his lot were no loss
to us. In fact we had a little piss-up, to celebrate
their demise. So you won't find anyone hassling
you for information or anything about the case.
Just as you won't if Jimmy North and his bunch
of scum get what they deserve.'

Phillip nodded his understanding, then said
quietly, 'But you are risking your career, your
pension, your freedom.'

The policeman looked piercingly at him. 'I
think not, Mr Ross. I doubt if wild horses would
drag from you the fact that I handed you official
information on a plate – conspired with you to
murder, if you like. I know you'll have destroyed
all clues to our previous . . . er . . . association,
and that you'll do the same with the North file the
moment you've memorized it. And if you don't
tell' – he smiled sardonically – 'neither will I.'

Hill stood up and went over to the window. His
back to Phillip, he said quietly, 'I don't tell many
people this, Mr Ross, but my father did all right
for himself. He was a workaholic long before the
word was invented. He was a builder, lived in
Battersea after the war when it was a real dump
of a place. He had a nice win on the football pools
and spent it on buying as many old houses as he
could get his hands on. Then, as the rents came
in, he bought more houses. He ended up owning

whole streets. Never spent a penny on himself, walked round looking like a tramp, did all the maintenance jobs himself. People thought that's what he was, the odd-job man. They never knew he owned one hundred per cent of the property company they paid their rent to. He died several years ago and left the lot to me. My monthly income in rents more than matches my salary as a copper, so I don't need a pension. But I do treasure my freedom – and that is now in your hands, Mr Ross.'

Phillip held out his hand. 'If those wild horses ever come along, they won't drag anything from me, Mr Hill, I promise you.'

The DCI gripped the proffered hand. 'Good hunting, Mr Ross. I'll see you out. Do keep in touch.' His eyes glinted, and he added, 'You look a bit pale, as though you could do with some sun. They say that Spain can be quite pleasant at this time of year.'

The two men went downstairs, chatting idly as they went, and said their goodbyes in the foyer. As soon as Phillip had left, Hill picked up a phone on the reception desk and rang Inspector John Thorpe. They agreed to meet in Hill's office in five minutes. The two had worked together for a long time – Hill had recently been instrumental in getting Thorpe his well-deserved promotion to inspector – and had few professional secrets from each other.

Hill was back in his office, ensconced behind his desk, by the time Thorpe entered, and he greeted him with a broad smile of victory. 'Ross has just left. He's going for it! He's going after North and his gang. Ross is off to Spain.'

Thorpe banged his right fist into the palm of his left hand. 'I knew it! I knew he would! That's the end of North and his band of scum. If he does the business on them like he did on Frank Chalmers and his boys, we won't be hearing from them again, and by God it's good riddance to vile rubbish, as far as I'm concerned.'

Hill became serious. 'For Chrissake don't breathe a word of this to anyone, will you, John? Not even to Jack Richards in the robbery squad. In fact, he's the last one to confide in – he'd feel duty-bound to tell the top brass about Ross. I know he's a mate of yours, John, but keep stumm, eh? What Ross is doing won't help Jack with his crime clear-up rate, but at least Jimmy North won't be committing any more robberies or shooting any more security guards or running down any more innocent pedestrians.'

Thorpe grunted. 'I won't breathe a word to anyone, George. This is bloody dynamite. If even a whisper got out that we knew about Ross's involvement, let alone helped him by supplying information, we'd both be for the chop – and a helluva lot worse. I promise you, I'm very, very well aware of that.'

'Any regrets? Any second thoughts?' asked Hill.

Thorpe shook his head. 'None at all. In fact I'd be more than happy if we could get Ross to sort a few more of the top villains, the ones we know are guilty as all hell but can't get convicted.'

'Yes, it would be great, and no one – not the villains, the public, not even our own boys – would suspect anything. If armed robbers and drug smugglers started to get their heads blown off, most people would think that one of their enemies or business associates had got pissed off and blown them away. There've been enough genuine gangland feud killings lately to make people believe that pretty easily, even if the villains yelled and screamed that it wasn't true.'

'With a man like Ross, we could create panic, and cut serious crime in just a few months,' said Thorpe happily. 'No villain would trust another. In fact, they'd probably panic and really start killing each other, to get their retaliation in first, so to speak.'

'If we could take out the brains and money behind the big drug operations, it would create a void. The smaller boys would fight each other for power, and then, once it all settled down in an accepted pecking order, we could simply chop off a few more heads and create turmoil again.' Hill chuckled evilly.

'One of our targets should be the main suppliers of ecstasy, the bastards who supply poison to young kids like those two in Manchester last week – the twelve-year-old's still in a coma, you know. And deaths and comas seem to be getting more and more common, don't they? It seems like every week or so we hear of another one.' Thorpe shook his head helplessly. 'I just don't understand how youngsters can pay good money for potentially deadly shit that's been mixed up in a filthy bucket in an even dirtier backstreet workshop, by an untrained, unwashed labourer who probably couldn't get a job in a soup kitchen. The pills are stamped out in machines that are rarely, if ever, cleaned. Then several pairs of unwashed hands handle and count them. Then some dirty bastard hides the pills in his underpants or his girlfriend's knickers because that's the last place we're allowed to search – or want to, for that matter.'

Hill finished it for him. 'Then kids from nice homes pop the pills in their mouths and swallow them, after paying ten or fifteen quid for the privilege. They know the danger, they know it can kill them, and they *still* take the fucking stuff.

'But that's not all, John. Who knows what long-term damage these youngsters are doing to their bodies and minds, taking untested contaminated drugs for short-term kicks? We could be in for a living nightmare a few years from now.' He lunged up out of his chair and paced restlessly round the room. 'If Ross does the business on North, I'm going to try to recruit him to work for me. If I can save just one young life, it'll be worth the risk.'

'Do you think he'll go for it, George? With Chalmers and North it's personal, because they both killed people near and dear to him. But would he risk his life and liberty again for total strangers?'

'Who knows? His whole life has been destroyed by villains. Apart from his son, he's got nothing left to live for, and from what he's told me it's

likely that the kid'll be brought up mainly by his
grandparents, anyway. I don't see how Ross could
cope with a tiny baby and earn a living at the same
time. And what sort of living could he earn, in any
case, that wouldn't drive him mad with boredom?
The army trained him to infiltrate, to attack, to kill
if necessary. It's what he's good at, what he knows
best. I'd love to get him to cooperate, be my "rod
of justice", if you like. I'd achieve more in a year
with a man like him than I have in all my years
in the job.' He sat down again heavily. 'We'll just
have to wait and see what he's got to say when
he gets back from Spain.'

Phillip lost no time before beginning his prepara-
tions. On leaving Hill's office, he drove directly
home to Farleigh, in Surrey, and phoned Peter
Russel at Hereford to arrange a meeting. In carefully guarded phrases he told Russel he'd located
the people he'd been looking for and was going
abroad to meet them. He'd need a new passport
and driving licence.
   'No problem,' Russel assured him. 'I'll get on to
it straight away. Should have them' – he thought
for a second – 'by the beginning of next week.
That be OK?'
   Phillip thanked him and suggested they meet
under the clock at Charing Cross station – 'Very
traditional,' said Russel ironically – at two o'clock
on Tuesday. He then settled down to study the file
on Jimmy North and his gang.
   He gritted his teeth and choked back bitter rage
as he stared at the photographs. He memorized

every detail of the five faces that stared blandly
back at him – the shape of nose, eyes and mouth,
a wart here, a scar there, freckles, hair and jawline,
profile and full face – until he was satisfied that
they were seared into his mind and he would
recognize each and every one of the men on
sight, anywhere, at any time. He knew their
height, weight, build, colour of hair and eyes,
which men had tattoos, what they depicted and
where on the body they were.

. By the time he closed the file and rubbed his
tired eyes, he was confident that he had absorbed
every detail, no matter how insignificant, that
might be useful when he came up against the
gang. He knew their birthdays, their star signs,
their likes, dislikes, favourite food, superstitions,
the names of their wives and all the other members of their families, the names of their known
associates, their habits, hobbies and vices, their
criminal records and the crimes they were known
to have committed but couldn't be charged with
for lack of hard evidence.

Closing the folder, he sat back wearily in his
armchair. His eyes closed and he fell into a
deep sleep.

Peter Russel was standing dutifully under the
clock at Charing Cross when Phillip arrived. They
went to a small coffee bar just off the Strand and
settled at a corner table. Phillip brought Peter up
to date with the intelligence he'd obtained on
the gang, though without divulging his source of
information. Peter was too professional to ask, but

as he'd advised Phillip to talk to George Hill he needed no help in putting two and two together.

When Phillip had finished, Russel slid a large brown envelope across the Formica table-top. 'Passport, driving licence and Visa card. There's a balance of five thousand quid in the Visa account. If it looks like you may need to go over that amount, give me a call and I'll top it up.' He frowned with concern and asked, 'Do you need any help or weapons, Phil? You haven't asked for anything.'

Phillip smiled grimly. 'No thanks, mate. This business is personal. Very personal. Those five bastards are going to rue the day they were born, let alone the day they murdered Julie. They're going to pay for what they've done, and the paying is going to hurt them. And they're going to know who's hurting them and why. I can't bring Julie back to life or undo the harm they did all those other people, but, by God, I can make them regret it.'

Russel nodded. 'I understand. But you might like to know that we've got a sub-unit working on a surveillance mission in the Barcelona area. So if you do find you need a pistol or some Semtex, it won't be a problem. Just ring me and I'll arrange everything.'

Phillip smiled gratefully, and said, 'If I need you, I'll call.'

Russel sensed that Phillip, now he had the necessary false documents, was impatient to leave and get on with his self-imposed mission. He leant across the table and slapped his friend

on the shoulder. 'Get going, my friend. Be first.
Be lucky.'

Phillip patted his pocket as he rose to leave.
'Thanks again for—'

Russel cut him short. 'No point in being with
the regiment if you don't make full use of the
facilities, Phil. Think nothing of it.'

Phillip took a deep breath and exhaled slowly.
'I've had my regrets in the past year, over leaving
the service. I miss the lads, and'—his eyes became
haunted — 'perhaps Julie and Gary would both
still be alive today if I hadn't made up my mind
to have a go in civvy street.'

'Don't think like that, Phil. It won't change a
damn thing, just drive you slowly mad. You go
and do what has to be done.'

The two men shook hands and separated for
their different journeys. Peter Russel returned to
Hereford. Phillip Ross travelled to Dover.

Phillip watched as his mother-in-law, Mary
Thompson, fussed over the baby with practised
hands. A lump formed in his throat as he looked
lovingly at his son and marvelled at the colour
of his bright eyes. Sea green, Thompson green,
just like his mother's; and she'd inherited them
from her father, Victor, who now came into
the comfortable sitting room carefully carrying
a baby's bottle full of warm milk.

With some relief, he handed the bottle to his
wife, saying, 'I've cooled it under the tap, but
you'd better check it's not too hot for the little
chap.'

Mary squirted a drop on to the back of her hand to test the temperature. 'That's just fine,' she said as she probed the teat into the open, searching mouth.

Victor sat down heavily on the settee beside Phillip and patted his son-in-law's knee. 'So you'll be away for two or three weeks, son?'

Phillip nodded. 'Yes, Dad. I've got some unfinished business to attend to.' He looked directly into the old man's eyes and knew that his father-in-law understood why he was going away and what he was going to do. He saw the mixture of pain and gratitude etched into Victor's face.

'Do what you have to do, son. But make sure that you come back safe.' He turned his eyes away from Phillip to hide the tears that were beginning to flood them, and stared at his grandson. 'We'll all be here when you come back.'

Phillip rose and crossed to his son. 'Let me take him for a moment, Mum,' he said, reaching for him.

'Mind his little neck,' Mary said protectively as she passed Gary to his father, making sure he supported the baby's head.

Phillip glanced at the watching grandparents as he fed the baby, pulling the teat from its mouth to release the vacuum.

Mary clucked approvingly, like a mother hen. The child had become their whole life since the death of their daughter only a year after they'd lost their son. Gary — and perhaps Phillip too, a little bit — was their only reason to carry on living.

God, Phillip thought, what would they have

done, if they hadn't the baby to care for, to take their minds off the loss of both of their children?

He put the baby back into Mary's eager arms and kissed them both goodbye. Gary smiled and gurgled happily, his chubby hands clutching at the thumb Phillip held out to him, his eyes bright and interested as he gazed up at his father. A lump formed in Phillip's throat as wondering love for this tiny, helpless son rushed up inside him. Thank God he doesn't know his mother's dead, he thought. Let him enjoy his innocence for as long as possible. He turned abruptly away, forcing a smile.

Victor walked with him to the front door and held out his hand in farewell. Phillip felt the strength of the old man's grip as he spoke. 'We don't believe in capital punishment, my boy. We're both devout Christians, as you know, and the Lord tells us that we must forgive, that we must leave vengeance to him. But sometimes I think the Lord needs a helping hand, if the law of the land can't touch murdering scum like that. Otherwise they'll kill more people and ruin more lives.'

There was iron in Phillip's voice as he replied, 'Don't worry, Dad, I'm on their case. They won't be killing or crippling anyone else. No one else will have to suffer the grief we've suffered because of them.'

'If I can help in any way, son . . .' The old man's voice trailed away.

Phillip knew that the young Victor had been

as tough as any man. He'd served with Number 2
Para, and had made sergeant. But he was old now,
worn down by grief and strain, only a shadow of
his former self.

'Yes, Dad, I know,' he said gently. 'In the
meantime, look after yourselves and Gary. I'll
see you as soon as I return. Bye, Dad.' He hugged
the old man and kissed his cheek, then turned on
his heel and walked away.

Chapter Three

The passport was in the name Edward Sydney Hutchinson, and bore the usual photograph making the holder look as if he'd just swallowed a red-hot chilli. Phillip handed it to the Spanish immigration control officer, who gave it a cursory glance and waved him through.

After collecting his baggage and clearing customs, he made his way to one of the many car-hire desks and handed over a driving licence in the same name. The attractive raven-haired young woman behind the desk smiled and handed him a form. 'Yes, we have a car for you, Señor Hutchinson. If you would please fill in the form, your car is waiting outside.'

Thirty minutes later Phillip was behind the wheel of a Ford Escort, following the signs to Lloret de Mar. On arrival there, he booked into a suite at the most expensive hotel he could find, showered and changed into light casual slacks and a polo shirt. As it was early June, the temperature was in the high seventies, many degrees warmer than in England.

Phillip strolled through the streets of Lloret until he found an estate agent. He professed interest in buying a villa in the development where the file had said the gang leader, Jimmy North, lived.

'Cala Canyelles?' The salesman raised his eyebrows. 'It is very exclusive there. Front-line, cliffside property.' He frowned, and asked delicately, 'How much do you wish to pay, *señor*?'

Phillip smiled disarmingly. 'Money is no problem, *señor*. I've recently sold my father's house in London for an extremely good price. Please be good enough to show me your most desirable properties.'

'Please take a seat, Señor Hutchinson. If that is the case I'm sure that we can find you a suitable property – in fact, I have several that may be of interest. Would you care for some coffee while I get you the details?'

When Phillip left the agency, he was clutching the details of six villas on the estate where North lived. They all boasted several en-suite bedrooms, swimming pools, large gardens and price tags that made him look twice to see whether they were in pesetas or pounds. They were in pounds, the least expensive being priced at £450,000. He had assured the salesman that he'd view the exteriors and locations of the properties and come back to him if he found them of interest.

He drove directly to the development, which from Lloret was in the direction of Tossa. Turning right into the estate, he drove round and round, studying a road map supplied by the agent. The

villas were large, white and expensive, standing
out starkly against the greenery of the pine and
palm trees that surrounded and protected them.
They all appeared to have magnificent sea views,
being tiered one above the other on a rising cliff
face, which curved round to form a secluded bay
lined with golden sand that was lapped by the
clear blue water of the Mediterranean. A small
harbour had been formed under the towering
cliffs, and in it fishing boats and pleasure craft
bobbed side by side to the swell of the waves.

Phillip slowly cruised the avenue where Jimmy
North's villa was situated. When he found it
he saw that it was set cliffside, with only the
terra-cotta roof in view from the road. He parked
in a small lay-by, walked back and peered through
the electronically controlled wrought-iron gates.
Three cars were parked by the house. Two of
them, both Mercedes, had British registration
plates, but the third, a Porsche, had a Gerona
tax-free plate. He walked on to the boundary of
the property, from where by leaning over the stone
wall he could see part of the terrace and the end
of a large swimming pool. He heard voices and
laughter, and splashings in the pool.

After an hour, he heard louder male voices
from the front of the villa. The gates jerked, then
opened silently. He stepped into view and saw
Jimmy North walking towards a white Mercedes
560 SEC, his arm round the shoulder of another
member of the gang, William Kincaid. Both of
them were braying with laughter.

As the two men reached the car, unaware that

they were being observed, Phillip strolled up the drive towards them, clutching the estate agent's brochures. Then, pasting on his silliest smile, he drawled in his best upper-class-twit voice, 'I say, excuse me, but do you gentlemen speak English?'

North and Kincaid swung round and eyed him suspiciously.

'Yeah, a bit,' said North.

Phillip waved the brochures. 'I'm looking for this property, which is up for sale. Perhaps you could direct me?'

North accepted the brochures. He read the address, then glanced down at the price and his eyebrows rose. He was clearly impressed – not surprising, really, because Phillip had passed him details of the most expensive villa of all.

North shot Kincaid a glance 'He's interested in that big villa on the Carrer de Italia.'

Kincaid looked puzzled.

'Behind El Trull,' North explained. 'The one that German bought and never used because he couldn't get his yacht into the harbour because it was too big.'

Kincaid nodded as light dawned. 'I know it.'

North looked back to Phillip, who was still grinning. 'Nice villa, that. Lotta money, though.'

Phillip looked nonchalant. 'Not really, not if one likes it,' he burbled. 'Property is so cheap in Spain, compared to England. I've got a few quid kicking around. My father died recently, and now that I don't have to look after the old chap any more I've decided to sell everything and come and live in the sun. It's taken over a year to sort out the estate.'

North scratched his head and shot Kincaid a sideways glance. Kincaid was staring at Phillip, thinking scornfully what a prat the man sounded and looked with his silly grin.

North gave him an encouraging smile and said, 'Why don't you come in for a minute? I've got a map inside. I'll mark out where some of these villas are. It'll make it easier for you to find them.'

'That's frightfully kind of you, old chap. I will indeed.' Phillip held out his hand. 'Edward Hutchinson is the name, Ted to my friends.'

North shook his hand warmly. 'Jimmy North, and this is Billy Kincaid, a friend and business associate.'

Kincaid held out his hand. Phillip shook it. It took all his self-command to maintain his foolish grin as he touched the flesh of the men who had mown down his wife in cold blood. The only way he could hide his revulsion and hatred was by retreating deep into the role he was playing and acting like a wally, a complete prat.

'Nice to meet you, Billy,' he said pleasantly.

Kincaid nodded and cracked a smile. 'Yeah, a pleasure, I'm sure.'

North smiled and said, 'Would you excuse me for a minute, Ted, while I see Billy off?'

'Yes of course, old chap. Nice to meet you, Billy. See you again sometime, I hope.' Phillip turned and wandered out of earshot, secretly appraising the two men as he pretended to admire the sea view.

North was forty-two years old. At six foot two, he was three inches taller than Kincaid. His broad shoulders were slightly offset by a beer paunch. A mop of curly light-brown hair framed a hard-boned, rugged face, in which his grey eyes were bright and alert. Kincaid was dark and good-looking, younger than North by several years. He looked in peak physical condition, muscles rippling smoothly under his white silk shirt.

North's voice was low and excited as he spoke. 'We might just have a nice little earner here, Billy. He's loaded and a complete wanker into the bargain. Most people leave their fucking brains behind when they come out here to buy property, don't they? If we can set the silly bastard up, it could be better than doing a fucking bank.' He shot a quick look in Phillip's direction, to check that he was still out of earshot. 'Come back about nine tonight. I'll invite him to a barbecue, see how it works out.'

Kincaid nodded, got into his car and accelerated away down the drive.

North waved at the departing Mercedes and called out, 'See you about nine then, Billy.'

He turned, smiling broadly at this new-found friend and sucker. 'Come on in, Ted. Come and have a nice cold beer, my friend.'

Phillip spent the next hour sitting on the terrace by the swimming pool chatting to North and his wife, Wendy. She was slightly overweight, but still looked good for a woman of forty. Her long dark hair curled as it fell over her shoulders framing a darkly tanned face. She looked Spanish until she opened her mouth and spoke in a strong East End accent. 'Another beer, Ted?'

He smiled and declined. 'I'd better slow down if we're going to be partying tonight.'

Phillip was feeling very pleased with himself. North had swallowed his story, hook, line and sinker: the hints of great inherited wealth, the fact that he intended to buy an expensive villa and would like very much to get involved in some kind of business to ward off boredom.

'But of course,' he drawled, 'I'll need to find someone with local knowledge to be my partner, someone who speaks the lingo and can take care of lawyers and accountants and all the other dreary people one has to deal with. After all, it'd be a bit damned silly to go mucking about investing two or three mill in property or whatever if one couldn't understand what everyone was saying, wouldn't it?'

Greed overcoming native caution, North said, 'I might have just the deal for you, Ted, just the deal.'

Phillip raised his eyebrows enquiringly.

'We'll discuss it tomorrow. Today we'll just have a good time. Tonight you'll meet a few of the local inhabitants. Nice people. You're going to like it here, Ted,' he purred, 'I'm sure of that.'

Phillip smiled and looked away. He rose and went to the edge of the terrace, leant over the wrought-iron balustrade and looked down. There was a sheer drop of two hundred feet to sharp,

jagged rocks below. The clear blue sea lapped
at the rocks forming a creamy foam that curled
round them, then ebbed away. He stepped back
and held the palm of one hand lightly against his
forehead as North walked to his side. 'God! It
made me feel quite dizzy looking down there.'

North chuckled and said, 'Don't like heights,
eh?'

Phillip shook his head and peered cautiously
down at the rocks below. 'It's a long way down,
Jimmy. I'd hate to get a bit tipsy and fall over the
railings.'

'Certain death, old son, certain death,' North
joked.

Phillip looked out to sea – and smiled.

The barbecue was a lavish affair. North had spared
no expense, ordering the most expensive delica-
cies from the local fish restaurant, El Trull. Lob-
ster, caviar, king prawns, squid and various other
shellfish were piled high on the damask-covered
tables round the swimming pool. Spiced steaks,
lamb chops, chicken drumsticks and marinated
spare ribs sizzled over glowing charcoal, filling
the air with a mouthwatering aroma. Champagne
corks popped, and the golden liquid flowed in
rivers. Red-jacketed waiters hired from the restaurant flitted among the guests, attending to
their needs.

There were over fifty guests, people who had
jumped at the opportunity to attend a party
thrown by Jimmy North, whose lavish hospitality
was legendary in the area. Phillip was introduced

to them all by North as a new friend who was
moving to the area and was interested in the
big villa on Carrer de Italia. He was instantly
accepted by the guests, and received numerous
offers of hospitality and assistance. Money talks,
he thought wryly as the offers flooded in.

Kincaid arrived with Cathy, whom he introduced as his wife. Phillip was aware from the
file on the gang that they were not married but
had lived together as man and wife for several
years. Cathy would not have looked out of place in
Baywatch: she was a stunning blonde with waist-
length hair and a figure like Pamela Anderson's.
Her long, grey, silky evening dress clung to her
body and shimmered as she moved. Her arm was
tucked through Kincaid's, and from time to time
she smiled adoringly up at him. Phillip had to
push to the back of his mind the fact that she
would soon lose the man she loved.

Harry Turner and Mike Lambert arrived with
their wives. They had travelled in the same car,
and had stopped off at a local bar for a drink.
Turner was already the worse for wear, unsteady
on his feet and with pink-rimmed eyes. Roger
Jennings came alone; his wife, Anne, didn't get
along with some of the people she knew would
be there, and had chosen to stay at home.

Phillip didn't refuse a single drink. But, as he
mixed with the guests, acting the part of an upper-
class berk who'd drunk too much champagne,
neither did he finish a single drink. Unnoticed,
he switched his almost-full glass for an almost-
empty one at every opportunity.

As the evening passed into early morning and drink washed away all inhibitions, the jokes grew louder and coarser, and the revellers staggered as they danced. Phillip's face ached from the fixed grin plastered all over it, but he mentally gritted his teeth and staggered and joked along with everyone else, laughing like a jackass as people jumped or were pushed into the swimming pool to the accompaniment of much merriment.

It all seemed about par for the course. The only thing that lit a warning light in his mind was the marked attention paid to him by Debby, an attractive, slightly built young woman in her late twenties. She was seldom far from his side, and kept asking him to dance, or fetching him drinks whenever she noticed his glass was empty.

'Are you married, Ted?' she enquired casually as she handed him yet another refill.

Phillip's grin faded. 'No, my wife died some time ago in a motor accident,' he said quietly. 'I don't like to talk about it.'

'Oh, I'm sorry,' she said quietly, laying a hand comfortingly on his arm. 'Then let's change the subject.' Her expression changed to one of puzzlement and she stared up at him. 'Have you been to Lloret before?'

'No, this is my first visit. A friend recommended it. Why do you ask?'

Debby shook her head and shrugged. 'Oh, no reason really. It's just that I keep getting a feeling that I've seen you before. It's probably just that you remind me of someone, but I can't figure out who.' She laughed lightly. 'It's silly really.'

She excused herself and disappeared inside the villa. Phillip thought rapidly. Was it possible they'd met before? He was certain they hadn't, but could she possibly have an inkling of who he was? He was almost as certain she hadn't: if she had, she'd surely have mentioned it to North, and the gang would be preparing to kill him, not inviting him to barbecues and involving him in dodgy property deals. He glanced casually round. There was no sign of North. Kincaid was chatting to Harry Turner and Mike Lambert. Hiding his unease, he wandered over to join their little group.

North was in the kitchen, filling an ice bucket from the ice-maker. Debby paused a moment in indecision, then went over to him.

North looked down at her and asked with a grin, 'How are you getting on with the toff?'

'I'm not sure yet,' she said hesitantly. 'He's recently lost his wife in an accident. He doesn't seem too interested.'

'Well, keep working on him. We want him to like it here.' North glanced at the ample breasts pushing against the thin cotton of her blouse, whose décolletage revealed enough to catch any man's attention. 'With your equipment,' he leered, 'it shouldn't be too difficult to make him forget her for a bit.'

Debby pulled away, frowning. 'He's a good-looking bloke, but his silly grin, and the way he talks' – she swung back to face him – 'he sounds just like Prince Charles. I don't know if I could get used to it.'

North slammed the ice bucket down and gripped her hard by the shoulders, making her wince. 'Listen, Debby, the fucking bloke's loaded – he's got millions by the sound of it. I want him to like it here. I want him around long enough to strip him of some of his dough.' He released his grip and patted her arm encouragingly. 'So do whatever it takes to make the geezer happy. Got it?'

Debby's gaze fell and she said almost inaudibly, 'Yes, Jimmy. I'll do what I can.'

He grinned broadly. 'Good girl. Now I've got to do a bit of circulating, so you get the hell back out there and make the toff happy.' He picked up the ice bucket, gave her a light slap on the cheek, and returned to the terrace.

North joined Phillip and the three gang members. 'Enjoying yourselves?' he asked jovially.

Out of sight of Phillip, Kincaid gave North a look of despair and rolled his eyes towards the sky. Phillip, acting the complete drunken wally, was boring the three men to distraction, making highbrow jokes way above their heads and laughing heartily at his own wit. The three villains just about managed to crack smiles and force the occasional laugh to humour him.

Phillip turned and slapped North heartily on the shoulder, his foolish grin wider than ever. 'Super party, Jimmy, absolutely super.'

North returned the grin and slung an arm round Phillip's shoulders. 'It's good to have you with us, Ted. We could do with a bit of new blood around here.' He looked round at the crowd of noisy revellers. 'Nice people. Know how to enjoy themselves.'

Phillip nodded and said with owlish enthusiasm, 'Yes, I'm a lucky chap to have found such a nice crowd of people – specially you, Jimmy. I think we'll get along fine.' He hiccuped, staggered drunkenly and almost fell.

'Careful, Ted,' North said genially, as he supported Phillip. 'You've had a bit too much of the hard stuff.' He winked at Kincaid and continued, 'I think you'd better stay here the night. We've got plenty of room, and I don't want you going and having a bloody accident.'

Phillip swayed artistically for a moment, then shook his head as though to clear it. 'You may well be right, Jimmy. I can hardly walk, let alone drive.' Giggling inanely, he groped for a chair and slumped into it.

'Look after our friend,' North told Kincaid, then left the group and crossed the terrace to where a cluster of guests, including Debby, were talking to Wendy North. He slid an arm round his wife's waist and gave her a squeeze. 'OK, my love?' he asked, smiling.

Wendy tossed her dark curls over her shoulder, her brown eyes glinting with amusement. 'How are you getting on with toffee-nosed Ted?'

North looked pleased. 'He seems to like us.' He glanced contemptuously back to Phillip. 'He's as pissed as a fart, so I've told him he can stay here for the night. So Debby, my girl' – his voice was suddenly vicious – 'go and do the business on him.'

Debby picked up her glass and, without looking at North, made her way through the crowd to where Phillip was lolling in his chair. She put her glass down on the table and pulled him to his feet.

'Come and dance with me, Ted,' she purred, staring into his eyes as she slid a supporting arm round his waist and led him towards the couples smooching to 'Moon River' beside the floodlit swimming pool.

Phillip wavered along beside her, then she turned, draped his arms over her shoulders and snuggled up close, her arms round his waist as she started to move against him in time to the music, gently massaging his back as she did so.

North joined Kincaid, Lambert and Turner. 'Well, what do you boys think of him?' he asked, nodding towards Phillip, who appeared to be enjoying Debby's idea of dancing.

'He's a complete dickhead!' said Kincaid sourly. 'I couldn't put up with too much of him.'

North grinned. 'Harry?'

Turner's broad, craggy face creased into a smile. 'I don't know how you find 'em, Jimmy. He's like something out of a fucking comedy film.'

'Mike?'

Lambert's hatchet face was expressionless, but his deep-set eyes showed a spark of amusement. 'If the wanker's got as much dosh as you say he has, I can put up with him for a while – at any rate, till we can nick a chunk of it.'

North grinned evilly. 'He wants to invest a lot of fucking money in local business, and I'm going to be his personal adviser.' He looked serious for a moment. 'I've been giving it a bit of thought. You know that development out on the old Gerona Road, the one where they put the roads in, but they never had the planning permission, so it got stopped and the investors lost their dough?' He paused dramatically. 'Well, I'm gonna sell him that. I'll tell him I've got an in with the local mayor and some geezers on the planning committee, tell him we can all make a fortune if we bung the right people and get permission to build the estate. He's the sort of tosser who'd think all foreigners are bent and bribable, so he'll buy that. And we'll just have to make sure he doesn't get a chance to talk to anyone who can tell him the truth. We could suck him along for months, keep squeezing more cash out of him till he squeaks.' He roared with laughter.

Kincaid said, 'He seems too fucking good to be true. I'm gonna check him out. See if he's all he says he is.'

The last thing that Phillip wanted or felt like was sex with a woman who was obviously out to seduce him.

Julie's face, with her laughing green eyes and long fair hair, was vivid in his mind's eye as Debby moulded her body against his and undulated in time to the music. He forced the vision to the back of his mind and reminded himself yet again why he was here and what he intended to do to North and his men.

He resisted the urge to push Debby away and

tell her he wasn't interested. If this was North's plan, he had to go along with it or risk their becoming suspicious. No man in his right mind would turn down the chance of going to bed with an attractive, sexy woman like Debby. And she definitely knew how to excite a man: her experienced hand and body had made his temperature rise by several degrees. Playing the idiot seduced by a *femme fatale* wouldn't be at all difficult . . .

Debby, aware of Phillip's arousal, became bolder. She ran the fingers of her left hand up his back and into his thick black hair and pulled his mouth down to hers as she pressed her groin against his hardening member. Phillip returned her lip-crushing kiss as her tongue searched his mouth.

She was starting to enjoy herself. It was a pity about the village-idiot grin and posh accent, but even so his clean good looks and lean, muscular body genuinely turned her on. She pressed harder against him as her excitement rose. She felt a flood of wetness as her juices flowed and the desire to feel him inside her became more urgent.

Phillip pulled away and held her at arm's length, his hands on her shoulders, as he gazed blearily at her. 'Gosh, Debby, what are you doing to me? I haven't felt like this since . . .' He waved his hand in a vague gesture of dismissal. 'Oh never mind. I need a drink.' He turned from her and reeled to the bar.

Debby followed, a small, private smile curving

her lips. I'm going to enjoy this after all, she thought.

Phillip sloshed champagne into two glasses and passed one to Debby. 'To us,' he slurred as he raised his glass. She raised her glass and clinked it against his. 'To us,' she repeated, smiling, and she stared provocatively up at him as she sipped.

North appeared beside them. 'You two seem to be getting along well together,' he said cheerfully.

Phillip grinned at him. 'Yes, I should say!' He turned his grin to Debby and raised his glass again. 'To a smashing and very lovely lady.'

North said, 'I'll drink to that,' and clinked his glass against Phillip's. He took a gulp of champagne, patted Phillip on the shoulder and said, 'I'll leave you lovebirds to it, then.' Into Phillip's ear he whispered, 'There's a double bed in every spare room, so take your pick, old son.' He winked knowingly, and wandered off.

The guests were leaving, calling out noisy goodbyes. Phillip took advantage of Debby's going to the toilet to ask North which room he should use. Hastily, before she came back, he slipped upstairs, found his room, closed the door behind him and leant against it with a sigh of relief. Peace at last! If Debby pursued him right into bed, he'd just have to pretend to have passed out cold.

He stripped off his clothes and slid between the sheets. After the noise of the party the stillness of the warm night was doubly welcome. He could hear the waves breaking on the beach two hundred feet below his window, which was open, the net curtains fluttering gently in the breeze.

He heard the bedroom door click open and through the slit of one eye saw Debby creep silently across the moonlit room and slip out of her clothes. Naked, she slid in beside him and snuggled up close. Her hand caressed his chest as she kissed his shoulder and flicked her tongue lightly across his skin.

He sucked in a deep breath and exhaled slowly, still feigning sleep. Her hand worked slowly downwards and lightly stoked the ridges of his stomach muscles then slipped between his thighs. She cupped him in her hands and gently squeezed and stroked him to erection. Then she slipped down under the sheet and, pulling back his foreskin, took him in her mouth, her lips hot and wet as she sucked and licked the length of his shaft. She eased almost the whole of him down her throat, then slowly, very slowly, drew away, caressing him with her lips and flicking her tongue the full length of his penis.

Unable to take any more, Phillip caught her head in his hands, pulled her up until her face was level with his and kissed her roughly. She straddled him and slowly impaled herself on his hard, hot flesh. She threw back her head, and with her hair flying and breasts bouncing, her tongue frantically licking her lips, she ground her pelvis against his groin.

Phillip threw her off him, turned her on to her back and, raising her legs over his shoulders, thrust savagely into her until he spurted inside her as she groaned and screamed and jerked in orgasm. They collapsed together, their sweat-drenched bodies stuck skin to skin as they lay panting in each other's arms.

Typically, Debby was the first to speak. She had raised herself to lean on one elbow, and was studying his face. She traced her forefinger along the deep scar below his left eye, and asked, 'How did you get that?'

Phillip thought fleetingly of those mad seconds in the Falklands when he and Gary had knocked out their first Argentine machine-gun post. A piece of shrapnel had stunned him, gashing him to the bone, but Gary had charged the post, drawing their fire and saving Phillip's life.

He smiled up at Debby. 'I fell off my bike when I was a kid. Lucky I didn't lose my eye.'

'You must have been scared stiff!'

He laughed. 'I was more than scared at the time. I thought I was going to die.'

Debby lay back down and snuggled up against him. 'I'm glad you didn't die, Ted,' she said drowsily.

They lapsed into a comfortable silence, and soon fell asleep.

Phillip awoke with a start and glanced quickly at the bedside clock, which informed him that it was eleven fifteen. Sunlight streamed through the window and the sound of voices and of crockery being gathered reached his ears.

Next to him Debby stirred and sighed in her sleep, as she shifted position and nestled closer

to him, reaching one arm out across his chest. He
turned his head to look at her: she was smiling.
His eyes strayed down the length of her body
to where the top sheet was crumpled around
her feet, a reminder of their fierce coupling
last night.

A wave of anger, guilt and revulsion swept
through him: it should have been Julie beside
him, not this little tramp. I'm sorry, Julie, my
love, he thought. It was only sex, nothing more.
I still love you, and I always will.

Pushing the thought aside, he carefully removed
Debby's arm and slid out of bed. He crossed
silently to the window and stared out across the
bay. The sand gleamed whitely and the clear water
reflected the sun's rays. The waves broke lazily
in white foam against the beach and outcrops of
jagged rock that formed the curves of the bay.

A lone swimmer was striking a path across the
bay. Swimming strongly, he reached the rocks the
far side of the bay, did a racing turn and headed
back again. Phillip judged the distance to be about
a thousand metres.

Glancing back at Debby's prone form, he crossed
to the bathroom, stepped into the shower and,
turning the taps on full blast, proceeded to
scrub away the guilt. As he stepped out of
the shower and started to towel himself briskly,
the bathroom door opened and Debby came in,
smiling broadly.

'I heard the shower going,' she said, 'and
thought it would be nice to join you. But it
looks as if I'm too late — or am I?' She pouted

suggestively as she slid her arm round Phillip and gently cupped his genitals in one hand.

Phillip recoiled, a pained look on his face. 'Not now, Debby, sweetie. I've got the most appalling headache. I had far too much champagne last night.' He rubbed his forehead. 'My head feels as if it's going to burst.'

'You were OK last night. I thought you were going to fuck my brains out.' She stopped, aghast, and clapped a hand over her mouth. 'Oops, sorry! I didn't mean to say that. But you were very good.' Her eyes dropped to Phillip's penis. 'You certainly know how to use that thing!'

Phillip shot her an embarrassed smile and looked quickly away. 'I was pretty drunk . . . and it's been a long time,' he said gruffly, not wanting his rejection to offend her.

Debby laughed and stepped into the shower. 'Then I'd better get you drunk again tonight,' she said as she turned on the water.

Phillip pulled on his clothes. He hated wearing the same clothes twice, but he hadn't expected to stay the night. He went downstairs, stepped through the French windows on to the terrace and eased himself into a lounger. He watched the lone swimmer cross the bay for the umpteenth time as he racked his brains for a plan of action. He wanted to get each man on his own and kill him slowly. He reckoned he could kill two of the gang before the remaining three became suspicious, provided he made the deaths look accidental. Once he had knocked off the third man, he was sure that North, whom he planned to save for last, would have no doubt that the 'accidents' were much more than mere coincidence. Phillip smiled cruelly at the thought of North finally catching on and trying to work out who was killing them and why.

Debby appeared by his side and admired the view. She was wearing crisp white shorts and a loose pink blouse and she was barefoot. She leant on the iron balustrade and watched the lone swimmer. 'He does that every morning,' she said.

'Who does what?' asked Phillip, puzzled.

'Billy.' She pointed to the swimmer, who had reached the rocks by the harbour and was climbing out of the water. 'He swims across the bay several times every morning, weather permitting.'

Phillip focused on the tiny figure of Kincaid as he scrambled over the rocks. 'I've been watching him. I didn't realize that it was Billy. He must be very fit.'

'Yes, he's a keep-fit fanatic. He's got a lovely body.' She looked admiringly at Phillip and reached out to touch his iron-hard biceps. 'But he doesn't look any fitter than you, Ted. You must play a lot of sport.'

'Yes, I play squash, jog, and do a bit with weights in the gym.'

'Do you like swimming? We could go to the beach,' she said hopefully.

'I'm not a very good swimmer,' he said, remembering with a flicker of amusement the army scuba-diving courses he'd passed with flying colours. 'But we could go to the beach. I could do with a nice tan.' He gestured admiringly at Debby, who had the deep golden tan that only sun-worshippers acquire. She was about to speak, but North appeared from inside the villa, his eyes squinting against the brilliant sunlight. He stretched hugely, then strolled over to join Phillip and Debby.

North's eyes were red and puffy, their colour all the more vivid against the white of his bath-robe. His fleshy face was pale and bloated. 'Cor, I feel bloody awful,' he said, leaning on the balustrade and rubbing his head as he tried to smile.

'Great party, Jimmy,' said Phillip brightly.

'Yeah, it must have been,' groaned North. He straightened and took a deep breath in an effort to pull himself together.

Wendy called out from the kitchen doorway. 'I'm cooking eggs and bacon. Anyone fancy some?'

'Yes please,' said Phillip.

'Leave me out, Wendy. I'll settle for black coffee,' said North, a pained expression on his face.

'I'll come and give you a hand,' Debby called to her. She flashed Phillip a smile and went off to join Wendy in the kitchen.

As soon as breakfast was over, Phillip left, saying he had to get back to his hotel and change to go villa-hunting.

Debby offered to accompany him, but he declined, explaining that he preferred to make up his own mind on the initial decision. He promised to show her the villa he decided to buy, the moment he'd made up his mind.

He went back to his hotel and changed into clean clothes, then, making sure he wasn't being followed, drove to the next town along the coast, Blanes. Once there, he parked in the harbour car park and spent a few minutes checking that he was still in the clear, while ostensibly looking at the pleasure craft and fishing boats bobbing to the swell of the sea and straining at their mooring ropes. Seagulls swooped and dived for scraps, screeching as they challenged and fought each other for the prizes.

Satisfied that all was well, he walked back towards the town centre, past the covered fish market where the crates of fish were set out in rows along the wet concrete floor, buyers and vendors pointing and shouting loudly at each other in Spanish as they bargained.

Just outside the harbour entrance, Phillip found exactly what he was looking for, a shop that specialized in water sports. He stepped out of the hot sunshine into the cool interior of the shop and looked around.

He was examining a scuba tank and regulator valve, when the young male assistant finished with another customer and approached him to offer advice and service. Phillip handed him a short list of goods and asked if he could supply them.

After a quick glance through the list, the young man smiled and looked up. '*Sí, señor*, no problem.'

Fifteen minutes later, Phillip headed back to his car carrying a large carton, a look of grim satisfaction on his face. He had decided whom to kill first, how he was going to do it, and when.

Chapter Four

The following morning, Billy Kincaid stripped off his brightly coloured shirt and Bermuda shorts and dived off the rocks into the calm water. His powerful strokes soon took him out across the bay. The sun was shining, there was a slight breeze, and a lone puffball of white cloud sat motionless in the powder-blue sky. Billy was happy and excited. His new car, a Porsche, had arrived at the dealer's, and he was to collect it that afternoon. It was great to be alive and have all the good things he had craved for, had done anything to achieve, even risking his freedom and his life.

Phillip watched patiently as Kincaid reached the far side of the bay, turned and headed back. He checked his air-cylinder gauge and turned the valve to the on position as he walked into the sea and disappeared below the surface in a cloud of bubbles. Visibility was good in the clear water as, arms at his sides, he propelled himself across the bay to where he judged by his converging course that he'd intercept Kincaid in the centre of the bay.

He reached the centre well before his quarry.
A gentle movement of his flippers was sufficient
to hold him stable several feet under the surface.
He spotted Billy's approach from a distance as
he trod water. He unhooked a coil of soft cotton
rope from his belt and opened the slipknot at
one end sufficiently to draw over the man's foot.
He secured the other end to his belt and waited
for Kincaid, now only a few yards away, to pass
overhead.

Kincaid, still swimming strongly and rhythmi-
cally, passed close by above him, totally unaware
of the menace that stalked him from below.

Phillip looked all round to make sure they were
alone, then, with powerful strokes of his arms
and rapid flipper movement, propelled himself
forward at speed, closing the gap rapidly. He
slipped the noose over Kincaid's right ankle and
yanked the slipknot tight.

Kincaid, puzzled and alarmed, stopped swimming and trod water as he swung round and
peered into the water below him. He saw a dark
shape swim rapidly away. Shark! was his first
shocked thought as he saw a wavering shadow
beneath him. He scanned the surrounding water
for bloodstains, in dread that something had
bitten his foot off. He felt no pain, but he had
read that a victim of a shark attack feels no pain,
just a thump or bump as the predator strikes.

In alarm he thrashed towards the shore and
safety. He had travelled only a few feet when
again he felt a snatch at his foot, more powerful
this time. Something had hold of his foot. It

stopped him abruptly, then yanked him below
the surface. He tried to shout for help, but as
soon as he opened his mouth water rushed into
it, gagging him. His eyes, wide with fear, searched
the water. Without the benefit of goggles or mask,
his vision was limited to only a few hazy feet. He
saw the shadow again and turned to swim away,
but something held him fast. His right leg was
trapped. He reached down to release it but it was
jerked straight and he was propelled backwards
through the water. The air he had gulped before
being pulled under escaped from his lungs in a
flurry of bubbles and sped to the surface several
feet above him. He turned and tried to kick his
way to the surface as the pull on his ankle slackened, but the thing holding him jerked tight again
and he was pulled in another direction. His lungs
felt as though they were going to burst. Sheer
panic took over as he realized he was drowning.
Red lights and starbursts filled his head as pain
racked his chest and water filled his lungs.

Suddenly his head broke through the surface.
His chest heaved as he sucked in air, choking
and retching as bile and salt water filled his
mouth. He sucked in more air and coughed
up and spat out more acrid fluid. He filled
his lungs again with fresh air, and flicked his
head to clear the water from his swollen eyes
and face. Blearily, he saw something bob to the
surface several feet to his right. He rubbed his eyes
and focused on the object: a man's head, a scuba
diver. The bastard was wearing a goggle-mask and
an aqualung.

'What the fuck are you playing at, you stupid cunt? You nearly fucking drowned me!'

Phillip removed his mouthpiece and grinned. 'Sorry, old chap.'

It took Kincaid a moment to recognize him. 'Ted?' he croaked, incredulously. He was about to launch into a tirade of enraged abuse, but Phillip replaced his mouthpiece and dipped under the water, leaving a burst of bubbles breaking the surface.

Kincaid searched the surrounding sea, his eyes straining to pierce the glistening surface. Then, taking a deep breath, he struck out for the rocky shore. He had taken only three strokes when he was again jerked violently under the surface and dragged backwards for several yards. His right leg was trapped and useless. He kicked out frantically with his left foot and made powerful strokes with his arms, but he was hauled relentlessly backwards, deeper and deeper. Air escaped his lips in great gouts of bubbles. His vision turned red and hazy as he opened his eyes and searched for his attacker. He bent double and groped at his ankle. He felt the rope, tried to release it, but his leg was yanked straight and he lost hold of the noose. Just as he was lapsing into unconsciousness, his head broke the surface and he gulped in life-giving air as he coughed and spewed up bile and sea water.

Kincaid's strength had drained away. It was all he could do to dog-paddle to keep afloat. He breathed deeply and slowly to recharge his blood and brain with oxygen.

The masked head burst through the surface, only a few feet away. Phillip slid his goggles up to his forehead and removed his mouthpiece. He smiled coldly as he appraised the spluttering Kincaid.

'I'll fucking kill you for this,' Kincaid gasped.

'Oh no you won't.' Phillip gave another tug on the rope, and jerked the struggling man under the water. But Kincaid was not finished yet. He fought his way to the surface and shook the water out of his eyes.

'Why are you doing this?' he choked.

'I came here to kill you.' Phillip smiled mirthlessly.

Kincaid gaped at him. 'Why? What the fuck for? I never even set eyes on you before yesterday.'

'Your last job, the Croydon bank robbery. You and your mates killed my wife. You ran her down like a dog, and left her lying dead in the road.' He pulled his goggle-mask down over his eyes and settled it comfortably. Holding his mouthpiece to one side, he said, 'Think on it. The next time I pull you under will be the last.' Then, slipping the mouthpiece into position, he dropped down out of sight in another flurry of bubbles.

Too late, in a last desperate bid for survival, Kincaid summoned all his remaining strength and dived after Phillip, trying to grab him. But a few deft flicks of his flippers kept Phillip easily out of reach.

Kincaid broke the surface and gulped in air. He swung frantically round in the water as he saw a shadow pass beneath him. He opened his mouth to scream in protest as he felt the rope tighten and drag him down. He flailed his arms and kicked wildly, fighting to stay above the surface, but his cries were cut off, stifled by the water that rushed into his open mouth. His lungs were on fire, his head bursting. He saw in his mind's eye the lovely fair-haired woman pushing the baby carriage in her frantic attempt to get out of the way. The terror on her face. The thud as the heavy car flung her high into the air and sped on. A voice, his own voice, screamed inside his head, 'I'm sorry! I wasn't driving! I didn't kill her! I don't want to die!'

Phillip held the rope fast until Billy Kincaid's body had stopped jerking and the last flurry of bubbles had sped from his open mouth to the surface. He swam up and round to look at the dead man. He was an eerie spectacle as he floated lifeless, mouth and eyes open, arms and legs splayed out in the clear water. Phillip swam to the sea bed, towing the corpse behind him. He slipped the noose from Kincaid's ankle and wrapped seaweed around in its place. A crab scuttled across an open patch of sand, disturbed by the intruders. Death rings the gong: dinner is served, he thought with grim satisfaction as, taking one last look at his victim, he spun round and swam towards the shore. One down, four to go!

'Where the fuck is Billy?' grumbled North. He glanced at his watch for the umpteenth time as he leant on the balustrade and stared out to sea. 'He knows we're playing golf this afternoon. If we don't set off soon, we won't make it all the way round.' He turned and managed to smile at Phillip. 'Sorry about this, Ted. Billy ain't usually late for a round of golf. Something must have happened. I'll give Cathy another ring – she might have heard from him.'

Phillip said, 'Don't give it another thought, old chap. We can always play another day.'

North strode off towards the villa. Left alone on the terrace, Phillip glanced down at the beach. A crowd of young bathers had gathered at the water's edge. A young man was swimming towards the beach, shouting in Spanish. He was dragging something behind him.

Phillip watched casually as the body was dragged out on to the sand. One of the young men started trying to pump water out of the dead man's lungs. Phillip smiled grimly. It's a bit late for that, he thought.

North came out of the villa and crossed the terrace to Phillip. 'Cathy ain't heard from him since he left for his daily swim. She says he might have got held up collecting his new car.' He grinned. 'Picking up a new Porsche today, our Billy is.'

Both men's attention was drawn to the beach by the arrival of a police car, siren wailing, blue light flashing. Two local policemen in their dark-blue uniforms ran to the crowd gathered at the water's edge. An ambulance with two white-coated attendants screeched to a halt beside the police car. The white coats hurried to the scene.

'What the hell's going on down there?' North screwed up his eyes against the reflected glare of

the sun, and tried to see what was happening. 'Get
my binoculars, Wendy,' he called. 'I think there's
been an accident.'

Wendy ran from the villa, carrying a large pair
of binoculars. 'It's not Billy, is it?' She sounded
alarmed.

'Don't be daft,' snapped North. 'He can swim
like a bleeding fish.' He focused the binoculars on the beach. The police were pushing the
crowd back to give the ambulance attendants
more room. One man was leaning over the body.
North couldn't see the prone man's face, but as he
studied the flaccid body, he let out a gasp. 'Christ
almighty! I think it *is* Billy!'

Phillip stepped forward, frowning with suitable concern. 'Billy? Are you sure?'

North passed him the binoculars. 'It looks like
him. I'd better get down there.' He hurried out
to his car, and Phillip heard the shriek of tyres
as North gunned it down the drive.

Wendy wrung her hands, silently praying that
it wasn't their friend.

Phillip watched through the binoculars as the
ambulance man stood up, shrugged helplessly,
and started to unroll a body bag. North's car
appeared and skidded to a halt beside the police
car in a cloud of sand and dust. He leapt out and
ran across the beach.

Phillip watched North through the binoculars.
He saw a look of anguish cross the man's face as
he recognized his friend, saw him slump to his
knees beside the body, his shoulders heaving as
he cried.

Yes, cry, you bastard, cry, Phillip thought coldly.

Wendy laid a hand on his shoulder and asked, her voice full of anxiety, 'What's happening? Is it Billy?'

Phillip lowered the binoculars. 'I think it is,' he said softly. 'You'd better phone Cathy. Just tell her you think there's been an accident and she should come over.'

'I'll go and fetch her. She'll be frantic if I tell her over the phone.' Wendy looked imploringly at Phillip. 'You're sure it's Billy? You're certain of it?'

'Jimmy's crying his eyes out down there, Wendy.'

Wendy nodded miserably and walked slowly to her car, too shocked to cry, dreading the task that lay ahead of her.

Phillip poured himself a long, cold drink of fresh orange juice and sat back to wait.

Within the hour, the Norths' villa had filled not only with the thieves and their women, but with several of the gang's friends, who had heard the bad news and arrived to comfort and console.

Phillip kept a low profile, offering assistance from time to time. No one doubted that he was appalled by the dreadful accident.

Debby arrived in a fluster, shocked and tearful. She spoke briefly to Jimmy North, then spent the next several minutes with her arm round the shoulders of Cathy, who sat weeping inconsolably. Phillip knew exactly how she felt. He pushed all feeling for her aside. She had lived a life of luxury at the expense of others, had happily spent the money her husband stole, not caring who was injured or traumatized to keep her in luxury. She'd not have thought twice about spending on fripperies the stolen money that had cost Julie her life, had caused injury and distress to the other victims, and destroyed his own happiness.

He visualized the men returning home after the robbery, jubilant at their success, sharing out the cash, handing bundles of notes to their wives, notes stained with Julie's blood and the blood of the crippled security guard, the injured pedestrians. No, he wouldn't let the wives' coming grief stand in his way. They, like soldiers' wives, lived with the knowledge that their men led dangerous lives and might come to a sticky end. What the four consoling wives did not realize was how close that sticky end was, and that their roles were about to be reversed.

Debby interrupted his thoughts. She sat down beside him and tucked her hand into his, like a child seeking comfort. Under the golden tan, her face was pale and drawn. 'I can't believe it,' she whispered. 'Billy dead.'

Phillip forced a sympathetic smile. 'I know how you must feel, Debby. It must have come as a great shock.'

She shook her head in bewilderment. 'If he'd died any other way I might have believed it, but he was such a good swimmer . . .'

'Perhaps he got a stomach cramp. It does happen, even to the best of swimmers.'

Debby said shakily, 'I suppose we'll never

know.' She buried her head in Phillip's shoulder
and sobbed unashamedly.

With Billy Kincaid dead, all thought of checking
on Ted Hutchinson, or even ripping him off, had
been pushed aside. Phillip stayed clear of the
North household for three days. He spent his
time acting out his part, looking over several
expensive properties and getting to know the
area better.

He returned to his hotel on the afternoon of
the third day to find a message from North,
inviting him to the villa that evening. Phillip
had made his plan and decided who was next
on his list. He'd been keeping Roger Jennings's
villa under surveillance. The man appeared to
lie in bed until noon each day, while in the
afternoon he pottered about the villa or garden, or went shopping. Phillip had watched
him drive off in his Jaguar and return with
Maso supermarket bags loaded with food and
drink. That was about all Jennings did during
the day. In the evening, he would emerge from
the villa between nine thirty and ten, drive off
down the hill and not return until the early hours
of the morning.

It had not been possible to follow him without
the risk of being seen, so Phillip wanted to know
where the man went in the evenings, if it was
a regular habit, whether he went to one place
or several, and how long he stayed at each. To
set up another little accident, Phillip needed to
learn a bit more about his intended victim's habits

and movements, so the invitation came at just the right time.

He arrived at the Norths' villa at eight, as requested. The door was opened by Debby, who flung her arms round his neck and said, 'Oh, Ted, it's so good to see you! The last few days have been awful.'

She took his arm and they went through the villa to the terrace, where North and the other gang members were sitting by the swimming pool. Phillip joined the group, while Debby went into the kitchen to get them both a drink.

North leapt from his chair and greeted Phillip with outstretched hands. 'Ted, it's good to see you.' He shook Phillip's hand vigorously. 'Sorry about the last few days, but things have been a bit difficult.'

'I understand perfectly, Jimmy,' said Phillip sympathetically. 'I felt I should stay out of the way for a few days, allow family and close friends time to grieve.' He shook hands with Turner, Lambert and Jennings, then turned back to North. 'How's Cathy bearing up?'

'She's totally devastated, but she's in good hands. She's gone back to England, to be with her family. I dropped them off at the airport this afternoon.' He glanced at his watch. 'Should be all settled in Hackney by now.'

'Did someone go with her?' asked Phillip.

'All the wives did,' said North. 'There's only us blokes left, so Debby's got her hands full looking after all of us.'

'What are the funeral arrangements? When

will Billy be buried?' Phillip assumed a look of sober gravity. 'I'd like to pay my respects, send a wreath.'

'Billy's being flown home. He always said he wanted to be buried on British soil.' North gestured vaguely with one hand. 'Me and the boys can't get to the funeral. We've got a big property deal on the boil, and if we're away for any length of time, we could miss out on it, and it's a big one.' He rubbed thumb and forefinger together in the international sign for money. 'Big bucks involved in this deal, Ted, millions.'

Mike Lambert spoke up. 'The wives will take care of the funeral in London. We'll go to the local church in Lloret and pay our respects there.'

Phillip guessed that North and his gang didn't dare risk returning to Britain so soon after the robbery. That was fine with him: it meant he'd have them where he wanted them for at least a week, probably more.

Debby arrived, carrying a tray of beers and orange juice. She put the tray down and handed the drinks round. Under cover of the activity, Phillip gave Roger Jennings a quick once-over. He was tall, lanky and taciturn. His hazel eyes were set a little close together and his lips were too thin for him to be regarded as good-looking. His pale, thinning ginger hair was swept straight back from a receding forehead. He rarely smiled.

You're next, arsehole, thought Phillip, with a smile.

North gave Phillip a friendly pat on the shoulder. 'Me and the boys have been having a business meeting. You know I mentioned a property deal? Well, we're all in on it.' He paused, then said sadly, 'So was Billy. Well . . .' He shrugged off his darker mood, and said briskly, 'Now, I've had a word with the lads, and they're all more than happy for you to take over Billy's place and have his share of the profits – if you're interested, that is?'

Phillip felt all eyes on him as he pretended to mull over the offer. He kept them waiting until he judged they were nicely on the boil, then said with a wide grin, 'I'd love to be part of the team, Jimmy. But' – he switched expressions: this called for serious thoughtfulness – 'of course I'd need to know a little bit more about the proposed development, look over the site and any proposed drawings et cetera. But in principle, count me in.'

'Great!' exclaimed North. 'We wouldn't invite just anyone to join in a deal as creamy as this one, Ted, but we all like you a lot, and think you'll fit in nicely. We can all go and look over the site tomorrow morning if that's OK with you.'

Phillip nodded and said, 'Fine. You name the time and I'll be there.' His eyes widened as though a thought had struck him. 'We could jump in a car and go and have a look at the site now. There's still plenty of light.'

'Calm down, calm down! There's no rush. But we will have to act fast when the time comes.' He cocked a questioning eyebrow at Phillip. 'You can come up with a large chunk of cash at short notice, can you, Ted? Because we're all transferring cash to a local bank in the next few days so we can slap a deposit down before anyone else tries to beat us to it.'

'How much are we talking about?'

'We're all putting up two hundred and fifty grand each as the initial fund, to cover deposits, licences and' – he winked knowingly at Phillip – 'the necessary bung here and there to the local mayor and councillors, all the people that matter.' North scratched his chin and did some mental arithmetic. 'Your total input would have to be about half a million quid. Not too strong for you, Ted?'

'No problem. I've got more than that on overnight call. I'll have it transferred to any bank you name. I'll do it tomorrow afternoon, as soon as I've seen the land.' He gave them one of his most fatuous grins. 'If the deal doesn't come off, I can't lose anything, can I?'

The four men smiled and nodded. 'You can't lose a tanner, Ted, not a tanner,' said North smoothly.

Jennings looked at his watch and hauled his lanky frame out of his chair. 'I'm off, then. See you boys in the morning. Half past ten, right?'

'Yeah, we'll all meet up here at half past ten and go look at the site. See you tomorrow, Roger. Be lucky, old son, and don't lose too much fucking money.'

Jennings ignored the remark, cracked a half-smile and departed.

North turned to Phillip and explained, 'He loves a gamble. Does well, wins quite a bit.'

'Horses?' asked Phillip.

'Horses, dogs, anything. He's off to the casino in Lloret, goes there every night at ten.' He laughed. 'You could set your watch by him. I always know where to find Roger when I want him. If he ain't at home, he's in the bleeding casino.'

Thank you for that information, Jimmy, thought Phillip. Now I know where to find the bastard, and when.

Chapter Five

Jennings's villa was set on the top of a mountain five kilometres inland from Lloret de Mar. A small rucksack on his back, Phillip sat in the darkness, hidden in the shrubbery that lined the driveway, and enjoyed the uninterrupted view of Lloret and Blanes. What seemed like millions of twinkling lights and a multitude of coloured neon signs set out the boundaries of the teeming nightlife below him, where thousands of carefree tourists were drinking and dancing the night away. Several laser beams, thin fingers of light, twirled and stabbed into infinity through the dark sky, reaching out to the stars from the roof of the Hollywood discothéque.

Brilliant headlights cut through the blackness as a car raced up the narrow mountain road, taking the bends at a reckless speed. The car sped past, its tyres losing grip on the loose gravel washed down the steep hill by recent rainstorms. Phillip ducked out of sight and shielded his eyes from the glare of the headlights as the Jaguar surged into the drive of the villa and braked to an untidy halt.

Jennings staggered slightly as he climbed out of the car, and walked with exaggerated care up the steps to his front door. He fumbled with his keys, opened the door and crashed it shut behind him.

Phillip watched patiently as lights went on and off, marking Jennings's progress through the villa to his bedroom. The front ground floor of the villa fell into darkness, then a light on the upper floor blinked on and stayed on, throwing a shaft of light on to the small wrought-iron-balustraded balcony outside the window.

He waited several minutes longer, until he was sure that all movement inside the villa had stopped, then slipped the rucksack from his back and set it on the ground. After a last quick look round, he ran lightly across the driveway and up the steps. With a flying leap, he grasped the edge of the balcony and heaved himself up and over the balustrade. He crouched into the shadows thrown by the light from the bedroom window and peered inside.

Jennings staggered out of the bathroom, naked, and dropped his clothes in an untidy heap on the floor. He flopped on to the bed and passed out almost instantly. A throaty, drunken snore filled the room.

Satisfied he was out for the count, Phillip slipped silently back over the balustrade and dropped to the ground. He retrieved his rucksack from the shrubbery and crossed to the Jaguar. He took a pair of thin rubber gloves from one pocket and pulled them on, then silently opened the

driver's door, leant in and released the bonnet
catch. From his rucksack he produced a long
piece of wire with a crocodile clip at each end.
He clamped one end to the live terminal of the
battery and the other to the coil. There was a
quiet click as the ignition switched on, and the
warning lights on the dashboard lit up.

Phillip set to work on the cigar lighter, bending
the retaining clips until they no longer held the
lighter in its socket as the element clicked out.
He tested it three more times. Each time the
lighter clicked out, it popped straight out of its
socket on to the floor carpet, glowing redly in
the dark interior of the car. Phillip removed the
hot wire from the battery and coil and pressed
the lighter fully home. With no current coming
from the battery, it stayed pressed in.

Next, he carefully removed from the rucksack
three bloated condoms, each one full of petrol
and with its neck tightly knotted. He tied nylon
fishing line round each one and slid them out
of sight under the passenger seat. He closed the
driver's door and walked round to the passenger
door, which he opened. He felt under the seat
for the loose end of the fishing line, took it up
and, unwinding more line to the outside of the
car, closed the door and tested the slack. The
nylon line slid easily through the rubber seals
of the door.

Backing up in a crouch and leaving plenty of
slack in the line, he tied the loose end to the
trunk of a stout tree. He returned to the car and
slackened off all four bleed nipples to the braking

system. He stepped back, peeled off his gloves and stuffed them in the rucksack as he checked round to see that all looked in order.

'*Bon voyage!*' he said quietly as he turned and made his way back into the bushes to wait out the night.

Jennings emerged from the villa to set off for his appointment with North and Ted Hutchinson. He squinted at the brilliant sunlight and donned a pair of aviator sunglasses as he walked to his car and settled behind the wheel. He slipped the key into the ignition and was about to start up when he was startled by the appearance of a man beside his car. The door was flung open and he looked up into the face of Phillip Ross.

'What the fuck are you doing here, Ted?'

Phillip produced a long-bladed hunting knife, and held it against the astonished man's neck. 'My name's Ross, Phillip Ross,' he hissed. 'I'm here to cut your throat, you murdering scum.' He pressed the blade harder and grabbed Jennings's hair, forcing his head back.

'Wha . . . ? What the fuck are you on about?'

'It was my wife you and your scumbag mates killed on your getaway from the Croydon bank job.' Phillip grinned savagely. 'Did you think Billy's death was accident? Wrong, Roger, wrong. It wasn't an accident. I killed him. And now it's your turn.' He released Jennings's hair and stepped back. 'Get out of the car,' he snapped, and took another step backwards to let Jennings out. As he did so, he tripped over the low curb at the edge of the drive and landed on his backside. Snarling, he scrambled to his feet and lunged at Jennings with the knife.

Jennings was fast. He slammed the door shut and pressed the central locking button as he frantically twisted the key in the ignition. Phillip was at the car window banging on it with the knife and shouting with rage.

The engine roared into life. Jennings slammed the gear-selector to 'drive' and stamped on the accelerator as he released the handbrake. The big car lurched forward, its tyres squealing as they fought for grip. His foot hard down, Jennings threw the car into a right-hand turn as he reached the road. The rear wheels skidded round until the tyres gripped and the car straightened and flew down the hill towards the hairpin bend and T-junction at the bottom.

Jennings had thought he was as good as dead when Ted or Phillip Ross or whatever his bleeding name was had grabbed his hair and pressed that fucking great knife against his throat. His terror had turned to a mixture of disbelief and hope as the man had released him and stepped back, ordering him out of the car. And when he'd tripped and fallen, then scrambled to his feet, thrusting the wicked-looking knife against the car window, Jennings had seen his chance and grabbed it with both hands. And he'd made it, he'd got away from that fucking lunatic. Once he was safely holed up somewhere, he'd have to ring Jimmy at once and warn him that so-called dickhead Ted was fucking dangerous, that he'd

killed Billy, that he was out to kill them all. Christ!
What were they going to do?

He hadn't noticed the soft plunking noise of the
nylon line ripping through the soft rubber of the
condoms, as the car raced down the drive. The
carpet was flooding with petrol and filling the car
with fumes, but he had no time to think of that.
The Jaguar was hammering towards the hairpin
bend at over seventy miles an hour. Jennings lifted
his foot from the accelerator and pressed hard
on the brake pedal to check his speed. Nothing
happened. His foot hit the floor as the car surged
down the steep hill, propelled by its own weight
and momentum with the automatic choke full
on. He pumped frantically at the brake pedal,
slammed the gear-selector to 'low' and hauled
on the handbrake, fighting to bring the car under
control.

The cigar lighter clicked.

Jennings glanced down in time to see it, glowing brightly like a firebrand, jump out of its socket
and land on the wet carpet. A flash of ignition.
Whoof! Searing heat and pain as the petrol flared,
filling the interior of the car with flames. He
raised a hand to protect his face as he yanked at
the wheel in a futile attempt to make the bend.

The last few seconds of his life played out in
slow motion as the heavy car smashed through
the crash barrier and became airborne. Jennings
screamed in pain and terror. In the last seconds
of his life, he saw Ross trip and fall, giving him
the chance to escape, and realized how he'd been
tricked.

'You bastard! You fucking bastard!' he screamed as the car plummeted to the rocky valley below. It crumpled on impact and exploded in a massive fireball as the petrol tank ruptured.

With ice-cold satisfaction, Phillip watched a pall of black smoke rise from the valley floor. Two down, three to go, he said to himself as he turned and made his way back to his hired car.

Phillip shook hands with Jimmy North. 'Awfully sorry I'm late, old chap,' he said apologetically. 'I overslept a bit.'

'No problem, Ted.' North checked his watch. 'It's only ten forty-five, and anyway Roger ain't here yet. He's probably overslept too. He stays at the casino till the early hours if he's on a lucky streak and winning.' He ushered Phillip through to the terrace. 'Harry and Mike are here, so come and have a cold drink. There's no hurry.'

Half an hour later North tried to ring Jennings, but got no reply. He swore, and told the group they might as well go and take a look at the land site anyway. 'Roger can catch us up later,' he said as he led the three men to his car.

The four of them spent the next two hours inspecting the four-hundred-acre site. The roads and services had been installed by the previous developer before the proper planning consents had been granted. In the course of a long legal battle, the developer had gone into liquidation and the shareholders had lost their investment.

Phillip asked North all the relevant questions about the density of the site, current building costs per square metre, architects' and agents' fees. He listened intently to North's answers and looked suitably impressed as the man explained the massive profits involved in such a venture.

Phillip then changed his expression to one of concern as he asked, 'What about the risks involved? It all sounds too good to be true, Jimmy.'

North burst into a loud peal of laughter, gave him a reassuring slap on the back and slung his arm round his shoulders. The man was all friendship and camaraderie.

'There ain't no risk to this deal, Ted, mate,' he said enthusiastically. 'We can buy the whole site for only a fraction of its true value. Provided we bung the right people, I can guarantee we'll get planning permission.' He winked slyly and lied, 'It just so happens that the mayor is a personal friend of mine, likes a good drink and ain't averse to accepting a few bob in return for a favour. Well, what do you think, Ted? Do you want in?'

Phillip said, equally enthusiastically, 'Count me in on this one, Jimmy. I know a good thing when I see it and this is certainly a money-spinner. How much do you think we'll make?'

North rubbed the back of his neck thoughtfully. 'I haven't worked out the bottom line yet. It all depends on whether we just sell on and make a fast profit or develop the site ourselves. But whichever way we go, we're on a winner.' He grinned happily. 'I'll get my accountant to work out some projected figures on both angles and we can all sit round the table and make our decision then. The important thing is that we get it all tied up quickly before one of the big building firms gets to hear about it, or we'll end up paying a lot more for the site.'

'I'll have my share transferred to a local bank immediately,' said Phillip.

'Good,' said North heartily, with a surreptitious wink at Lambert and Turner. 'Our cash is either in place or on its way, so we're in a position to act fast the minute we get the green light.' He rubbed his hands together. 'Come on, lads, let's go home and have a nice cold beer.'

Phillip was lounging beside the swimming pool, sipping a cold Estrella and discussing the property deal when a distraught Anne Jennings rang.

Debby answered the call on the terrace extension, and it was soon clear that something was very wrong. Now she came running over, calling, 'Jimmy! Jimmy! Oh God, Jimmy, it's Roger. He's been killed in a car crash! It's Anne on the phone. She left her London number with her housekeeper like she always does, and the Lloret police have just rung her there to tell her. It can't be Roger. Oh God, it *can't*!'

North leapt to his feet in shock. 'I don't fucking believe it,' he groaned. He shook his head and repeated, 'I don't fucking believe it. First Billy, now Roger. All in a few days. Where, how? What the hell happened?'

'Anne's still on the phone. She wants to talk to you. She said the police will call round to see you.'

His back bowed, North walked heavily over to the phone and held a long, distressed conversation in which he assured Anne Jennings that he'd take care of everything and that he'd phone her back the minute he learnt all the details and confirmed that it really was Roger who'd been killed.

'He rang me this morning before he left home to meet you,' Anne sobbed. 'It must have been him.'

'Yeah. He didn't turn up, love, so we went to look at the site and left a message for him to catch us up. I thought he'd just made a night of it last night and overslept.'

Debby interrupted him. 'Jimmy, the police are here.'

North nodded acknowledgement and said into the phone, 'I've gotta go, Anne, love. The Bill are here now. I'll call you back when I've got any news. Bye for now, and I'm so sorry, Anne. I don't know what to say. Bye.'

He put the receiver down and leant against the wall for a moment, visibly trying to pull himself together. When he spoke his voice was flat and lifeless. 'Debby, you'd better take the Bill into the lounge and see if they want a drink or a coffee or something. I'll be with them in a minute.' North turned to Phillip. 'Sorry about all this, mate. I can't quite grasp it yet. I'll see what these geezers want, and I'll be with you in a tick. Help yourself to more beer or anything you want.'

Phillip thanked him and watched him go inside, shoulders slumped, eyes brimming with tears. He flipped the top of another beer and smiled as he looked across the bay.

Ten minutes later Debby joined him on the terrace. She sank into a lounger and gave a long, tearful sigh. 'I've been phoning round to let Jimmy's friends know about Roger. Some of them are coming straight over.' She reached with shaking hands for a handkerchief. 'Oh God, Ted, it's all too much. I can't imagine what Anne must feel like, comforting Cathy one moment, then finding herself in the same horrible position so soon afterwards. She adored Roger, idolized him. He was her whole life. And now he's gone.'

'Yes, I know exactly how she feels,' he said flatly. 'I suffered the same loss when my wife was killed in a motoring incident. I'll never get over it, never.'

North appeared, holding a large brandy glass filled to the brim. He took a swig from it as he crossed the terrace and leant heavily on the balustrade. 'He drove straight over a bloody cliff just a few hundred yards from his villa. The car burst into flames, burnt to a fucking cinder.' He stared blindly out across the bay. 'I asked to see the body, but they said I wouldn't recognize him. They wanted to know the name of his dentist. Said the only way to get a positive ID was from a dental X-ray.'

Phillip went over to join him, the image of sympathetic concern. 'Where did he have his teeth dealt with, in England or Spain?' he asked.

'In Lloret. We all use the same dentist, so it won't be long before they get an ID. The Bill are on their way to the dentist now to pick up Roger's X-rays.'

'Any other vehicle involved?' Phillip asked.

North shook his head. 'Not as far as they know. Anyway, no one's come forward.' His voice took on a vicious edge. 'If I found out that some bastard was involved and never even stopped to see if Roger was hurt or needed help, I'd kill him. I'd tear him apart with my bare hands.'

'Yes, I know exactly how you feel,' Phillip agreed. He looked down at the jagged rocks below and the sea swirling round them in a white froth. 'I know exactly how you feel,' he repeated.

By that evening the terrace was filled with friends who'd heard the bad news and come over to find out what had happened and share the sorrow. Phillip had already been introduced to most of them at the party and on the occasion of Billy's death. Harry Turner and Mike Lambert were among the crowd of shocked mourners. The mood was solemn and subdued as they formed little groups and stood or sat talking quietly.

Phillip studied Lambert and Turner. The two men were deep in a quiet but heated discussion. Phillip caught the odd word and watched their mouths form words. From what he could make out, they were not only upset by the deaths of their two friends but also angry that the gang had been depleted: if the big job North had promised cropped up, they'd be short-handed and unable to carry it out.

As he watched them, he felt his anger and

hatred renewed, and his resolve hardened, by their naked greed and self-interest. One of them would be the next to die (North, he had decided, would be the last), and die soon. But from now on he would have to be cautious and quick. The two seemingly accidental deaths had been accepted without question, but a third would cause concern and possibly panic – certainly suspicion. Deep in thought, he strolled to the edge of the terrace and looked down at the bay. The sea was now inky black and reflected the moonlight and the lights from the nearby harbour.

A hand placed gently on his arm startled him out of his reverie.

Debby looked pale and drawn. She smiled weakly as she spoke. 'It's been quite a night – in fact, it's been quite a week. Like a nightmare that doesn't end when you wake up.'

Phillip put a comforting arm round her shoulders. 'Yes, troubles seem to come all at once.' He felt a pang of regret and guilt as they stood silently looking out over the bay to the horizon, where an ocean liner stood out against the skyline, its lights twinkling in the distance. He was using this young woman to get closer to North, and at the same time causing her grief by his acts of retribution. He was certain that North was using Debby in the same way, to draw him into the web. But there was an open innocence in her demeanour. Either she was a very good actor, which could well be the case, or she genuinely liked him.

He derived no satisfaction from the knowledge that she would end up hurt, whichever was the

case. The fact that Julie was dead had not stopped
Phillip loving her, and he knew he never would.

Debby snuggled closer and let out a long sigh
as she relaxed against him. Phillip glanced down
at her and brushed a wisp of hair away from her
eyes. She smiled up at him and said, 'I'm glad
you're here, Ted.' She hesitated, as if searching
for the right words, but before she could speak,
North joined them.

His eyes were red-rimmed and looked sore. 'I'm
sorry about all this, Ted. It takes quite a bit to
shake me up, but losing two good mates in one
week . . .' His voice trailed away.

Phillip smiled inwardly.

'You couldn't have turned up at a worse time,
mate,' North went on. He managed to crack a
half-smile. 'But don't judge us by all this. We're
usually a carefree, happy bunch.'

Phillip patted him on the shoulder. 'Don't even
think about it, Jimmy. I understand perfectly. It
must be terrible what you're going through, and
I think you're holding up superbly, old chap,
superbly.'

More visitors arrived and North went over to
greet them.

Debby was staring intently at Phillip, a puzzled
frown on her face.

'Penny for your thoughts,' he offered, smiling.

She smiled back and said, 'Oh, nothing much.
It's just that, like I said, I'm sure I've met you
before somewhere. You know what it's like when
you can't quite remember something – it's driving

me crazy trying to place you or remember where I've seen you.'

Phillip laughed to cover his concern. He thought rapidly, but could come up with not one place or occasion when they could possibly have met. 'You also said it's probably just that I remind you of someone else. I certainly wouldn't have forgotten meeting a girl as good-looking as you.'

Debby shrugged and said, 'Oh, I expect I'm mistaken. Anyway, if I have met you before it'll come back to me. It always does.' She glanced over at North, who was talking to the new arrivals. 'I'd better go and say hello and get them drinks.' She started to move away, but then swung back and looked imploringly into Phillip's eyes. 'Please stay with me tonight, Ted, I can't face the thought of being alone. If you don't want stay here again, we can go back to your hotel – whatever you like. Just, please, say you'll let me be with you.'

Phillip smiled down at her and saw her face lighten in relief as he said, 'I'd like that.'

As he watched her greet the new arrivals, hugging them and kissing them on both cheeks, he racked his brains again over where Debby might have seen him. He was pleased that she wanted to be with him that night. From now on he intended to stay very close to her, just in case she had a sudden return of memory.

He walked over to join Turner and Lambert, who were now talking quietly together in a corner of the terrace. Time was almost up for one of them, and he had to decide which to slot first.

*　　*　　*

North held open the lounge door and ushered in the two remaining members of his gang. He closed the door securely and seated himself in a white leather armchair. Turner and Lambert sat opposite on a matching sofa. Sunlight beamed through the picture windows that looked out across the curve of the bay to the cliffs beyond.

'I've called this meeting, lads, because we've got serious problems. The deaths of Billy and Roger aren't only a great personal loss to all of us. They've also put us out of business. And now, on top of that, I've got to tell you that Delta One wants out.' He paused to let the news sink in. 'So we're three down, not two, and we can't do a sodding thing until we've replaced them all.'

'Delta One wants out?' Lambert was amazed. 'Why?'

North shrugged. 'Ain't been the same since the Croydon job. Seeing the guard shot and those people the Jag hit and that bird laying dead in the road is what's done it. Been having nightmares about it.'

'Fuck me!' exclaimed Turner. 'It was bad enough to have to find replacements for Billy and Roger. Now we need a fucking lookout as well. Can't you make Delta One change his mind?'

'I've had a call from my snout about another blag,' said North. 'Says it's worth four or five hundred grand at least.' He grinned fiercely. 'We need to do every job we can, while we can get the inside information, 'cos it won't bleeding last for ever. Our bloke's been getting a bad time from the Bill. He's stood up to it OK so far, but it sounds like he may be getting a bit nervous. Richards from the robbery squad has been leaning on him heavy. Keeps telling him he knows it's him involved and when he gets the evidence he's on a murder charge and facing thirty years, unless he spills the beans now and does a deal for four or five years and be out in two.'

'He's a lying cunt, that Richards,' snapped Turner. 'It's up to a fucking judge to decide who gets what and how long. Richards can't promise fuck all.'

'I've told my snout that, just to stop him even thinking about it,' North said viciously. 'I've also told him it ain't the police he's got to worry about or how long he'll serve in prison if he grasses. It's a case of how long he's got to live.'

'Let's do one more job, and then have him shut up for good just in case he cracks,' suggested Turner. 'You can never trust a bloke that's been honest all his life not to crack and grass everyone to save his own precious skin.'

'Can't the three of us do one last job, if we can talk Delta One into it?' asked Lambert.

'What, just two of us in a bank to control both sides of the counter, while you sit in the fucking car?' North shook his head. 'Five hundred grand means it's a big branch, with lots of staff and fuck knows how many customers. We've got to be five up, plus a lookout.'

Turner agreed. 'If you're the only one, public or staff side of the counter, some dickhead will get all brave and play the fucking have-a-go hero, but if four of us are screaming our fucking heads off and letting rip at the ceiling and the cameras with shotguns, no one ever gives it a thought. They're too busy being shit-scared, and keeping their heads down and doing like they're told.'

'We've got to get back up to full strength,' said North. 'Delta One will be here soon. You boys are about to discover who it is.' He laughed softly at their puzzled expressions. 'Perhaps you can put the pressure on. There's no better person for the job – knows exactly what to look out for, don't attract any attention from anybody. No one's ever suspected Delta One of being involved in anything. Not even the Old Bill has caught on.'

He grinned mockingly. The two men looked questioningly at each other and shrugged in bafflement. North turned serious. 'I would never have told you if it weren't for the fact that we need them to do at least one more job. Give us time to find a replacement.' He threw up his hands in exasperation. 'I ain't been able to talk 'em round. Maybe you boys can. Oh, and by the way there's something else. Tony Pacetti phoned me from Miami. He's flying to London for a few days, then coming down to Marbella. He's got a problem. Someone's ripping him off, nicking his gear, or providing the information to some of the toerags in Marbella so they can do it. He ain't got a clue who it is, but he reckons it could well be one of his own boys so he can't trust anyone of his own to sort it. He wants someone from outside, so he's asked me to take a couple of boys that ain't

known on the Costa del Sol to have a sniff round
to see who's crossing him.'

'What's his problem, Jimmy?' asked Lambert.

'Two big consignments of resin from Morocco
have gone walkies, and, like I said, Pacetti thinks
it could be one of his own boys that's at it. He's
mighty pissed off, I might tell you. Said he'd pay
us really well if we could sort it.'

'What about Ted the toff?' asked Turner. 'He's
got half a million quid on its way here. I thought
we was going to nick it off him.'

'We are,' said North. 'I've put Pacetti off for a
bit, said we was busy on a nice little tickle. I
told him we'd get there as soon as we could.
He said there was no hurry, but the sooner the
better.' He held up his hands in frustration. 'It
comes either all at once or not at all, and here
we are short-handed.' He thought for a moment
or two. 'If we can nick Ted the toff's cash, then
nip down to Marbella and sort Pacetti's problem
out, perhaps we'll meet up with some of the guys,
and if they've got a good pedigree, we can sign 'em
up for the bank job.'

There was a knock at the door and it opened.
Debby came in, carrying a tray of cold beers. 'I
thought you boys might be thirsty,' she said.

North laughed and said, 'We've just been talking about you. Come and sit down. Harry and
Mike want a word with you, Delta One.'

Turner and Lambert's mouths fell open in
astonishment.

Lambert swung round to North. '*She's* Delta
One?' he demanded.

North smiled and accepted a cup of coffee from Debby. 'I told you you wouldn't believe who it was. This young lady is the best lookout in the business, ain't you, Delta One?'

Chapter Six

It was just after midnight when Harry Turner got back to his villa and climbed wearily into bed. He had phoned his wife, Laura, from North's villa after the meeting; all three men had spoken to their wives and asked after Anne and Cathy, whom they were comforting.

Turner tossed and turned for ages, unable to sleep. He missed Laura lying beside him. It was a depressing time for all of them: Billy and Roger had been good friends for many years. No one had come to terms with their sudden deaths. It would take a long time.

At two a.m. he checked the time and reached for his sleeping pills. He swallowed two and lay back to await the sleep that had eluded him. His mind was troubled. Nothing had gone right since the Croydon bank job. All the gang's previous blags had gone smoothly, with no injuries, let alone fatalities. It had seemed that they had the perfect MO and the perfect team to carry out the raids.

Now two of them were dead and Delta One had dropped out. The three men had tried for ages to talk her round, until it finally got through to them that she had made up her mind and was going to stick to her decision. The thrill and excitement of being a bank robber and an important part of the team had been swept away with the shooting of the guard, the death of the young woman and the injuries to the other pedestrians. She couldn't take any more, no matter how much money was involved. She was having nightmares, endlessly reliving the violence and death. She wanted to forget that it had ever happened, or that she had been part of it. 'I block it from my mind,' she'd said. 'I can't allow myself to think about it or I'd go mad.'

The three men had accepted her word that she would never let them down or speak to anyone about her involvement. She was from the East End. She'd been brought up from babyhood not to tell tales, and never under any circumstances to grass to the Old Bill. Grasses were hated and reviled, almost as much as nonsense merchants.

Turner woke with a start from a deep sleep. He peered into the darkness, wondering what had disturbed him. He tried to move his arms but couldn't. He felt with his fingers and sat up in alarm. His hands had been tied together in front of him.

He looked up and in the darkness could dimly see the tall silhouette of a man standing at the foot of his bed.

'What the fuck? Who the fuck are you?' he demanded as he attempted to break the binding.

'You're staring death in the face,' answered Phillip.

'Ted? *Ted*?'

'Ross. My name is Phillip Ross.'

'I don't understand.'

'I'm here to kill you, Harry.'

'Kill me? What the fuck for? I don't even know you. I never set eyes on you till Jimmy's party.'

'That's correct, but you met my wife. You bumped into her in Croydon.'

'Croydon?' A puzzled frown.

'Yes, Croydon. The day of the bank robbery.'

'Oh no!' Realization dawned on Turner as he remembered the blonde bird they'd knocked down during their getaway. The television news had said she'd died and named her as – oh Christ!

Turner swallowed hard. 'Listen, Ross, it was an accident. And anyway I wasn't driving the fucking car.'

'Neither was Billy or Roger.'

Turner's mouth fell open. 'Billy and Roger? You mean . . . it wasn't . . . you *killed* them?' His eyes flicked round the darkened room as he searched for something to say that might save him.

'They both knew it was me before they died. Before I killed them,' said Phillip unemotionally. 'I wanted them to know why they were dying.'

Turner started to panic. 'Look, Ross, isn't there anything I can do, anything I can say? We didn't mean to hurt anyone.'

'Nothing.' Phillip tossed a loop of nylon rope over Turner's head and snapped the noose tight, jerking the man's head sideways.

'You ain't going to hang me?' His voice trembled.

'Hanging's too good for scum like you,' said Phillip icily, 'but it will have to do. You're feeling so bad about Billy and Roger's deaths that you're going to commit suicide.'

'No one will believe it. I ain't the type.'

'The Spanish police will believe it, Harry. As for North and Lambert, they don't count. They'll both be dead before they can find out what really happened.'

Phillip stepped to one side and pulled on the rope. Turner tumbled out of bed, naked. He scrambled on to his hands and knees and tensed himself to charge Phillip, head-butt him and bash him with his balled fists. He was desperate, he had to try. He launched himself head first into the attack. Phillip stepped nimbly aside and met the man's charge with a roundhouse kick to the ribs. Turner gagged as the wind was violently expelled from his lungs, and collapsed to the floor, fighting for breath.

'Not even a good try, Harry,' said Phillip contemptuously. He tugged on the rope. 'Get up. It's time to die.'

Turner struggled to his feet, his face twisted in pain and hatred. 'You bastard, Ross! Jimmy and Mike will fucking kill you for this.'

'Better men than them have tried and failed. I'm not easy to kill. Now get outside.' He nodded towards the French windows that led to the balcony and yanked hard on the rope.

Turner lurched to keep his balance and dragged

slowly to the door. His legs felt wobbly, he felt sick, he didn't want to die. It all seemed unreal, a terrifying nightmare. He opened the door and stepped out into the cool night air. Fingers of light stabbed into the sky from the east as the sun promised to show itself over the horizon. 'It's going to be a nice day,' he whispered quietly to himself: he realized he wouldn't be alive to enjoy it.

The balcony faced south under an overhanging roof. To one side were two white plastic chairs and a small table. Phillip moved one of the chairs until it was directly under a stout timber rafter. He threw the free end of the rope over the rafter and stood back, drawing on the rope to take up the slack.

'Turn round,' he ordered.

Turner turned to face the man who was about to kill him. He could see Phillip's face now. It was no longer the idiotic grinning face he'd become accustomed to over the past few days, but hard, pitiless, the face of a driven man. 'You sucked us all in. Made us all think you was a complete prat, with millions.'

Phillip smiled coldly. 'Greed is a deadly sin.' He gave an encouraging tug on the rope. 'Now get up on that chair.'

Turner resisted. 'Look, hang on a minute, there's got to be another way. I had fuck all to do with your wife's death, I was only a passenger in the bloody car. I'm sorry, Ross. I felt terrible about it.'

'Too late for all that, Harry, and I can assure you that you didn't feel half as bad as I did.'

He pulled on the rope. Turner staggered towards the chair.

'No one will believe I topped myself,' he said wildly as the rope tightened.

'They'll believe you're dead. That's all that matters to me. Now you can climb up or be hauled up. Take your choice.'

His legs shaking, Turner climbed on to the chair. 'You can't do this,' he said, his voice cracking in desperation. 'You can't just kill me.'

'Oh yes I can, Harry, just as easily as you killed my wife.' Phillip tied the free end of the rope to the wrought-iron railing of the balcony, leaving a little slack, and produced a knife from his waist. The long thin blade gleamed balefully in the dawn light. Keeping to one side, he cut the soft bandages binding Turner's wrists and slipped them into his pocket. Turner rubbed his wrists. He was a pathetic sight standing there naked with the rope round his neck.

'You thought you'd got away with murdering my wife and injuring all those other people. You thought that out here, where the British police can't touch you, you'd be safe. You thought you were safe from justice.' There was raw hatred in Phillip's voice. 'Well, here's your justice, Harry Turner.' He kicked the chair from under Turner's feet, and it skidded across the balcony. Turner screamed, but his scream was abruptly cut off as the rope snapped taut and bit into his neck. The stricken man kicked in the air, clawing frantically at the rope as his eyes bulged and his tongue protruded from his mouth. Then, with a final gargling moan, he went limp. He hung there, twisting slowly in the light of the rising sun. All that broke the silence was a splattering as his bladder and bowels voided themselves and the contents trickled on to the ceramic floor.

Three down, two to go, Phillip told himself as he turned and made for the door.

Turner's housemaid discovered the body just after nine that morning. She ran hysterically into the street. Three hours later two senior police officers were banging on Jimmy North's door.

North's shock and grief turned to misgivings and self-concern when one of the policemen asked, 'Señor North, do you and your colleagues have enemies capable of crimes such as these?'

'What? What the hell are you getting at? What are you telling me?' North was astounded.

The policeman shrugged. 'Well, one fatal accident, a simple drowning, is not surprising – these things happen. Then Señor Jennings's car goes over a cliff. A coincidence, yes? And now we have an apparent suicide. All three men are connected. They are friends, they work together.' He shook his head. 'Possible, but unlikely.'

'Are you telling me that my mates have been murdered?' demanded North.

The policeman shrugged again, and opened his hands, palms up. 'I am telling you nothing, señor. I am simply making comments and asking questions as they enter my mind.' He paused, and stared hard-eyed at North. 'We are aware that the British police are most interested in you and your colleagues,' he said evenly. 'You have committed no known crimes in España, so we are not that concerned for the moment, but it has now crossed my mind that these deaths, the deaths of your friends, may be connected in some way with your activities in other countries.'

North dropped his head into his hands and thought it through. He looked up. 'Have you found evidence of foul play?' he asked. 'Do you believe they were murdered?'

The policeman flicked his hand dismissively. 'No evidence, only a suspicion that there may be more to this than meets the eye.'

North said, 'You could be right. Harry Turner wouldn't have topped himself. He was really upset about Billy and Roger – we all are, we're gutted – but never in a million years would Harry have hung himself. He had too much to live for. Lovely wife, money in the bank, nice home. And besides all that, he was a tough, hard-minded bastard.' He shook his head emphatically. 'No way.'

'Well, we shall see about that. We have special investigators on their way from Barcelona to look into the affair. We must wait for their conclusions. Until then we can only treat the affair as a simple suicide.'

After asking about North's whereabouts and movements during the previous several days, the policemen departed.

North immediately rang Mike Lambert. 'Get the fuck over here,' he yelled. 'Harry was found hanging on his balcony this morning. He's dead.' There was a gasp of astonishment from Lambert.

North continued, 'It was made to look like suicide, but the police aren't buying that. They think Billy, Roger and Harry might have been murdered.' He slammed the phone down.

Fifteen minutes later Lambert was knocking on the door.

'This is very worrying, Jimmy, very worrying indeed.' Lambert's hatchet face showed no emotion as he spoke, but his deep-set eyes darted from place to place. 'No way would Harry have hung himself.'

'If someone has bumped 'em off, we must be next on the fucking list – that's what's worrying me at the moment, Mike. Now we've got to find out who it is, and do the fuckers.'

The two men made their way to the terrace, talking as they went. North grabbed two beers from the fridge and handed one to Lambert.

'But who the fuck could it be? Who the fuck have we upset enough for them to send a hit squad after us?' He scratched his chin as he ran through a mental list of possibles. 'Not the banks or the British police, surely? And the Spanish government might be up to it, but they've got no cause: we've kept our noses clean over here.'

'No, we ain't terrorists or anything like that. Governments only go after terrorists like this. They gun 'em down, and make an example of 'em.' North shook his head adamantly. 'No, if someone's out to get us, if the others *have* been topped, it's personal. Only villains take the law into their own hands like this.'

The two men slumped into sun loungers and

stared out to sea as they swigged their beer and searched their memories for the villains they had crossed over the years.

'What about Barry Mead?' asked Lambert. 'We slipped it up him good and proper. Done him up like a kipper, and he got fifteen years into the bargain.' He thought for a moment. 'That was eight years ago, so if he was a good boy while he was inside, he'd be out and about by now.'

'Nah,' said North. 'Last I heard, he was a wreck. Had boiling fat chucked in his face, for trying to fuck one of the young lads in the shower at Parkhurst. I don't think we even have to consider him. Besides, he had a lot of bunny when he was surrounded by hard cases, but no bottle on his own.'

'I never heard about the boiling fat.' Lambert screwed up his face in mock sympathy. 'I bet that made his eyes water a bit.'

North said, chuckling, 'Turned him right off sex for a while. They put him in with the nonses under rule forty-three, but none of 'em fancied him with his face and hands all scarred and fucked up like that.'

Lambert brightened as a thought struck him. 'How about Kevin Seymour? He was mouthing off about getting even over that currency scam. Reckoned he should have had a share in it, because it was his idea.'

North grinned. 'Yeah, it was his idea, but we did it. He only mouthed off about it.'

'He went stark staring bonkers when he found

out Billy'd been shafting his bird. He swore he'd
kill him for it.'

North dismissed the idea. 'No, if he was going
to do anything about it, he'd have done it long ago.
Besides, it ain't his style. He's a sawn-off-shotgun
merchant, or else he'd bash your brains in with
a baseball bat when you had your back turned.
He ain't clever enough to operate the way this
bastard does.'

The two men thought deeply for a while.
Then North asked, 'Have you seen anything suspicious? Anyone hanging around, or following
you?'

'No, nothing like that. Why?'

'Well, whoever it is must be pretty fucking close
to us. They must spend a bit of time planning
and sorting it all out.' He chewed nervously at
his thumbnail. 'They knew exactly where to find
Billy and Roger and now Harry. Whoever it is also
knew when and where they'd be on their own.' He
took a long swig at his beer and lit a cigarette. He
blew the smoke out slowly and said thoughtfully,
'New faces. What new faces have appeared on the
scene?'

'What about Ted the toff? He's the only new
bloke around.'

North considered the idea for a moment, then
his face cleared and he grinned. 'Don't be fucking
stupid, mate! The man's a complete prat, a total
wally. He couldn't kill a bleeding spider.'

'He's a fit-looking bastard,' persisted Lambert.
'Looks like he could handle himself.'

'Yes, I know that. So he plays a lot of tennis and

squash. But he's a public-school toff, educated and all that, and he ain't a killer, he ain't the type. He probably ain't never had a fight in his life, would bottle out, run a mile at the first sign of trouble.'

'Why don't you have a word with Debby? She's been bonking him, spent more time than anyone else with him.' He looked back at the villa. 'Where is she, anyway?'

'Went to the market this morning. She don't know about Harry yet.' North looked at his watch. 'Should be back soon.' He stared down at his hands for a moment, then said, 'I've got some phoning to do. I've got to tell Laura that her old man's dead. I ain't looking forward to that. The women will wonder what the fuck is going on. Anne and Laura went off to England to take care of Cathy and help her bury Billy. Now all three of them are bloody widows. I can't believe it's all happening. It's like something out of a fucking horror film.'

'Are you going to tell the girls that the lads may have been murdered?' asked Lambert.

'No, not yet, not until it's been proved. I don't want to scare the pants off Wendy and your Amy. It'd worry them to death and they'd be back here like a shot. If there is any danger, I want the women left out of it.' North climbed out of his chair. 'I'm going to phone from the lounge. Let me know when Debby gets back. I need to talk to her.' He disappeared inside the villa, leaving Lambert deep in thought.

Debby arrived fifteen minutes later. Lambert

helped her unload several bags of shopping from her car and carried them into the kitchen. 'Jimmy's in the lounge. He wants a word.'

'What about? I'm not going on any more blags,' she said defiantly.

'No, it's not about that.' He hesitated. 'Jimmy'd better tell you himself. I'll go and tell him you're here.'

As he went out, Debby called after him, 'I've bought some cream cakes. I'll make a pot of tea and come and join you.'

She switched on the kettle and began to lay the tray, wondering with a touch of anxiety what North wanted. When she joined the two men in the lounge, North waited for her to pour out the tea and sit down before he spoke.

'Harry's dead.'

'*What*?' Debby was stunned. She sat and stared at North in disbelieving horror.

'He's dead, love. He hung himself. Or at least he was found hanging on his balcony at home. They found him this morning. The police have already been here.'

'It's bad karma,' she whispered. 'Nothing's gone right since the Croydon job. We're all paying for it now.'

'What the fuck are you on about?' asked Lambert angrily.

She looked at him, her face white and strained. 'It's all happening to us because of what we did to those people in Croydon. Shooting the guard, and injuring those others, and killing that young mother.' Her voice rose high in her distress. 'She had a baby, and we killed her, so we're all paying for it now. It's God's way of paying us back.'

'Oh, don't be fucking stupid!' Lambert snapped. 'Someone might be killing us. But it ain't God, that's for sure.'

'What do you mean, someone might be killing us?' she asked nervously.

The two men exchanged glances. North answered her. 'The police think there's something fishy about three of us dying all of a sudden like. They're looking into it.'

'Oh my God!' Debby breathed. 'Not Billy and Roger?'

'We don't know for sure,' said North. 'But it's all a bit suspicious, so we've got to look out for ourselves, just in case there's some bleeding maniac out there knocking us off, one by fucking one.'

'But who? Who would do that?' Debby sounded as scared as she looked.

'We've been discussing that,' said Lambert. 'We ain't got a clue, really. The only strange face around here lately is Ted Hutchinson. Jimmy don't think it's him, but I ain't too sure. What do you think, Debby? Could it be him? What do you make of him? You know him better than we do. You've been screwing the geezer.'

'Ted? No, he's too kind. He's too silly.' Her expression changed to an irritated frown. 'I'm sure I've seen him before somewhere, though.'

'What?' North jumped out of his chair. 'You've seen him before? Where the fuck was it? When? Come on, girl, spit it out!'

'I don't know. I'm not sure. I just have this

feeling in the back of my mind that I've met him somewhere, that's all. It's been driving me crazy trying to remember.'

'Well think, for Christ's sake. This could be important, you stupid cow!' shouted North.

'It could have been years ago, for all I know,' she said defensively. 'I might be wrong, I could be mixing him up with someone else. Oh, I just don't *know*.'

North sat down again. 'Well keep thinking on it, love, because if it's him, I'm gonna rip his bleeding heart out. Tell you what, I'll invite him over and we'll all get to work on him. I'll tell him I want to discuss the property deal and I need to see some bank documents to prove he's transferred the cash. I'll tell him that I've been asked for references by the people selling the land and that they want to know who they're dealing with and we've gotta prove we've got the cash available for an immediate purchase. If Ted fucking Hutchinson can't prove he's who he says he is' – he clenched his fists – 'he's fucking dead.'

'Spring it on him that Harry's dead,' suggested Lambert, 'and we'll all watch his reaction. If he don't react convincingly, I say we kill him there and then.'

Debby leapt to her feet. 'Don't you kill him while I'm around!' she shouted. 'I don't want any part of it. I can't take it. I've seen enough blood to last me a lifetime. I can't stop seeing that security guard shot down and that poor woman laying dead in her husband's arms – oh my God!'

She buried her face in her hands and said, almost inaudibly, 'Oh Christ, it's him, it's her husband. That's where I've seen him.'

'Whose husband? Seen who?'

Debby didn't answer.

North lunged at her, grabbed her by one shoulder and slapped her face hard. 'What the fuck are you on about?'

'It's him, it's Ted. I saw him in Croydon. That woman, the one who was killed, he was with her, he was holding her in his arms as she died. His face was half hidden in her hair, that's why I couldn't place him before. But I just got a flashback. The black hair and the angle of his chin and the set of his shoulders. It's him, I swear it's him.'

North let her go and turned to Lambert. 'So that's what it's all about. We killed his wife, and he's come after us. All of us.'

'Yeah, and he's already done three of us. We'd have been next, Jimmy. Thank fuck Debby remembered the geezer.'

'What about me?' asked Debby fearfully. 'He'll kill me as well.'

'He ain't going to kill anyone, darling,' said North. 'It's his turn now. His fucking card's marked.' He studied her thoughtfully. 'He don't know about you, that you're part of the gang. He wouldn't have fucked you, not if he intended to kill you.'

'I was really getting to like him.' Debby was close to tears. A thought struck her abruptly and she said, 'He even told me his wife was killed in

a car accident. I never put two and two together.
Well, I had no idea. Billy and Roger, it looked like
they had both died accidentally.'

North slumped back into his chair. 'This is one
hard-minded bastard we're dealing with. He ain't
the wanker he made himself out to be, not by a
long chalk he ain't. For him to track us down and
then waltz in here and calmly bump us off one
by one, look into our eyes and smile, while all
the time he's planning to kill us . . . This is one
hard sonofabitch. Yeah, and come to think of it,
how the fuck *did* he track us down? How did he
know it was us, and how did he find us?'

'He can't be on his own, can he?' said Lambert.

'No, he ain't doing all this on his own.' North's
forehead wrinkled as he thought. 'That's a bit
worrying. It might not be just a case of knocking
him off, and forgetting it. There could be more
than him down here. He could have some help.'
He sat forward in his chair. 'We've got to play
this carefully, think it all out before we just leap
in and kill him. We've got to find out if there's
anyone helping him. Someone's put him on to
us. We need to know who, and why.'

'I say we kill him first and worry about the rest
later,' said Lambert. 'He might come leaping over
that fucking wall in five minutes and shoot the
lot of us, for all we know.'

North shook his head. 'No, not while Debby's
here. He don't know she's involved, I'm certain
of that. If even you and the others didn't know
she was Delta One till I told you, no one else

knows, that's dead sure. It's been our best-kept
secret, one of the main reasons we've never been
caught on the hop.' He looked across at Debby
and smiled. 'She ain't a known bank robber,
and no one suspects a woman of casing a bank
and being a lookout. So we've never walked
into a trap, like so many others have done.'
He stood up. 'Get Dave Taylor on the blower.
He's from south London, works down Croydon
way. He always knows what's going on, or can
find out. He owes us a favour for putting him
on to that post-office blag. Him and his mate
made thirty grand out of that. See if he knows
anything about the woman who was killed in
Croydon, and find out what you can about her
husband.'

'He's bound to ask why we want to know,' said
Lambert.

'Tell him you just found out about it and
think you know the husband.' North smiled
unpleasantly. 'Tell him you want to send your
condolences.'

Lambert picked up the phone and dialled
from memory. He spoke for several minute and
replaced the receiver. 'He's going to phone back.
Says he knows someone on the *Croydon Advertiser*. They did a big piece on the robbery and the
woman getting killed. He asked if it was us. I told
him not to be so fucking silly and to be careful
what he says.'

'Good,' said North. He picked up one of the
cakes and bit into it. 'Make us another pot of tea,
Debs. There ain't much we can do till Dave rings

back and we know a bit more about what we're up against.'

Two hours later the phone rang. Lambert snatched up the receiver.

'I've had a bit of luck, said Taylor. 'My contact at the *Croydon Advertiser* actually covered the story. It was a bad business. The woman's name was Julie Ross. She was married and had a kid. Her husband was burnt out of business and his partner murdered by Frank Chalmers and his boys over a year ago. But rumour has it that they came a bit unstuck. Ross is ex-SAS. Some people reckon he killed the whole gang. Anyway, Chalmers and eleven of his men are dead and buried. This Ross bloke was a war hero. He won a medal in the Falklands war for charging and knocking out Argie machine-gun posts. Some people say if it was him that done Chalmers and his boys he should get another medal. How's Jimmy, by the way?'

'He's fine. Thanks, Dave. I'll talk to you later.' Lambert dropped the handset back into its cradle. He was as white as a ghost as he turned and relayed Taylor's words to North, who listened in deathly silence.

'That's all I fucking needed to hear,' said North finally. 'Sounds like we're in a bit of trouble, specially if he's got some of his mates with him.'

'What're we going to do now, just sit here and wait for him?'

'Are we, bollocks!' North jumped up. 'We need to get the fuck out of here and have a bit of time to reorganize, get some bodies round us as protection. There could be a whole fucking squad of SAS men planning to come after us.'

'Where we gonna go?' asked Lambert.

'First stop, Marbella. We can get tooled up there, and Pacetti's got a lot of muscle round him. He asked us to go down and help him, so he's expecting us to turn up.'

'He won't be very happy if we involve him in all this,' said Lambert.

'We don't necessarily have to tell him, do we? Besides, Ross won't have a clue where we've gone, and by the time he finds out we'll have moved on.'

'What about Wendy and Amy? They'll be worried sick.'

'Better than being widows like the other poor cows,' said North. 'We'll tell them a big job's cropped up and we've gotta move fast. We'll explain it all later. Come on, let's sling a few things in the Porsche and get the fuck out of here.' He turned to Debby, who had sat silent, as though in a daze, as she listened to the two men. 'Debby, you stay here and act dumb,' he ordered. 'I want you to throw Ted, or Ross, or whatever his fucking name is, off the scent. Send him on a wild-goose chase. Tell him that we've decided to go to the funerals after all and that we'll be in London for at least a week, maybe two.' He glanced across to Lambert. 'If he turns up in the East End, there'll be plenty of volunteers to knock him off, after what he's done to Billy, Roger and Harry.' He turned back to Debby. 'Did he say when he'd see you again?'

Debby nodded. 'He said he was spending the
day in Barcelona. He's got to go to the bank
and then he's going to look at another villa. He
said he'd call round for a drink about nine this
evening.'

'Lying bastard could be out there watching us
right now,' said Lambert uneasily.

North nodded. 'Yeah, we leave here empty-
handed, like we was just popping into town for
a drink. We can buy all we need on the journey,
or when we get to Marbella. We'd better get off
now. And Debby, I'm relying on you to put Ross
off the scent and give us a bit of time to get
organized.' He stared menacingly at her. 'So play
him along, right? Don't give him any clues about
what's really happening, or I'll be fucking angry.
You get my point, girl?'

Debby nodded. Yeah, she thought, fuck off and
leave me to face the man, all on my own. Aloud,
she said obediently, 'I'll take care of it Jimmy. Be
careful, won't you?'

North's expression softened and he stepped
forward and kissed her on the cheek. 'You can
do it, Debs, can't you?'

She nodded and forced a smile. 'I can do it. Go,
now, before it's too late.'

The two men hurried from the room, leaving
Debby with tears of worry and fear in her eyes.
To wait for Phillip Ross.

Chapter Seven

Several of North's friends called at the villa during the early evening. The news of Harry Turner's suicide had spread through the small British community at the usual wildfire speed. Debby spoke to them at the door, explaining that North had gone to London and would be away for at least a week.

The visitor she dreaded turned up promptly at nine. Phillip rang the bell and waited. Debby opened the door and stepped back to let him inside. Unsmiling, she turned and walked into the kitchen, where the kettle was boiling. Phillip followed her through.

'I'm making tea,' she said, avoiding eye contact. 'Would you like a cup, or would you sooner have a beer?'

'Tea will be fine, thanks. Is Jimmy at home? The Porsche isn't in the drive, I noticed.'

'No, Jimmy took it. He's gone to London.'

'Why didn't he fly? It's much easier — and quicker.'

'He's dead scared of flying. That's why he lives

in this part of Spain. He can drive from here to
Calais in ten hours. Jimmy wouldn't get on an
aeroplane to save his life.' Her mouth twisted
as she realized the irony of what she'd just said.
She still didn't look at Phillip, but concentrated
hard on keeping her hands steady as she poured
tea into two bone-china cups. 'Have you heard
about Harry?'

Phillip watched her closely as he said, 'Yes, it's
awful, isn't it? I didn't think he was the type.'

'He wasn't. At least we didn't think he was.'
She turned to face him at last and handed him a
cup of tea, which rattled in its saucer.

'You're shaking, Debby. What's wrong?' Phillip
set the cup down and put an arm comfortingly
round her shoulders. Debby flinched at his touch
and looked into his eyes only fleetingly before
turning quickly away.

'What's wrong?' he asked again. 'You're acting
like a frightened rabbit.'

She buried her face in her hands and started to
sob, her shoulder heaving. 'You're damn right I'm
frightened. That's three of us dead. I can't take
all this.'

Phillip gently removed her hands from her face,
crooked a finger under her chin and tilted her
face up to his. He knew something serious was
up: it was clear that she was afraid of him, and
North had made a sudden and hasty exit. He bent
his head and kissed her gently on the lips. She
responded by throwing her arms round him and
holding him tightly as she returned his kiss with
a desperate urgency.

She had been brought up with hard, dangerous men and in that world successful villains were glamorous, powerful and exciting. She'd slept with some of them, and the knowledge of what they were like gave her a thrill not unlike the excitement she'd felt when doing a blag. The man now in her arms was not the grinning idiot he'd pretended to be. He was a killer, a man not afraid to take the ultimate revenge on those responsible for the death of his wife – and she was one of those people. She was afraid, but at the same time she wanted him, wanted him to take her as ruthlessly as he had before. Her desire rose as she clung to him, kissed him and explored his mouth with her tongue. She felt his response, pulled away and led him by the hand silently to the bedroom they had shared. Phillip knew this was not the time to ask questions. He'd get more out of her after he'd satisfied her desire.

Without a word, they both stripped naked and slipped under the top sheet. At once, trembling with mingled excitement and nerves, Debby began to stroke Phillip's chest and belly, pressing her groin against his, feeling his cock pulsate and expand as she slowly rubbed its length in the wetness between her legs. She slid down under the sheet and took him in her mouth, caressing him with her lips and tongue as she knew he liked. When she judged he was close to orgasm, she wriggled up to the head of the bed and stretched out to grip the sides of the headboard, face down and raised on to her knees. 'Take me from behind,' she said huskily.

Phillip knelt behind her, spread her buttocks and entered her slowly, forcing himself deep inside her. She moaned with pleasure and pushed against him for maximum penetration as he thrust harder and faster, slamming his thighs against hers. She reached between her legs, took his balls in her hand and squeezed and stroked them in time with his thrusts until she sensed he was about to come. She pulled away and spun on to her back underneath him. Her knees raised high and open wide, she pulled him into her and drove her pelvis up against his as her orgasm built deep inside her. She felt him spurt into her, felt the flood of wetness as his penis jerked. He gave one last thrust and held himself deep inside her as he spent himself and relaxed on top of her trembling, sweat-drenched body.

They lay panting in each other's arms. Debby kept her eyes tightly closed for several minutes, then opened them and stared up at the ceiling, wondering what was going to happen next. She knew Phillip must be suspicious. She had tried to act normally, but had been afraid of him at first, until he kissed her and took her in his arms. She lay still beneath him, afraid, waiting for him to speak.

But Phillip too lay in silence as he wondered how to play it. She knew. He was positive of that because of her fear of him. But then she'd let him seduce her again. Was it a desperate bid for her life? Was she afraid because she thought he was going to kill her? Should he in fact kill her if she knew too much, to stop her going to the police?

But if she did know the truth, why hadn't she been to the police already? Or told Jimmy North so that he and Lambert could set a trap for him? All the different possibilities flashed through his mind. He was puzzled and unsure what action to take. Anyway, how to broach the subject?

Characteristically, Debby led the way. 'You're going after them, aren't you?' she said quietly.

He rolled off her and lay on his back beside her, not touching her. 'Yes,' he said. 'I have to.'

'What about me? Are you going to kill me too?'

He didn't answer straight away. He looked at her for a while, then asked, 'Why didn't you go to the police and tell them about me?'

'We can't, I can't. We don't do that. It's not the way it's done where I come from.'

'Explain that to me, Debby. I don't fully understand.'

'Well, it'd be grassing for a start, and cowardly.' She smiled wryly. 'It's instilled in you as a kid. You don't snitch, not ever, not about anything, and you take care of your own problems for better or for worse.'

'Is that why Jimmy didn't set the police on me?'

'Jimmy'd never go to the police for help. He'd sooner die. Besides, he understands what you're doing and why. We all do. Because it's what we would do if it'd happened to us. If you'd killed one of us and just pissed off, we'd have been after you like a pack of hounds.'

'I've killed three of you. I don't hear any barking.'

'It's different. Just deserts. Anyway, Jimmy was going to sort you out till he found out you're ex-SAS. Then he thought there might be more than just you. So he cleared off, to get more help.'

'How did he find out?' Phillip hid his surprise.

Debby hesitated, to give herself time to think. The last thing she would be was disloyal. She'd sooner die.

Phillip could see her turmoil. 'I have to know, Debby. It's very important to me,' he said quietly, like a schoolmaster speaking to a nervous child.

'Mike phoned a mate in south London, got him to check you out.' She realized she was being dragged in deeper. Each answer was leading to another, more difficult, question.

'Check who out? He must have had a name. How did he get it?'

Debby was frightened now, and it showed in her eyes. If she answered him truthfully, he'd find out that she had been there, that she was part of the gang. She was afraid of what he might do. She wanted to cry, but forced the tears back. 'I don't know how to tell you,' she said in a choked voice.

Phillip put a hand on the side of her head and stroked her hair. 'Best to tell me the truth, Debby. I'll know if you're lying.'

She turned her head away and said bleakly, 'It was me. I was there. I saw you in Croydon. I've been having nightmares ever since. Your poor wife. And you holding her. And the baby carriage lying in the gutter.'

Phillip was astounded. 'You were there? What were you doing there?'

She gritted her teeth, lifted her chin and said, 'I was the lookout. I was outside the bank. I saw that guard shot. Billy just shot him. I couldn't believe it. I jumped on my bike and chased after them. I was behind the police car, and when it stopped I did too, and I saw you.' She turned her face into the pillow and let the tears come. 'I just want to die,' she wept. 'I can't live with all the grief, all the guilt.'

'When did you realize it was me? You did say a while ago that you'd seen me before sometime, but you couldn't remember where.'

'Only today, this morning when Jimmy and Mike asked me. I've been trying to blank it all out. Every time it comes into my mind, I refuse to think about it, it was all so horrible. Then this morning Jimmy forced me to think back and relive it, and I saw your face, and I realized that it was you. Your face was half hidden in your wife's hair. That's why I didn't realize before.'

'So Mike phoned, and checked me out through the death of my wife,' he said slowly, nodding as it all clicked into place.

'Your name's Phillip Ross, not Ted Hutchinson, isn't it?' She managed a watery smile and added, 'Well, at least I can stop calling you Ted. Ted the toff, we called you.'

'Where have they gone?' he asked. 'North and Lambert?'

Debby shook her head. 'I don't know, and I wouldn't tell you if I did,' she said stubbornly.

'That would be terrible. Jimmy's been good to me. My parents were killed in an air crash a few years back, and Jimmy and Wendy took me in. He's my friend, whatever he's done.'

Phillip realized he'd have to torture her to get it out of her, and no way could he do that. Besides, she wouldn't go to the police, he was certain, or she'd have done so already. She'd had plenty of time to have him arrested if she'd been so inclined.

Her next words shocked him. 'I've fallen in love with you . . . Phillip.' She hesitated over his real name, as if afraid he might be angry with her for using it. 'I don't want you to kill Jimmy and Mike, but I'm afraid for you. I don't want them to kill you either.' She took his hand and held it tightly. 'I'm so confused,' she whispered.

Phillip felt slightly confused himself. Here he lay, naked, having just had sex with a woman who'd been involved in the death of his wife. Yet he didn't hate her as he felt he should. He was certain that her remorse was genuine and that she'd suffered, knowing herself guilty. Instead of hatred, what he felt for her was something like pity. But he knew, too, now North had learnt who he was, that it was a case of kill or be killed.

'It's the way it has to be, Debby. None of us can stop until it's over. What will be, will be, whatever the outcome. It's gone too far. I won't stop until the job is done, or they get me first.'

'Make love to me. Do it again. I want you again.' She pressed against him, stroking his chest, gently biting his nipples.

Phillip felt a sexual stirring and responded. This time he was more gentle. He didn't love her, he couldn't. He was still in love with Julie. And he knew that Debby wasn't in love with him. Infatuated maybe, but love takes a little longer. It grows stronger with every year and even separation by death cannot destroy it. But Debby seemed to find his pity an acceptable substitute for love, and she was almost pathetically eager to please him.

They made love for over an hour. Then Phillip slipped out of bed and showered and dressed. Debby remained in bed. She looked lonely and anxious as he said goodbye.

'Come back to me,' she said forlornly as he paused in the doorway. 'I'll be here, I'll wait for you. And please, Phillip, please be careful.'

He smiled, then turned and made his way out to his hired car, thinking over what she'd told him. He wondered if he'd ever see her again.

Phillip drove straight back to his hotel, checked out and drove to Barcelona Airport, where he returned the car and booked a seat on the first flight to London. He now had the task of finding North and Lambert. With the help of a senior police officer at New Scotland Yard, it shouldn't be too difficult.

He doubted that the gangsters would return to London so soon after the robbery: the police would undoubtedly hear of their arrival and pull them in for questioning. He decided, however, not to return to his home, just in case North had set a trap there for him. The man appeared to travel freely to and from Britain whenever he wished to carry out a raid, so he must have false passports or a back door that he could slip through unnoticed.

Phillip took a black cab into central London and booked into a small private hotel in Victoria, in the name of Hutchinson. He slept soundly until his alarm woke him at eight the next morning.

Immediately after breakfast he phoned George Hill at New Scotland Yard. They arranged to meet at a pub in the City, where Hill, being Met rather than City of London Police, was unlikely to be recognized; they both felt they shouldn't be seen together in places where either of them was known.

Hill was already there when Phillip arrived. He was seated at a corner table with two pints of bitter in front of him.

'I took a guess,' he said with a smile as he stood and held out his hand in greeting. 'If you want something different, I'll drink both of them.'

Phillip gripped the policeman's hand and sat beside him. 'No, that's fine, thanks.' They raised their glasses, said, 'Cheers,' and took a swallow of their beer.

After a careful look round to make sure they couldn't be overheard, Phillip filled Hill in on the events of the past couple of weeks, and on the fact that North and Lambert had slipped anchor.

'Shouldn't be too difficult to find,' said Hill. 'They'll run for cover where they've got friends. No doubt about that. I'll put the word out. Men

like them can't hide anywhere. Too well known
among the criminal fraternity, and there isn't
a British copper anywhere in the world that
wouldn't recognize them on sight.' He took
another swig of beer and smiled. 'We've got
eyes everywhere. Wherever there's a bunch of
expat villains, we've got someone keeping an
eye on them. Even retired coppers make reports
when a well-known villain like North turns up.
They know we'll be interested and pleased to hear
about it.'

'Once a policeman, always a policeman, eh?'
said Phillip.

Hill smiled again. 'Something like that,' he
said. 'Leopards rarely change their spots.'

The two men finished their drinks and parted
company. Hill promised to let Phillip know the
minute North and Lambert surfaced.

Phillip returned to his hotel and telephoned the
Thompsons. He was missing Gary, and thought it
would be a good opportunity to spend some time
with him while he waited for Hill to come up with
information on North and Lambert. He decided
that it would be too risky to go to their home, just
in case the house was being watched. Instead, he
and Victor agreed that the Thompsons would
take Gary to Canterbury the following day, and
he would meet them at the bus station there.

Antonio Pacetti leant over the stern rail of his 150-
foot yacht, *Charlene*, and watched the holidaymakers wander along the quay. Puerto Banús was
busy. People from all over the world flocked to

the port to see the huge yachts, and to admire
the Rolls-Royces, Porsches and Ferraris lined
up along the quayside and outside the plush
restaurants where only the wealthy could afford
to wine and dine.

He turned and called to his second in com-
mand, Salvatore Morino, who was lying on a sun
lounger in the shade of a large beach umbrella, a
magazine over his face. 'Hey, Sal, wake up! I want
you to get some girls.'

Morino removed the magazine from his face
and squinted up at his boss. 'I thought you was
going to do some paperwork today. You said it
was important.'

Pacetti scowled. 'Not so important that it won't
wait till tomorrow. I've had enough of it today. I
want to enjoy myself.' He grinned. 'We're going
to have a party, so arrange some pussy. I'll phone
round and invite some of the boys.'

Morino clambered out of the lounger, stretched
and yawned. Both men looked typically Italian:
short and stocky, olive-skinned and with thick
black hair. Morino was the taller of the two, at
five foot nine, and thicker set. They had both been
born in the East End of London, to Italian parents
who had emigrated to England after the Second
World War, in search of work and a better life.

As a boy Pacetti had heard from cousins in
the USA about Al Capone, John Dillinger, 'Legs'
Diamond, Machine-Gun Kelly and the other glam-
orized thugs who had ruled America by fear and
the gun during the twenties and thirties. He
devoured books and articles about them, and

they became his heroes. From them he learnt that the quickest way to fast cars and fast women was through drugs, gambling and prostitution, and that in order to frighten a thousand men you needed to kill only one. By the time he reached his teens he had a close-knit gang of young toughs with similar ambitions. Most of them were immigrants' kids, but one of his most loyal mates was a tall, hard-faced native Londoner called Jimmy North.

'The only people you can really trust,' Pacetti had once said, 'are the ones you've known all your life. If they've never let you down in twenty years, they ain't never going to.'

Morino was on his way into the lounge to phone an escort agency and several girls he knew who liked to party, when Pacetti let out a howl of delight and called to him as he saw the 911 Porsche turbo pull up on the quay and Jimmy North step out, accompanied by Mike Lambert.

Pacetti ran down the gangway to greet them. He threw his arms round North's shoulders and kissed him on both cheeks. 'Hey, Jimmy, it's good to see you, my friend. It's been a long time. Too long.' He shook hands with Lambert. 'Great to see you too, Mike. Welcome aboard, both of you. Come and have a drink. Salvatore and me, we was just planning a party. Now it's in your honour, Jimmy. We celebrate you and Mike coming to see us. We do some business and we have a good time as well.'

The four men settled in *Charlene*'s luxurious

lounge and exchanged small talk while a stewardess opened a bottle of champagne and filled four glasses. She set out a selection of savoury canapés, then retreated to the galley.

'Now we can talk business. Afterwards we go to Silk's and have a meal, then we come back here and party.' Pacetti grinned delightedly. 'How does that sound to you boys?'

The three men nodded and smiled their agreement. They all knew the type of party Pacetti threw. Everything would be on offer, every known variety of drug and booze, and every size, colour and nationality of beautiful women, who for their fee would do anything to please their clients.

'Firstly, I want to thank you for coming so soon, Jimmy. I wasn't expecting you for another week, at least. Did you get your business sorted OK?'

North nodded. 'Yeah, I'll tell you about it later. When you phoned and asked me to come down I thought it would take longer, but things changed.'

'OK, I'll fill you in on my little problem. I've had two big shipments of drugs go missing. We've recovered one and dealt with the people concerned. But we didn't find out who made the snatches. Someone's getting just the right information at just the right time, so it could be one of my guys is mouthing off. The fact is there's a guy or guys out there, sitting on my stock, and they've got to find a buyer. That's where you come in, Jimmy. I want you and Mike to put the word round that you're in the market for a big buy.'

'But everyone knows that we're good mates from way back,' said North.

'Yeah, that's right,' agreed Pacetti. 'So tonight at the party, we have a big row. Throw a few fucks and threats at each other, and we stop talking. You go round the town calling me a cunt and telling everyone you won't deal with me so you need a new supplier.'

'And if we get approached, do you want us to sort it?' asked Lambert.

'No, Mike, I want to deal with this guy personally. Just give me the nod. Then' – he winked at North – 'I'll throw another party, and we make it up, settle our differences and no one will know any different.'

'How did you get the first shipment back?' asked North.

'I contacted every distributor in every city that I knew was big enough to buy a large consignment, and told them I'd kill the guys who bought my missing load. I offered them all a hundred grand reward if they reported to me the minute they was offered my goods and could name the guys selling it.'

'So you got a call from one of them?' asked Lambert.

Pacetti laughed out loud. 'I got a call from *all* of them. I'd sent my own people out to each of them and offered the exact same consignment to every one of them at half the going rate. All of them phoned me, the minute my men left, and told me the names of my guys offering them my stock. All except one. He didn't phone. He agreed to buy but said he needed time to come up with the cash. He said he'd just bought a big consignment and needed a bit of time to recover his outlay, so my guys agreed to wait.

'A couple of days later, I sent two potential buyers to this guy. They showed him a suitcase full of fifty-quid notes to prove they had the buying power and he arranged to show them the goods. *My* fucking goods. A meet was arranged. They took my guys and the money back to the farm where the goods were stored. There was three of them, all big guys, all looked like fucking Schwarzenegger.' He smiled. 'My guys were only small Italians, so they felt in control after they'd frisked them and knew they weren't carrying.' He looked over at Morino. 'You tell 'em the rest, Sal, you were there.'

Morino said, 'We'd had these guys followed from the minute we suspected them, so we already knew about the farm and guessed that was where they kept the drugs. It was pretty isolated and you had to drive down a single-track lane to get to it. I waited in the lane by the entrance gate to the farm. When they arrived and one of them got out to open the gate, I let the fuckers have it with a pump-action twelve-bore. They didn't know what hit them. What little brains they had were spread all over the inside of the car like strawberry yoghurt.'

'Did you get all the merchandise back?' asked Lambert.

Morino nodded. 'There was a little bit missing, but nothing to worry about. The main thing is, we made an example of them three arseholes. There ain't going to be too many willing buyers for the consignment that's still missing. The people sitting on it have a problem. If they contact one of the usual buyers, we'll get a phone call, so they have to find someone that don't or won't deal with Tony Pacetti.' He grinned at North. 'So you and Tony had better make it look good, give each other a little slap before we break it up. Mike, you pull Jimmy off, and I'll hold Tony. They've gotta make it look good, as if they want to kill each other.'

Pacetti stood up and lifted the champagne bottle out of the ice-bucket. He topped up all four glasses and, smiling at North, said, 'Make sure you pull the punches, Jimmy. Don't mark me.' He stroked the side of his face with his free hand. 'I'm a good-looking guy and I want to stay that way.'

North chuckled. 'I'll try.' He turned serious and asked, 'Can you let me have a couple of handguns, Tony? I've got a little problem of my own needs sorting.'

'No worries, Jimmy. Salvatore will take care of that, won't you Sal?'

'Sure. Anything you need, I can get you. I'll sort it this afternoon. Two nine-millimetres and a hundred rounds be OK?'

North gave him the thumbs-up sign. 'That'll do nicely,' he said.

'Sounds a bit serious, Jimmy,' said Pacetti. 'If you need any help, we've got plenty of muscle.'

North thanked him and went on to describe the events of the past two weeks. Pacetti was shocked to hear about the deaths of North's men. He'd known and liked all three of them.

'Hey, this guy's fucking dangerous,' he said. 'But don't worry, I know how to deal with him.' He turned to Morino. 'Spread the word I want a contract on this guy. Twenty grand – and let it be known that Tony Pacetti picks up the tab.'

Chapter Eight

George Hill listened intently to his informant. They were sitting on a bench near the pagoda in Kew Gardens, where they were unlikely to be seen: few villains take much of an interest in horticulture.

Benny Gibbs was a well-known small-time crook, accepted without question in the criminal fraternity. He'd been in and out of prison most of his life, usually for petty theft, though he'd once served five years for armed robbery. Five years before, he'd been involved in a building society robbery in which a security guard had been seriously injured. Hill had discovered Gibbs's involvement and given him a choice: twenty years plus, or turn grass and stay free. It was no choice: unable to face the thought that he might well die in prison before his sentence was up, Gibbs had turned. Five years on, Hill still held him on a tight leash and, whenever he wanted to know what was going on amongst Gibbs's associates, gave it a tug.

Terrified that Hill would let it be known that

he'd grassed, Gibbs always obliged. Now sixty, fat, balding and almost an alcoholic, he was no longer used on blags, so the money Hill paid him came in useful when cash was short and he was desperate for a drink.

Hill had worked hard for over a week trying to find out where North and Lambert were. He'd used all his informants from the East End who knew the two men from the old days, and eventually Gibbs had been suggested as someone likely to know where they were – he'd recently been overheard in a pub talking about them.

'So tell me about Jimmy North,' prompted Hill.

'I'd had a nice little tickle,' Gibbs said, 'so I nipped down to Marbella for a couple of weeks to see the lads. Apparently Pacetti threw a party on that fucking great boat of his, and North was invited, along with his mate Mike Lambert. At the end of the evening, when things had hotted up a bit, Pacetti and North had a right set to – throwing punches, yelling that they wanted to kill each other. They had to be pulled apart before they did each other some real damage. It was the talk of the town down there for a while.'

'Did you find out what it was all about?' asked Hill.

Gibbs shrugged. 'The word is that Pacetti's lost a couple of consignments of drugs and he thinks North might have had a hand in it.'

'North's never been involved in drugs. He robs banks and security vans,' said Hill, surprised.

'Well, he's into it now. He's been putting the

word out that he wants to make a big buy, and he don't want to deal with Pacetti.'

Hill leant back. 'Well, there's a turn-up. I didn't think North would have got involved in drugs. Not his style.'

'They all do it in the end, Mr Hill. Too much money involved, can't resist it. One big consignment and they ain't never got to worry about money ever again.'

'Is that it? Nothing else?' pressed Hill.

'No, it all happened at the end of me holiday, so what's going on now I ain't got a clue.'

Hill passed him a packet of twenty Benson & Hedges. Gibbs opened the pack and took one out. As he lit the cigarette he inspected the notes tucked into the back of the packet. He thanked Hill and slipped the packet in his pocket. 'I'll be on my way then, Mr Hill.' He stood up and was about to set off towards the main exit from the gardens, when he had an afterthought. 'Oh, talking of Pacetti, have you ever heard of a bloke called Ross, Phillip Ross?'

Hill was shaken, but kept his face impassive. 'No, why? Should I have?'

Gibbs shrugged. 'I don't know. But when I got back to the smoke, I heard a whisper that Pacetti's put a contract out on him for twenty grand.'

'When did you hear that?' The hairs on the back of Hill's neck stood up.

'Couple of days ago, I was talking to a bloke in the Kingsland Road, and mentioned I'd been down Marbella and was talking about the bust-up between North and Pacetti. It wasn't a big deal. He just mentioned it, that's all.'

Hill stood up. 'I've got to go. I'll be in touch.' He turned and made his way quickly out to Kew Road. He hailed a black cab and told the driver, 'New Scotland Yard, quick as you can.'

As soon as he arrived, Hill hurried into his office and rang Phillip Ross at his hotel in Victoria; he was awaiting word from Hill about North's whereabouts. Phillip answered almost at once, and Hill said, 'Wait in your room. I'll be there in thirty minutes. I've found North.'

He next summoned John Thorpe urgently to his office.

'What's up, George?' Thorpe could tell immediately that this was something important.

'Sit down, John.' He waved to the chair opposite his desk. 'I've found Jimmy North, and guess what.' He brought Thorpe up to date with the new developments.

Thorpe whistled when Hill told him of the contract on Ross's life. 'That should make it interesting. Now Ross hasn't got a lot of choice. He's got to work with us.'

Hill nodded. 'It looks that way. I was worried that he'd call it a day once he'd taken care of North and his gang, but now he'll have every thug on our books after him, and the only way he can get the contract lifted is to kill the paymaster. He's got to go after Pacetti. Get out on the street, will you, John, and find out what you can. See if you can find out whether anyone's taken up the contract. It sounds open to me, as though the first one to kill Ross gets twenty grand. But that sort of money will attract the professional hit men.' He got up and strode to the door. 'I'm going to see Ross now and warn him he's in a lot of danger.' He slammed the door behind him and hurried to the lift.

Phillip took the news calmly. 'I need to know everything about this man Pacetti and his gang. He was mentioned in your file on the North gang, but I'll need lot more than that. He must be a good friend of North's to have done this.'

'They grew up together, went to the same school.' Hill rubbed the back of his neck thought-fully. 'You know, something about the whole thing smells fishy to me. You're North's enemy, not Pacetti's, and Pacetti could only have got your name from North. Those two have a big falling out, and then a few days later Pacetti puts out a contract on you. Why the hell would he be doing North a favour now that they're enemies? It doesn't make sense.'

'If you have a big falling out with someone, you don't usually offer to pay someone else twenty thousand pounds to kill their enemy,' agreed Phillip. 'He can't be short of a bob or two if he can pay that much to have someone killed for double-crossing a friend.'

'A friend he's supposed to have fallen out with,' Hill reminded him. 'Oh, and by the way, he's a bit more than not short of a bob or two. He is rich, I mean seriously rich. He's one of the biggest criminal operators around, and he's got connections in America, Italy, Russia, you name it. He owns a string of nightclubs and casinos, but his real money comes from selling whole consignments of drugs, and he uses the casinos and nightclubs to launder the cash from his drug deals.' He scowled. 'We know what he's up to, but we've never been able to get anything on him. He never dirties his own hands, of course, oh no. He's got a whole string of thugs, flunkies and front-men to do the dirty work for him.'

'Can you get me a full dossier on him?'

'I'll work on that first thing in the morning. We've got reams of paper on him. He's got one of the biggest "suspected of" files in the Yard. He's got a record, but only minor stuff from years ago when he was young and green. Handling stolen goods, petty theft. The most serious thing was a charge of GBH with intent, but the victim refused to testify so we couldn't get a conviction. Then he got into drugs and went big-time, and since then he's kept well out of our reach.'

'Well, he's not out of mine. He's put out this contract on my life, so now he's my personal enemy. All his money and friends won't help him. He may be rich and powerful, but he's not bulletproof.' Phillip smiled sardonically and formed his fingers into an imaginary pistol. 'Two in the chest, one in the head, you're dead. No matter who you are. But I agree that it's a different ball game now. This Pacetti character won't be so easy to get at, and it looks like I'll have to eliminate him before I go for North and Lambert.' He rubbed his chin thoughtfully. 'I'm going to need some special equipment from my mates in the regiment to give me a bit of an edge, and I'll need expenses. It costs a bloody fortune travelling and staying in posh hotels. I'm getting through my cash at a rate of knots.'

'I will pay you twenty grand to get Pacetti.'

'*What*?'

'I'm a rich man,' said Hill. 'You need an income, and I am going to provide it. Tomorrow, I'm going to put you on the payroll of my property company. "Estate manager" will be your title. You'll be on thirty-five thousand a year, plus expenses, and on top of that I'll pay a bounty on the head of every top villain you put out of action. If you can get them into my hands, together with evidence that will give us watertight cases against them, that'll be great. But if it comes to a fight, and one or two of them don't make it back here alive, I shan't shed many tears. If you accept my offer, you'll have an office and all the facilities you need, and we'll have a legitimate reason for being in regular contact.' He paused to let what he had said sink in. 'Or you can go back to selling washing machines and we'll both forget we ever had this conversation.'

'You really hate them, don't you?'

'I loathe and despise the bastards. Prison's too good for most of them. Capital punishment isn't the answer – it doesn't work: look at the murder rate in countries like America which still have it. And all these new vote-catching gimmicks that have been brought in recently, they don't work either. The only thing that really deters crime is the criminal's knowledge that he's not going to get away with it. But we're so short of manpower and resources that the clean-up rates, even for crimes as serious as murder, are way below what they should be, so the villains carry right on and laugh in our faces. They know damn well the odds are in their favour. It makes me sick to the pit of my stomach. Violent robberies, rapes, stabbings and shootings used to be rare, but now we have to deal with them almost every day, and I reckon most of them are drug-related. It's got to stop. Somebody has to do something about it. These thugs can't have it all their own way for any longer.'

'I must admit, I like the idea of it a lot better than selling washing machines,' said Phillip. 'Let's give it a try, boss.' He stood up and held out his hand.

Hill gripped it tightly in both his. 'We'll give 'em hell,' he said, grinning broadly. 'We'll give 'em absolute hell.'

The moment Hill left, Phillip phoned Peter Russel in Hereford and arranged a meeting the following day at the café off the Strand where they'd met before. He brought Russel up to date with the latest developments and handed him a list of equipment he'd like to 'borrow'.

Russel scanned it quickly. 'No problem,' he said. 'I'll arrange for this little package to be delivered to you in Marbella. Could take a couple of days, though.'

'That's no sweat – it'll take me a few days to get settled and sorted, anyway. Thanks, Peter, thanks a lot. I'll phone you from that area, once I'm settled, to let you know where to contact me.'

'Be careful, mate. These sound like dangerous men.'

Phillip's eyes glinted. 'Yes, I like it. It's a bit like the old days. I'm starting to come alive again. There's nothing like a bit of danger to keep the adrenalin running and the mind alert.'

'When do you fly out?' asked Russel.

'First flight to Málaga tomorrow morning. I want to surprise those bastards. They think they've lost me, but' – he smiled angelically – 'I'm going to turn up like a bad penny and make their worst nightmare come true.'

Russel looked at him resignedly. He'd seen Phillip in this mood before, and knew that all hell was about to break loose and that someone, somewhere, was about to wish, very earnestly indeed, he'd never been born. 'Just remember, Phil, if the going gets too heavy and you need some help, don't hesitate to phone me. If I can't get away myself, there are always a couple of the lads due some R and R and they'd be only too willing to give you a hand.'

'Thanks, I know that, and I'm grateful for the supply of the gear I need. But I want to keep the regiment out of this if I can. I'm a civilian acting on my own at the moment and I'd like to keep it that way – if the sky falls in, there's no way anything can be traced back to you guys to cause embarrassment.'

Phillip said goodbye to Russel and made his way back to his hotel. There was a package waiting for him at reception. Inside he found five thousand pounds in cash, a file on Antonio Pacetti and several of his gang, and a note from George Hill, which wished him luck and explained the cash as 'an advance against expenses'.

He packed his suitcase in readiness for an early departure and spent the evening studying the file, making coded notes and memorizing the names, faces and descriptions of Pacetti and his associates. When he'd finished, he tore each page into tiny shreds. Pacetti had thrown down the gauntlet. Phillip had no choice but to pick it up.

He had, though, one great advantage. The last thing Pacetti expected was for Phillip to go straight at him, and cancel the contract.

North and Lambert were sitting in the shade of an awning outside a café on the quay of Puerto Estepona, luxuriating in the heat, but grateful for the slight sea breeze that stirred the rigging of the yachts bobbing at anchor in the small harbour.

Lambert wiped the sweat from his brow with the palm of his hand and inspected it before drying it on his Bermuda shorts. He took a long swig of his beer. 'I wonder where that bastard Ross is,' he said as he searched the faces along the quay.

'Stop worrying,' said North. 'He's not going to find us here, is he?'

'He found us in fucking Lloret. How did he do that? I keep thinking on it, but can't come up with the answer.'

'I'm buggered if I know. A lot of people suspect it's us keep popping over and doing the banks, but no one really knows. Perhaps someone pointed

the finger. They all know we live in Spain.'
North waved the thought away. 'Anyway, the
thing we've got to worry about is where he is
now. He ain't turned up in London. Debby told
him we'd gone there to attend the funerals, but
the girls ain't seen hide nor hair of him. I phoned
Wendy again this morning and then I phoned
Debby. No one's seen him.'

'The word must be out by now that Pacetti's
put out a contract on him for twenty grand. It
don't take long to get round, not with that sort
of wonga on offer,' said Lambert.

'The word's got round,' said North with a sickly
smile. 'Oh shit. I've had so much on my mind that
I forgot to tell you Morino phoned while you were
down having your breakfast. He wanted me to run
over Ross's description and tell him where he was
likely to show up. So I told him where the girls
are staying in Hackney and about the funerals.
I also gave him Dave Taylor's number. Said he
could probably find out where Ross lives.'

'Why did he want to know all that?' asked
Lambert.

'Tony's had a couple of phone calls. Two very
serious geezers have contacted him to ask if the
word about the contract is kosher, 'cause if it is
they want a crack at it.'

'I bet every villain in the Smoke's looking out
for him,' Lambert replied with some satisfaction.

'Trouble is,' said North, 'he ain't a known face.
I wish we'd taken a picture of him at the party, but
we never expected anything like this to happen,
did we?'

Lambert shook his head and lapsed into a morose silence, until he saw a familiar figure approaching along the quay. 'Here comes one of Pacetti's boys. Luigi, ain't it?'

North looked up. 'Yeah. When he sees us, he'll probably blank us.'

Luigi spotted the two men and stopped dead in his tracks. He carefully surveyed the quay in both directions, then walked over and sat at the table. Grinning, he said, 'I shouldn't be seen talking to you guys.'

'Then why are you?' North's tone was unfriendly.

'I just think it's sad. You and Tony have been good mates for years. If I can help you both make it up, just say the word.'

'There's fuck all to say,' snapped North. 'The man's a cunt of the first order. I'll piss on his grave before I ever speak to him again.'

Luigi looked up and down the quay again. 'Can we go inside? I don't want to be seen talking to you, but I've got a proposition, a business proposition.'

North and Lambert exchanged glances. Then North nodded and led the way inside to a table in the far corner of the café. The others followed and sat down, Luigi with his back to the entrance.

'If we're seen, we make out that I'm trying to get you to make it up with Tony, right?'

North nodded and asked, 'What's this business proposition?'

'I hear you're looking for a purchase, a big one.'

'Yeah. I don't want to fuck about. I want to do
one big one, and retire for life.'

Luigi licked his lips nervously. 'I could put you
on to a good deal, but Tony mustn't get to hear
that I helped you.'

North nodded in understanding. 'I'm listening.'

'There ain't too many people deal as big as this,
you understand. This geezer don't want anyone
to know it's him selling the gear, so he asked me
to approach you.'

North smiled. 'You're just doing him a favour,
like?'

Luigi nodded eagerly. 'Yeah, that's right Jimmy.
I'm just the go-between.'

'Not interested,' snapped North with a note of
finality.

Luigi looked aghast. 'But you're looking for a
deal. A big one.'

'I'm looking for a deal, yeah, but I deal with
the mechanic, not his oily rag, old son. So get
this Mr Big to contact me direct, and I'll be only
too pleased to discuss it with him.'

'He won't do that. He'll only deal through me.'

'Then there ain't no more to talk about, is
there, son?'

'Why? I can set it all up, Jimmy. You'll earn a
fortune.'

'What if it all goes wrong? I lose me money,
and don't even know who ripped me off.' North
leant back and smiled nastily. 'I wouldn't have
anybody to shoot except you, Luigi. And you're
only the messenger boy.'

Luigi pulled a white handkerchief from his pocket and mopped his brow and the back of his neck before stuffing it back in his pocket. He was fidgety and nervous as he thought it through. 'OK, there ain't nobody else. It's my shit. I'm the one selling.'

North smiled knowingly at Lambert, then said to Luigi, 'Now we've got the bullshit out of the way. Tell me about the deal.'

Luigi breathed a sigh of relief and said eagerly, 'I can do you the best deal of your life, but Tony mustn't hear about it or I'm dead. You understand?'

'He'll be the last one to hear from me. So spell it out. What have you got to offer that I might want to buy?'

'Two tonnes of cannabis, a hundred kilos of pure cocaine, and a million ecstasy tablets.'

North whistled. 'Nice! How much, and where is it?'

Luigi hesitated, then said, 'It's in this area. You can get an artic up to the loading bay, so it's easy to collect. I want five million quid for the whole lot.'

'That's a lot of cash,' said North.

'You said you wanted a big buy. In the Smoke, it'll fetch over twenty-five million on the street.'

'I ain't going to be standing on street corners selling eighths and quarters – or Es and fucking grams of charlie, for that matter,' said North sarcastically. 'I want to get it in, and sell it on in one lot. And if I buy this little lot, I take the risk of losing it at fucking Dover or wherever.'

'Send it in split loads. If you send five consign-ments, it's odds-on that four will get through – if not all five with a bit of luck.'

'I don't work on luck. I work on percentages, which means I'll probably lose twenty-five per cent of my goods.' said North. He studied Luigi coldly for a moment, then asked, 'Is this one of the loads your boss lost?'

Luigi shifted in his seat and looked from North to Lambert and back again. 'If he finds out it was me, he'll fucking kill me. That's why I came to you, Jimmy. He fucking hates you. He flies into a rage if anyone so much as says your name. No one's allowed to mention you or Mike. He just sounds off about what he's going to do to you.' He grinned. 'You must have really upset him.'

'Not half as much as you have, nicking two loads off him,' said Lambert with a chuckle.

'I lost out on the first consignment, didn't I?' said Luigi angrily. 'I let the sodding buyer have it on a pay-later basis. Tony tracked him down and sent Morino after him. He blew him and two of his mates away. I ain't taking that chance again. It's got to be cash on delivery. I can't risk nicking any more off him. Besides he keeps it well safe now. Armed guards round the clock.'

'What made you do it? asked North. 'I thought Tony was good to you boys.'

Luigi shrugged. 'Yeah, he's OK. But I ain't never going to get rich working for him, and I'm sick of running around for him. "Get this, Luigi, get that, Luigi." I've had enough of it. I want to be my own man.' He looked at the two men questioningly. 'Well, have we got a deal?'

'Let me work some figures out,' answered North. Lambert passed him a ballpoint and he spread a paper napkin flat on the table and scribbled down some numbers. He spoke aloud as he wrote. 'Two tonnes of resin, say. A grand a kilo. That's two million. One hundred K of charlie, say fifteen grand a K. That's one and a half million. Plus a million Es at fifty pence each.' He tossed the ballpoint on to the table. 'That only adds up to four million, old son.'

Luigi shook his head. 'You're working it out at shit prices. This stuff is all high-grade. The resin is Moroccan gold, the charlie is pure cocaine. You can easily cut it three to one with glucose. Then add some billy.'

North looked puzzled. 'What's billy?'

'Speed, amphetamine. Everyone's doing it. Billy's a fraction of the cost of charlie and glucose costs fuck all. When you've cut it all together, it'll fetch twelve hundred quid an ounce from a punter.' He grinned. 'And they love it.'

'What about the ecstasy? What brand's that?' asked Lambert.

'Omegas. They're one of the best. They fetch a tenner each on the street.'

North screwed up the paper napkin and slid it into his pocket. 'I'll pay you three million in cash, for the lot. You can have the money in three days,' he said bluntly.

'You're robbing me, Jimmy. It's worth more than that.'

'Not to me, old son. The minute I buy it, I'm
in the same position with Tony as you are. He
might hate me now, but if he finds out I bought
his missing consignment' – North sliced his forefinger across his throat – 'we're all dead.'

Luigi thought on it for a moment, then made
up his mind. 'OK,' he said reluctantly, 'we've got
a deal.' He held out his hand and North shook
it. 'I'll meet you here at midnight on Friday. You
show me the cash and I'll take you to the stash.
You can lay on transport, but not while I'm there.
I don't want anyone else to know that I sold it
to you.'

'Fine by me, Luigi. We'll be here with the cash,'
said North.

Luigi stood up and went quickly to the door.
After a careful look round the quay, he walked
back in the direction he'd come from.

North and Lambert grinned at each other.

Lambert spoke first: 'Do we tell Pacetti?'

'Of course.'

'Why not just blag it off Luigi and then bump
him?'

'We don't know he's got it.'

'What?'

'Tony might be trying us out.'

'Shit! Fuck me, I never thought of that.'

'Tony don't trust anyone at the moment. There's
so much money involved, it could cross his mind
that even we might get greedy, so he could be test-
ing us out.' He looked meaningfully at Lambert.
'If Tony sent him, and don't get a phone call in
the next half-hour, we're in deep shit, old son.'

Lambert stood up. 'Let's go and find a fucking phone.'

North looked at his watch. 'We've got time to get back to the hotel. We'll phone from there. Just in case Luigi's hanging around to see what we do next.'

The two men strolled out to North's Porsche, which was parked on the quay, climbed in and headed back to their hotel. North phoned Pacetti from reception. He spoke briefly, then turned to Lambert and told him, 'He's coming straight over. He said to wait in our suite.'

The two men walked towards the lift.

'Did you tell him who it is?' asked Lambert.

North grinned happily. 'No, I just told him we'd located his stock and we've just had a meeting with the dealer.'

'So it wasn't a try-out, after all.'

'No, he was shocked. He didn't expect a result so soon. He just said he'd be right over, and slammed the phone down.'

Lambert chuckled. 'He's in for a shock when he finds out that it's Luigi who's crossed him.'

North shrugged. 'Just goes to show, don't it? You can't trust anyone these days.'

North poured himself and Lambert a stiff drink and settled down to wait. Pacetti and Morino turned up within half an hour.

'Who is it?' were the first words out of Pacetti's mouth as he sat back with a drink in his hand.

'Luigi,' North answered. 'He approached us and tried to make out he was putting us on to the deal. But he finally came across and admitted it was him. He agreed to sell us the lot for three million.' He ran through the list of drugs Luigi had offered him.

The blood drained from Pacetti's face. 'Fuck me,' he exclaimed. 'I never suspected him. I trusted the guy.' He looked at Morino, who shrugged. 'He was a fucking waiter. I took a liking to him and brought him into the fold. Treated him like a son. Made him a somebody. Showed him the good things in life.' He finished his drink in one gulp and slammed the glass down.

'When's the deal being done?' asked Morino.

'He's meeting us at the port, Estepona, midnight on Friday. He's taking us to where he's got the drugs stashed.'

Pacetti said viciously, 'You follow them, Sal. Take one of the boys that you can trust. I'll leave it up to you. You know what I want. A closed coffin. I don't want anyone seeing his face again. Not his mother, his father, not his brothers or sisters. No one. Destroy it.'

Chapter Nine

Phillip whiled away the flight from Heathrow to Málaga by chatting to the passenger next to him. He was one of a group of eight young men on a golfing holiday, and Phillip was soon as involved as he cared to be in their talk of birdies, bunkers, the Open and so on. Time passed.

The aircraft landed smoothly and taxied to a halt. The doors opened and a blast of hot air filled the cabin. Phillip stayed with the group while they collected their baggage and golf bags, and passed through immigration and customs chatting to them. He reckoned he'd attract less attention as part of a group than as a lone traveller.

Once clear of the arrivals hall, he made for the nearest exit and took a cab to Marbella. The taxi driver recommended an excellent small private hotel, owned by his cousin.

Having showered and changed, he walked through the town until he found a public phone, and made two calls, the first to Peter Russel and the second to George Hill. He gave both men his phone and room numbers at his hotel and warned them both, 'Only small talk on that line. I'll call you back from a phone box to discuss business matters.'

He found a car-hire company and hired a white Seat hatchback. His next stop was a chemist, where he purchased peroxide bleach and blond colouring. He returned to his hotel and set to work on his black hair.

At eight that evening, a very different-looking Phillip Ross drove from the hotel to Puerto Banús. Wearing sunglasses that covered the distinctive scar under his left eye – even with a little skin-coloured make-up he couldn't be too careful – and with his hair now blond, he was sure that neither North nor Lambert would spot him in the crowd should he chance on them. And, with a rucksack on one shoulder and a camera hung from its strap round his neck, he looked the typical tourist out to see the sights as he strolled along the quay.

He spotted Pacetti's yacht, *Charlene*, backed up to the quay in a line of large yachts. He wandered over to a low mooring bollard, sat down on it and watched. Three crewmen were coiling ropes and hosepipes, having just scrubbed and hosed the decks. The captain appeared from the bridge and made a quick inspection. He spoke briefly to the crewmen and returned to the bridge. One of the crew stayed on the after deck, while the other two ran down the gangway to the quay and walked away towards the bars and cafés that lined it. Phillip followed them into Sinatra's Bar. He sat up at the bar, with his back to them, waited

while they ordered two beers, and called for one
for himself.

He listened to the two deck hands chatting and
laughing about the day's work and the two girls
they were going to meet later. He was about to
engage them in conversation, so that he could
pump them for information about their boss,
when another young hand joined them. He was
unshaven and very drunk. He swayed as he
clapped a hand on the taller crewman's shoulder
and slurred a greeting.

'How you doing, boys?'

'Hi, Bob. You fixed up with a job yet?'

Bob staggered, regained his balance and said,
'Not yet, Johnny. I was hoping Miller might take
me back on. He's looking for another deck hand.'

'No chance there, mate. Not after the mouthful
you gave him.'

Bob chuckled. 'Yeah, I told that shit what I
thought of him, didn't I?'

'Do you want a drink, Bob?' offered the shorter
deck hand.

Bob smiled gratefully. 'Yeah, I'll have a whisky,
Paul. I'm a bit skint at the moment but I'll pay you
back, I promise.'

Paul handed him the whisky and said, 'If you
get hungry, mate, call by and I'll nick a bit of grub
out the galley for you.'

Bob raised his glass. 'You're a real mate, Paul.
I won't forget you.' He took a large gulp of the
whisky, spilling some down his chin. Paul stood
up. 'Here, take my stool. Sorry, but we've got to
go, mate. We've got a couple of birds lined up,

and we'll be late if we don't leave now. Come on, Johnny, time to go.'

They drained their glasses, said goodbye to Bob and left. Bob dragged the vacant stool close and sat on it, leaning heavily on the bar.

Phillip waited until he'd drained his glass, then patted him on the shoulder. Bob turned and stared blearily at him.

'Hello, Bob. How are you doing?' said Phillip. 'Can I get you another drink?'

Bob held his glass out. 'I'll have a whisky, ta.' He peered at Phillip again. 'Do I know you?'

Phillip smiled. 'Sure. We got drunk together a couple of weeks back, with Paul and Johnny. I'm Alan – you remember.'

'Oh yeah, Alan, that's right,' he agreed. 'Nice to see you again.' He belched. 'Alan, yeah.'

Phillip called for a whisky, then asked, 'Have you found another job yet?'

'No. There isn't much about at the moment.'

'What was the name of the yacht you used to work on? *Charlene*, wasn't it?'

'Yeah. I fucked up with Captain Miller and the cunt sacked me.'

'Nice yacht. How big is she?'

'Hundred and fifty feet.'

'How many berths?'

'She's got seven guest cabins, which sleep eighteen, plus crew's quarters for eight.'

'No,' said Phillip disbelievingly. 'She can't have that many.'

'She bloody well has,' retorted Bob. 'I should know. I worked aboard her for nearly a year.'

'Could you sketch it for me? I'd love to see how they fit that many berths on a yacht that size.'

'Yeah, I know the layout by heart. Give us a bit of paper.'

Phillip reached along the bar for a paper napkin and produced a ballpoint from his rucksack. 'Here you go.'

Bob spread the napkin on the bar and started to sketch the lower deck. Phillip was surprised how adept he was, even in his fuddled state. Some of the lines were a bit wobbly, but the man was evidently talented. 'You're good at drawing,' he commented.

Bob smiled, pleased at the praise. 'Yeah, it was the only thing I was any good at at school. Wanted to be a commercial artist, but it didn't work out.' He handed the finished sketch to Phillip. 'That, my old son, is how you get so many berths on a yacht the size of *Charlene*.'

Phillip took the drawing and studied it for a moment. He pointed to the rear cabins. 'Are they very comfortable?' he asked.

'Not half! The bloke that owns her is a multimillionaire. A spaghetti-cruncher, an Italian.' He looked round to make sure he couldn't be overheard. 'He's a fucking gangster, so they say. Always surrounded by bodyguards.'

'Really? I've heard rumours,' said Phillip. 'Which is his cabin?'

Bob pointed to the rear master cabin. 'That one. Luxury like you've never seen. He's got stereo systems and video and colour TV. He's even got his own cocktail bar in there, not to mention a mirrored ceiling. He's a right dirty bastard. Likes a brass, he does.'

'Really? I bet he has some great parties.'

Bob rolled his eyes. 'Oh, you wouldn't believe it! Drugs, high-class brasses, the fucking lot, he has. He always slips anchor and cruises or anchors offshore when he's having a shindig.'

'I bet you had some really good times at the parties.'

'Not bloody likely. The crew are always sent forward to their quarters and told to stay there, before the fun starts.'

'Didn't you creep forward to have a peek at what was going on?'

'We talked about it, but it was too dodgy. Morino used to post armed guards on deck while it was all going on, so we didn't fancy it.'

'They've got guns, have they?'

'I've seen them all with guns at one time or another. No kidding. They're real gangsters, especially that Morino. He's a nasty fucker. I wouldn't want to cross him.'

'Who's Morino?'

'The boss's right-hand man. He's in charge of the other heavies.'

'Has he got his own cabin?'

Bob pointed to a starboard cabin, next to Pacetti's. 'That's his cabin there.' His finger moved to two port-side cabins. 'The other three monkeys sleep in those two. It's so no one can get to the boss without going past his heavies.'

'He likes a bit of security, then. I suppose

he's got video surveillance all over the yacht, has he?'

'No, only on the gangway. There's a monitor on the bridge, and an alarm pressure-switch on the gangway. The minute someone steps on the gangway to go aboard, a buzzer sounds on the bridge. If the crew are watching telly or chatting, they hear it and they check the monitor to see who's coming aboard.' Bob drained his glass and looked at it sorrowfully.

Phillip caught the barman's eye and pointed to the empty glass in Bob's hand. The barman nodded, scooped more ice into a glass, poured a generous measure of Bell's over it and set it on the counter as he accepted the thousand-peseta note Phillip handed him.

'Have another one, Bob,' Phillip said, pushing the glass towards him.

'Thanks, Alan. It's very kind of you. I'll buy you one back once I've got myself a job.' He belched and hiccuped simultaneously. 'I'm as pissed as a fart, but I couldn't give a fuck.' He poured more whisky down his throat.

'So if you were late returning on board, you always got caught, I suppose,' prompted Phillip.

Bob giggled, and whisky dribbled down his chin. 'Not fucking likely, or I'd have been sacked long ago. And so would most of the other hands.'

'Oh? How did you manage that?'

'We used to board the blue yacht two to port of *Charlene* and climb over the bows, then slip into the crew's quarters through a hatch on the foredeck. That wanker Miller used to sit waiting to catch us coming back late, and there we were, tucked up in our bunks, laughing our bollocks off.'

Phillip folded the paper napkin and slipped it into his pocket. 'I've got to go, Bob. Nice to see you again. I hope you get fixed up soon.'

'Yeah, thanks for the drinks, Alan. We must do it again some time. I'll have some cash by then.' He turned to wave goodbye to his friend Alan, lost his balance and fell off his stool. By the time someone helped Bob back up, Phillip had gone.

He made his way back to the yacht. Captain Miller was on the bridge with two of the crew. Otherwise, the yacht looked deserted. Phillip hung around for over an hour but Pacetti and his gang did not appear, so he went back to his hotel. He was relieved to find a different girl on reception when he asked for the key to his room, just in case the clerk who'd checked him in noticed the change of hair colour.

'There is a message for you, Mr Hutchinson.' The receptionist gave a professional smile and handed Phillip his key and a folded piece of paper. He read the message. 'Please telephone Peter Russel. Any time.'

Phillip thought for a moment. At this time of the evening it would be best to ring Russel at home, rather than at the regiment.

Russel answered after two rings.

'Hello, Peter. Sorry it's late, but I've only just got your message,' said Phillip.

'Glad you rang, Phil. I've got a couple of

guys on their way to you with the stuff you wanted. They're driving down overnight from Barcelona. Their ETA in Marbella is oh nine hundred hours tomorrow. They'll phone me for instructions when they arrive. So where and when can you rendezvous?'

Phillip thought quickly. He still didn't know the area that well. 'I'll be in a bar called Sinatra's in Puerto Banús at ten hundred hours. I'll wait for them to approach me. If there's no contact by twelve, I'll phone you at your office.'

'OK, fine. Anything to report?'

'No, but it's early days yet. I've located Pacetti's yacht, but haven't set eyes on him yet.'

'Any sign of the two from Lloret?'

'No, but I've got someone working on that.' His coins were disappearing down the slot at an alarming rate; the last one dropped. 'Look, I'm running out of change. I'll phone you as soon as something happens.'

'OK, I'll—' The line went dead.

Phillip made a mental note to get plenty of change for his next call. He decided to call it a night. He walked briskly back to his hotel and, after a long, cool shower, flopped into bed and fell fast asleep to the humming of the air-conditioning and the pleasing thought that tomorrow he would have the tools to do the job.

Phillip strolled into Sinatra's at 9.45 the next morning. There were about a dozen customers. He ordered a *café con leche* at the bar and took it over to a table in the corner furthest from the door.

He casually surveyed the customers, looking for two likely lads, but nothing clicked.

Two men and a pretty brunette left the bar, calling noisy goodbyes to their friends. They looked more like workers than holidaymakers, with their deeply tanned bodies and cut-down jeans.

Two long-haired young men came in, one of them carrying a plastic supermarket bag. A bread stick and a bottle of Coke stuck out of the bag. They ordered drinks and, after a look round, chose the table next to Phillip's. They ignored him, and chatted quietly in strong Geordie accents. Phillip studied them. They were dressed in football shirts, shorts and trainers. He'd seen more fat on a chip. They were both about five foot ten, thickset, with muscular arm and legs. Fit men, he thought.

The one nearer him turned to face him and asked, 'D'ye speak English, mun?'

Phillip smiled and said, 'Yes, I am English.'

'Thank fuck for that. Too many foreigners here. We've only just arrived, and we're looking for cheap digs. D'ye you know anywhere?'

Phillip shrugged. 'Sorry, pal. I haven't been here long myself.'

The young man held out his hand. 'I'm Mark.' He jerked his thumb towards his mate. 'He's Tommy.'

Phillip shook his hand. 'I'm David, David Stirling.' It was a name that any SAS man would recognize instantly, but that would probably mean nothing to the average citizen. David Stirling was the regiment's venerated founder,

whose brainwave back in 1941 had led to its
formation. Their eyes locked in recognition and
understanding.

'In that case, do you mind if we join you?' Mark's
Geordie accent had suddenly disappeared.

Phillip smiled warmly and said, 'Advance,
friend.'

The two men picked up their drinks and sat
either side of him. Tommy put the shopping bag
on the floor between himself and Phillip and said
in an undertone, 'You'll never guess where we've
just come from.'

'Barcelona?' suggested Phillip.

'Good enough.' Tommy relaxed and sat back.
'We didn't have a clue who we were looking for.'
He grinned at Mark. 'Before we came in here, I
said I bet it'd be the bloke sitting in the corner
with his back to the wall.'

'Gets to be a habit, doesn't it?'

'Would you like to run through what we're
supposed to deliver, just to make sure we've
brought the right gear?' asked Mark.

Phillip checked to make sure that no one
was paying them any attention. 'Two Brownings,
silencer, spare magazines, some PE and two radio
transmitters.'

Mark said, 'It's all in the shopping bag.' With
his foot he nudged it closer to Phillip. 'There's a
crystal tuned receiver in there as well.'

Phillip gave him a thumbs-up sign. 'Cheers,
mate.'

If there's one thing you learn in the SAS, it's
not to ask questions. It was obvious to Phillip

that these two hadn't been told who he was or what he was up to. They'd simply been briefed by Peter Russel to deliver certain equipment to 'one of us' in the Marbella area. Russel had stuck to the 'need-to-know' rule, and told them no more than was required for them to deliver the goods.

The three men chatted about things in general. Phillip offered to buy them another drink. Mark declined.

'Thanks all the same, Dave, but we've got to turn round and head straight back to Barcelona. It's a long drive, but we take it in turns, so it's not that bad.'

The three of them left the bar together, Phillip carrying the shopping bag. They walked to the corner, shook hands, wished one another luck and went their separate ways. Phillip went straight back to his hotel room to inspect the goodies.

There was another message for him at reception. 'Phone Mr Hill.'

He went up to his room, stashed the carrier bag in the wardrobe, then went out to the phone booth.

Hill sounded very pleased with himself. 'We've found out which hotel North and Lambert are staying at. One of our undercover drug squad boys heard that North was putting the word round that he wanted to make a big purchase, so he's been keeping an eye on them. He followed them to their hotel in Marbella.' He read out the name and address of the hotel. 'They're in room number four twenty, on the fourth floor. North is driving his red Porsche.'

Phillip thanked him and said, 'Right, leave

the rest to me, George. Can you get the drug squad man pulled off? I don't want North under surveillance for what I've got in mind.'

'Already taken care of. He's been told that North is already under investigation, and to stay clear of him.'

'Great,' said Phillip. 'I'll be in touch. Thanks, George.'

He went back to his hotel room and inspected the delivery. He stripped the two nine-millimetre Browning automatics. They were well oiled and in perfect condition. He loaded three of the six magazines, thirteen rounds in each, and set them aside with one of the pistols, the silencer and the two radio transmitters. He packed the remaining equipment in his suitcase, locked it and stacked it on top of the wardrobe. That evening he planned to board *Charlene* and plant the listening devices. Thanks to Bob the drunk, he knew the way to board her unseen and where to plant the bugs.

At 10.30 that evening Phillip was in position on the quay, observing the big yacht. He was dressed in whites similar to those of the crew in the hope that he could pass as one of them, or make out that he was looking for work – he knew Captain Miller wanted another deck hand to replace Bob – should he be discovered on board. Miller was on the bridge with two of his crew, making out a new rota and studying marine charts. The lights were on in the forward crew's quarters and two of the deck hands were sitting on the foredeck, smoking and chatting. A steward and stewardess were setting a dining table for ten people on the after deck, which led Phillip to think that Pacetti was due back on board at any time.

The level of activity on the yacht made it impossible for Phillip to board her unseen. He decided to stay where he was and see who the table was being set for, and, if necessary, wait until most of the occupants were asleep in their cabins before stealing aboard.

He didn't have to wait long. Twenty minutes later, two big Mercedes limousines crawled along the crowded quay, the drivers blowing their horns and flashing their lights to disperse the pedestrians. They parked alongside *Charlene*, and Phillip saw for the first time the man who had taken out a contract on his life.

Pacetti got out of the first Mercedes, accompanied by Morino and two attractive tarts. Luigi climbed from behind the wheel and locked the car doors, before following his boss up the gangway.

The two men who alighted from the second car Phillip recognized, from photos in the file George Hill had supplied, as two more of Pacetti's heavies. He didn't recognize the three women with them, but if they weren't tarts they certainly dressed like them, in clothes that revealed more than they hid. The women giggled and tottered as they removed, under orders, their high-heeled shoes, before going aboard.

Phillip moved to another vantage point. The crowds were thinning out, and he didn't want to stand out by staying in the same place too long. He found a free table at a café from where

he could see the quay and *Charlene*'s gangway.

Two hours later he again walked the quay, passing by *Charlene*. Pacetti and his guests, having
finished their meal, were drinking coffee and
liqueurs. Two crewmen were on the bridge. There
was no sign of Captain Miller, but some of the
forward portholes in the crew's quarters showed
lights.

Phillip decided to go for it while Pacetti and
his friends were busy getting drunk on the after
deck. He turned on his heel and walked directly
to the blue yacht two along to port of *Charlene*.
He walked straight up the gangway as though
he owned the boat, or at least was entitled to
board her, and made his way along the port-side
walkway to the bow. After a quick look round,
he vaulted lightly over the safety rail on to the
next yacht and crossed to the starboard side, his
rubber-soled trainers making no sound.

He ducked down and froze behind a locker as
the door leading to the crew's quarters opened
and the deck hand named Johnny stepped out.
The sound of pop music emanated from the open
door. Johnny lit a cigarette and looked idly out
across the harbour at the twinkling lights of the
other yachts and the cafés and restaurants that
lined the *puerto*.

The music changed and a voice from inside
called out, 'Come on, Johnny, the film's started.'
Johnny flicked his cigarette butt into the black
water, and went back inside, shutting the door
behind him.

Phillip stepped over the safety rail on to the deck of *Charlene* and crouched in the darkness, watching and listening for movement or sound that would signal that he had been seen or heard. All was quiet. He walked to the door through which Johnny had appeared, opened it and stepped inside. He found himself in a narrow walnut-veneered passage with skirting-board lighting and several doors on either side leading to crew cabins. Only the hum of the air-conditioning and the sounds of shooting and police sirens from the crew's video broke the silence. It was blessedly cool.

A toilet flushed and a door further down the passage opened. Phillip ducked into the near-est cabin and pulled the door almost shut. He watched as a deck hand came out of the toilet. The dimly lit passage filled with light and sound from the video as he opened the door of the cabin opposite and went in.

Behind Phillip, there was a rustle of sheets as a body turned in a bunk and a sleepy voice asked, 'That you, Paul?'

He took a chance. He said quietly, 'Yeah, it's only me,' and stepped back out into the passage, closing the door softly behind him. He made his way aft until he came to the door separating the crew's quarters from the guests' and owner's cabins. He opened it and listened. Raucous laugh-ter wafted down a spiral staircase from the rear deck. At the end of a long passage was the door that Bob had said led to Pacetti's suite.

Phillip cautiously climbed the spiral staircase

until his head was level with the deck. An open
door led into the lounge, which was in semi-
darkness. The only lighting was at skirting-board
level and from deck lights that shone through the
windows from the walkways and the after deck,
where Pacetti and his guests were still drinking
and smoking.

He crossed to the lounge door and peered
round. He could see the revellers through the
windows at the rear of the lounge. The big room
was expensively furnished. Two four-seater white
leather settees faced a heavy carved walnut coffee
table in the centre of the lush carpet. A well-
stocked cocktail bar was built into one starboard
corner and two matching carved walnut cabinets
faced each other across the room. Using the settees as cover, Phillip crouched low and crawled
to the port-side cabinet. He produced from his
pocket one of the miniature bugs and concealed
it at the rear of the cabinet. The door from the rear
deck opened. Phillip rolled up tight against the
back of the settee in time to see Salvatore Morino
come in.

Morino went over to the bar and picked up a
long silver canister. He shook white powder from
it on to the glass top, divided it carefully into two
with a razor blade and formed the two halves into
lines. He took a fifty-pound note from his wallet,
rolled it into a straw and sniffed up both lines.
He tossed the fifty on to the bar and then, wiping
the traces of cocaine off his nose, he turned and
went out to rejoin Pacetti.

As soon as the door had closed behind him,

Phillip retreated quickly to the lower deck and made his way to Pacetti's suite to plant the second bug. He fixed it behind the padded headboard of the king-size bed, then quietly opened the door and slipped out into the passage.

A voice boomed from the darkness, 'What the fuck were you doing in Mr Pacetti's cabin?'

Out of the next cabin stepped one of the heavies Phillip had seen sitting on the after deck with their boss. This one had obviously nipped down to his cabin for more cigarettes. He held a freshly opened pack of Fortuna, and an unlit cigarette hung limply from his lips. Not taking his eyes off Phillip, he slipped the Fortuna into the breast pocket of his shirt and took out a lighter. As he lit up, the flame illuminated his face enough for Phillip to recognize him as one of the thugs in Hill's file: Giovanni Vicci.

Vicci drew hard on his cigarette and grinned menacingly at Phillip. 'You're in deep shit,' he said. 'Crew ain't allowed down here unless they're summoned.' Clearly confident from coke and booze that he could handle any deck hand, he took a step forward and grabbed Phillip's arm to pull him out of the shadows.

Phillip hit him.

The cigarette flew out of Vicci's mouth as Phillip slammed a foreknuckle fist into his larynx. His brief grunt of shock and pain became a shriek as Phillip snap-kicked him in the balls, and he doubled up in sweet agony. A powerful hook punch took him on the side of the head. He was out cold before he hit the deck.

Phillip dragged the man's limp body back into his cabin, and closed the door. He flicked on the light and paused to think things through. He was annoyed that Vicci had discovered him on the yacht. It would arouse Pacetti's suspicions and he would be bound to step up security. He might even order a search, and find the bugs. Phillip decided to make it look like a burglary so Pacetti would think it was simply another out-of-work deck hand looking for cash or valuables. He proceeded to ransack the cabin, making as much mess as he could in the few seconds available. He pocketed a handful of jewellery, then returned to Pacetti's cabin, where he repeated the procedure, strewing the contents of drawers and cupboards over the floor, stripping the bed and ripping not only the mattress but the pillows: down spiralled round the room as it was caught in the current of the air-conditioning. It was like being a naughty kid again. Fun. Something told him Mr Pacetti was going to be a mite unhappy.

He stuffed more valuables into his pockets, then made his way back to the crew's quarters. The sound of the video reassured him that they were still engrossed in their film. He opened the door and stepped out of the air-conditioned coolness into the hot night air, praying that none of the crew had stepped out on deck for a smoke. All was clear, the deck deserted. After a careful look round, he stepped over the rail on to the next yacht, ran across her foredeck and leapt on to the second yacht. He paused just long enough to throw the stolen valuables into the harbour, then returned to the quay. Several couples were promenading along it, but none of them took any notice of a deck hand coming ashore from a yacht.

Phillip strolled casually back to his car, glad to have the bugs in place. He hoped Pacetti would put the intrusion down to a mere burglary, but the moment Giovanni came to, he knew, they'd be looking for a man dressed in crew's whites.

He got into the car and switched on the crystal tuned receiver. It looked like a radio cassette player, complete with matching head-phones. There was no sound from Pacetti's cabin. He switched to the bug in the lounge. Laughter and a medley of different voices came over the air. Then Pacetti's voice rose above the din: 'Where the fuck's Giovanni? Someone go and find him.'

'Interesting,' said Phillip. He reached under the passenger seat and pulled out a carrier bag. From it he took a dark-blue tracksuit, which he pulled on over his whites. Zipping up the jacket, he decided to go back and watch the balloon go up – and see whether they found the bugs.

He sat on a bench only twenty-five metres from *Charlene* and waited. Not for long. He heard a man yell, 'Tony! Tony, we've been robbed! Giovanni's out cold!'

'S-search!' bellowed Pacetti, almost stammering with rage. 'Search the fucking boat. The bastard may still be on board.'

Amused, Phillip watched *Charlene* erupt into frenetic activity, crewmen dashing round the deck, dashing below, dashing topsides again, shouting importantly to each other the while. An hour later it had all quietened down again, so he went back to the car to have another earwig.

Pacetti and Morino were trying to question Giovanni Vicci, but he was having trouble talking and could manage little more than a hoarse whisper. 'I thought I'd caught one of the crew snooping round your cabin, boss,' he croaked. 'I grabbed him, but he hit me with a cosh or something. Maybe there was two of them.'

Pacetti's fury was less noisy now, but twice as deadly. 'I want the fucker caught,' he said venomously. 'Offer a reward. If he tries to sell the stuff, we'll get him. Break his arms and legs, break his thieving hands, break every fucking bone in his fucking body. Nobody steals from Tony Pacetti. Nobody!'

Phillip decided it was time to get some sleep. He'd come back in the morning. He still had North and Lambert to deal with, but Pacetti came first. That contract on Phillip's life must be made null and void.

Chapter Ten

North sat drinking coffee as he waited for Luigi. He checked his watch. Luigi was late. Estepona *puerto* was still busy. People sat outside the cafés and restaurants, and others strolled up and down the quay.

Luigi appeared, looking flustered. 'I had to finish a job for Tony. I couldn't get away any sooner.' He looked round. 'Where's Mike?'

'Guarding the cash,' said North. 'We'd look silly dragging two fucking great suitcases through all these poxy tourists.'

Luigi nodded. 'I've got to see the cash before I take you to the gear,' he said with some embarrassment. 'It's not that I don't trust you, Jimmy, but I can't be too careful.'

'Well I don't fucking well trust you, Luigi.' North patted his side under his armpit. 'We're both carrying, and we know how to use them. No tricks, understand? If there's any trouble, you get the first bullet.'

Luigi threw up his hands, hurt. 'Hey, Jimmy, this is a straightforward business transaction. I only want the money so I can fuck off out of here and have a good life.'

'Who's guarding the stuff, and how many of them are there?'

'I've got four spics from La Linea. They're OK. They've worked for me before. I can trust them.'

'Guns?'

'Naturally. We're in a funny business. We've got to protect ourselves.' Luigi grinned. 'That's the fucking trouble with this business. Everyone wants to fuck you. The police, the customs, the people you buy from, and the people you sell to.'

North grinned back. 'And the people you nicked it off.'

'Christ!' said Luigi in horror. 'I'm finished if Tony finds out. That's why I came to you. He fucking hates you.'

'He won't find out.' North took a long look along the quay, checking for familiar faces. 'I'll go on ahead. You follow.' He climbed out of his chair, waved a casual goodbye and strolled off towards the car park. Luigi followed at a discreet distance. He quickened his pace to catch up as North approached his Porsche.

'Where's Mike? Where's the cash?' he demanded.

North pointed to a curtain-sided truck in the far corner of the car park. 'He's in the truck. We're taking the stuff with us, seeing as we're paying for it.'

'I've got to see the cash before we leave here, or the deal's off.'

'No problem. Come on.' He went over to the truck. Mike Lambert was at the wheel.

North cocked a thumb at Luigi. 'He wants to see the money.'

Lambert got out of the cab, went round to the rear and slid up the rear roller-shutter door. The three men climbed in.

There were two large suitcases and a stack of wooden crates on pallets at the rear of the truck. Luigi looked at the crates suspiciously. 'What's in those?'

'They're empty,' said Lambert. 'We brought them to stack the gear in for shipping.'

Luigi inspected the top crates. He lifted the lids and checked that they were empty. He banged on the sides of the bottom crates.

Lambert opened the two suitcases and stood back. 'This is what you're interested in, ain't it?'

Luigi stepped forward and picked a wad of fifty-pound notes out of the first case. He flicked through it, picked another two bundles at random and examined those as well. He checked another two bundles from the second suitcase, then said, with satisfaction, 'OK, let's go.'

'You come in the Porsche with me, Luigi. Mike will follow in the truck.' North jumped off the back of the truck. 'How far is it?'

'About an hour.'

Luigi watched Lambert close and lock the two suitcases, close the rear door of the truck and snap a padlock into place. 'Take care of that money, Mike,' he laughed. 'That's my future.'

No it ain't, mate, thought Lambert. You ain't got one.

Luigi directed North on to the Cadiz road. They

drove for forty minutes, then took a right-hand turn inland. The road was full of potholes and North cursed as the Porsche bottomed out. 'What sort of fucking road's this?' he complained.

'It isn't far now, Jimmy,' said Luigi. He pointed to a narrow lane branching off to the right. 'Down there, and it's about a mile.'

North signalled, and checked in his rear-view mirror that Lambert was following. He slowed to allow the truck to close the gap, then turned into the lane. A mile along it they came to a pair of rusting wrought-iron gates. The Porsche's headlights shone through the gates on to a group of dilapidated farm buildings and an old tractor.

Luigi pointed to a big old barn. 'Park to one side of the doors. I'll tell Mike to back up to them, and I'll get them opened.' He climbed out of the Porsche and opened the gates for the two vehicles to enter the yard, then closed and locked them, before sprinting after the truck.

Lambert backed the truck to within a few feet of the barn doors. Luigi ran to the doors and knocked four times. 'It's me, Luigi,' he said quietly.

A few whispered words were exchanged through a crack in the door and then Luigi said, 'It's OK. They've got the money. I've seen it.'

The doors swung open, floodlights blazed on and two men, one holding a Kalashnikov AK 47, the other a Savage pump-action twelve-bore shotgun, walked into the light.

North stepped behind Luigi and shoved his Beretta pistol into his ribs. 'Tell them to put the guns down. We came here to do a deal, not have a fucking war.'

'OK, OK. Put the guns down. These guys are friends of mine.'

The two Spaniards looked at each other for a moment, then sullenly obeyed, and leant their weapons against the barn door.

'Where are the other two?' demanded North.

'Inside. Don't worry, Jimmy. I'll fetch them out.' He called through the open door, 'Paco, Jordi, come on out.'

Two men appeared, each with an automatic pistol slung at his belt. One man carried an Uzi machine pistol, the other a Skorpion 61 sub-machine gun.

North gave Luigi an encouraging nudge with the Beretta. 'Tell them to lose the weapons and start loading the truck.'

'What about the three million? I get that before we start loading.'

North called to Lambert, 'Get the suitcases out of the truck, Mike, and give them to Luigi.'

Lambert climbed into the back of the truck and tossed the heavy cases on to the ground, sending a cloud of red dust into the air from the sun-baked soil.

'Get those cases inside and start loading the truck,' ordered Luigi. Paco and Jordi leant their guns against the door with the others and carried the suitcases into the barn. One of the Spaniards threw a switch and the barn was flooded with light. On a loading platform, stacked high, were plastic-wrapped bales of cannabis resin, cartons containing kilo bags of cocaine, and sacks of ecstasy tablets. North whistled as he surveyed the stolen consignment.

Luigi opened one of the suitcases and started to count the bundles of fifty-pound notes.

'Back the truck up to the loading bank,' North told Lambert.

Lambert backed up tight to the platform, switched the ignition off and leant on the horn as he jumped out of the cab.

The horn-blast was the signal for Morino to release the two bolts holding the side of one of the lower packing cases in position and swing the case open. He crawled out of the confined space gripping an Uzi machine pistol in his right hand, which he used to give the packing case next to his a light tap. The side panel opened and Vic Morelli crawled out, Uzi in hand. He hauled himself to his feet and stretched his cramped limbs.

The two men walked to the rear of the truck and stood watching the group of men examining the packets of drugs.

Morino smiled at Morelli and gave him the nod. They both pulled back the cocking levers of the machine pistols and let the blocks slam back into the firing position.

North and Lambert stepped quickly to one side. Luigi and his four men swung round in surprise, and stared wide-eyed at the two men who stood there covering them with their Uzis.

Morino leapt on to the loading bay and shouted. 'OK, get it loaded. It's going home.'

Luigi, pale and trembling with fear, stuttered, 'S-S-Sal, we can work this out.'

Morino smiled wickedly. 'There ain't nothing to work out, Luigi. This consignment belongs to Tony Pacetti. It's going back. Now get humping.'

Jimmy North stepped forward. 'Do you need us any more, Salvatore?'

Morino shook his head. 'No, thanks, Jimmy. You did good, you and Mike, but your work's finished now. Just take the money and go back to the yacht. Tell Tony we've got the gear and are taking it back to the warehouse.' He looked back at the five frightened men. 'We'll take care of this bunch.'

Luigi stepped forward and frantically grabbed North's arm. 'Don't let him do this to me. He's gonna kill me.'

North pulled his arm away. 'You knew the risk when you crossed Tony. It ain't my problem.'

'You set me up, you bastard,' Luigi shouted after North as he and Lambert collected the suitcases. 'You never fell out with Tony, did you? It was a fucking set-up.'

'Yeah, we dangled the carrot, and you went for it, sucker.' North shook his head in contempt. 'You should have had a bit more loyalty. Tony was good to you, and you shat on him. Now you get what's coming to you.' He turned and walked out to the Porsche, followed by Lambert.

Morino stepped close to Luigi and ordered, 'On your knees.' He raised the Uzi to Luigi's head.

Luigi dropped to his knees. Hands clasped together against his chest, he pleaded, 'No, Sal.

Let me speak to Tony. We can work something out. I'll make it up to him, I swear.' Morino walked behind the trembling man and held the machine pistol close to the back of his head. 'No open coffin for you, you little rat.' He squeezed the trigger.

The barn was filled with a roar like thunder. Luigi's face blew out in a red spray of blood and bone fragments as the burst of nine-millimetre steel-jacketed slugs ripped through the back of his head and out through his face. His body thudded to the dirt floor, his face gone, leaving a sticky red hole the size of a saucer seeping blood and grey matter into the dry ground.

One eye, hanging on a partly severed tendon, swung from the upper side of his face and stared up vacantly at Morino who laughed and called to Morelli, 'Ay, ay! I think he got the message.' He turned his Uzi to the four men who looked on in sick horror and fear.

He told them in Spanish, 'Get working, unless you want the same.'

The men hastily started carrying the bales of cannabis to the truck and dumping them into the empty crates.

Morino and Morelli sat watching silently and unconcernedly while the men worked as though their lived depended on getting the truck loaded quickly. Once they had finished, the four men jumped down from the truck and waited nervously to see what the two Italians had in mind for them.

Morino nodded towards the open doors. 'You can go,' he said.

The men hesitated, still unsure. They had to pass the Italians to get to the open doorway.

Morino and Morelli stood with the Uzis hanging at their sides.

'I said you can go,' Morino snapped in Spanish.

The four men edged past them and made for the door, glancing back nervously. Morino and Morelli raised their guns. The men ran for their lives. A hail of steel-jacketed bullets from the two Uzis sliced them down like a sickle cutting grass. The thunderous roar from the machine pistols drowned their screams as their bodies jerked and danced to the muzzle flashes of brilliant light.

Morino drew a pistol from under his jacket, walked over to them and casually fired a bullet into each head. 'Can't be too careful,' he said to Morelli. 'Come on, let's get out of here.' He climbed into the truck, fired up the engine, waited for Morelli to climb into the passenger seat, and pulled away, whistling 'Ten green bottles'.

Phillip was sitting on a dockside bench, apparently listening to the cassette player slung on a strap over his shoulder, when he spotted the Porsche as it crawled along the quay towards *Charlene*. He covered his face with a hand and brushed his blond hair forward as North drove past and pulled up. North jumped out and ran up the gangway.

Pacetti came out of the rear lounge to greet him. He knew from the smile on North's face that things had gone well. He threw his arms wide and laughed. 'Jimmy, we did it.' He hugged North warmly and kissed him on both cheeks. 'Come in, come in and have a drink. Let's celebrate our success. But where's Mike?'

'He's in the car with the cash. He's guarding it.'

Pacetti told Giovanni, who was sitting in the lounge watching television, to go and help Lambert bring in the two suitcases, then turned back to North. 'We've been robbed enough lately. Two men will be safer than one.' He went to the bar, threw ice cubes into two tall glasses, poured a generous amount of J&B whisky over the ice, then topped it up with dry ginger. He handed one to North. 'You and Mike just earned yourselves half a million quid.'

North started to protest. 'I don't want a reward—'

'I insist, Jimmy. That shit's worth five million to me. Ten per cent's fair for what you just did.' He raised his glass and clinked it against North's. 'I'd have paid you that just to nail that thieving rat Luigi.' His smile faded. 'I liked that little shit. I'd never have believed it of him. I trusted him. I had big plans for that guy.' He waved the problem away. 'Never mind, it's over now. Sit down, Jimmy, sit and be comfortable.

'Well, that's sorted my problem,' Pacetti went on, when they were ensconced on one of the settees. 'All we've got to do now is nail your Phillip Ross. Salvatore put the word out last week that I want the man dead. And with twenty grand on offer it shouldn't be long before things start to happen.'

Phillip, sitting on his bench fifty yards along the quay and listening intently through his headphones, fully agreed. 'No, it won't be long now, Pacetti,' he murmured aloud.

He watched as Lambert and Vicci struggled up the gangway with the heavy suitcases and turned the bug's volume up slightly to ensure he wouldn't miss anything. He wanted to know what North and Lambert had been up to and, more importantly, what they were going to do next.

He heard North describe the way he'd set up Luigi and the drug deal, and tell Pacetti that Salvatore was moving the consignment back to the warehouse. He heard Pacetti laugh loudly, and say, 'I told Morino to blow Luigi's face away, so that no one could look at it again. His coffin will be closed at his funeral. Everyone will get the message.' He gave another high-pitched laugh. 'Tomorrow night I'm going to throw a big party to celebrate. We'll cruise the yacht and anchor off Victor's beach, and have a real shindig. I'll get Sal to lay on some tasty girls. We'll cast off at nine, so be here well before then.'

That was enough for Phillip. In his head he reran part of what he'd heard. He was filled with icy anger at the men's flippancy over their drug-dealing. It wasn't just that the kids themselves were dying or ruining their health. Their families and friends suffered terribly too, sometimes for years. And all to make scum rich. Pacetti's high-pitched laugh as he boasted about the death of another man rang in Phillip's ears. He wondered if the murdering swine would find his own death equally funny. He walked back to his car smiling to himself. There'll be an unwelcome guest at the party, he thought, with a nasty surprise.

He reached his car and slipped the key in the door lock. He was about to turn the key when a leather-clad figure on a Virago motorcycle roared up and skidded to a halt beside him. He swung round in surprise. The rider kicked down the stand and leapt off the machine to face him. He couldn't make out the face through the tinted visor. He turned and was about to open the car door, when the rider called his name and pulled off the crash helmet.

Debby shook out her hair and smiled. 'I knew it was you. The blond hair fooled me for a while, but the way you walk, the shape of your body . . .' She ran to him, flung her arms round him and held him tightly. 'I missed you, I've been worried sick.'

Worried that she might be seen and recognized, Phillip panned the car park as he put his arms round her and hugged her. 'How did you find me?'

'I guessed that wherever Jimmy and Mike were, you'd turn up sooner or later.'

'Get in the car quickly, before you're spotted by someone who knows you,' he said. 'We need to talk.'

Debby ran round and jumped into the passenger seat. She gripped Phillip's hand. 'I told you, I love you. I haven't been able to sleep. I couldn't stop thinking about you, and worrying about what Jimmy will do to you if he catches you.'

'How long have you been here? When did you arrive?' he asked.

'Yesterday afternoon. I saw you once. You were sitting on the quay, and there were lots of people walking about. I didn't give you a second glance at the time because of the blond hair.' She laughed and ran her fingers through it. 'I like it. It suits you.' She ran a finger lightly along the scar below his left eye. Skin-coloured make-up rubbed off on to her fingertip. 'Can't see the scar, even from quite close up.'

Phillip smiled. 'Jimmy and Mike drove straight past me the other day. They were within three feet of me, and didn't give me a second glance.'

'How did you find them so quickly?' she asked admiringly. 'Jimmy phoned me the other day to check on things, and we talked about you. He said you'd never find him. He told me Tony Pacetti's put out a contract on you for twenty grand, and that you'd be dead before the week was out.' She bent over and put her head in his lap. 'That's when I knew I had to find you, to warn you.' She stroked the inside of his thigh as she whispered, 'I love you, Phillip. I can't let anything happen to you.'

Phillip ran his fingers through her hair, touched by her concern. He glanced out the window at the motorcycle. 'Did you ride all the way on that bike?'

She looked up at him and grinned. 'It took me fifteen hours. But I panicked when I heard about the contract. So I just slung a few things in the saddle-bags and kept going till I got here.'

'Where are you staying?'

'A small *pension* on the way to San Pedro. It's cheap, and there are a quite a few bikers staying there, so I don't stand out.'

'Where does Jimmy think you are?' Phillip's mind was racing. How would Debby's unexpected arrival affect things?

'I told him I had to get away for a few days. I said I didn't know where I'd go or where I'd end up, so if I do bump into him, I'll tell him I've just arrived and was looking for him.' She sat up and unzipped her leather jacket. 'I must get out of this. It's OK while there's air passing through it, but now it's boiling.'

Phillip pulled at the sleeves to help her out of the padded leather. Underneath she wore a thin white T-shirt. It was damp with sweat and moulded to her breasts like a second skin. Her nipples showed clearly through the thin material.

'You're soaking wet, Debby,' Phillip said as he cupped one of her full, rounded breasts and toyed with her nipple, which hardened and swelled at his touch.

'Let's go to the beach,' she said. 'I've got clean clothes and a towel in my saddle-bags. It's such a lovely night, I'd like to swim in the sea for a while.'

'I haven't got a costume with me,' said Phillip.

Debby laughed. 'The beach won't be crowded at this time in the morning – and anyway I've seen all of you before.'

She opened the car door and stepped out.
'Follow me. I know a lovely beach that's right
out of the way. It's four or five miles along
the coast.' Without waiting for an answer, she
pulled her jacket back on, tugged her helmet on,
leaving her hair loose at the back, and skipped
round the car to the Virago. She roared out of
the car park. Phillip had to drive hard to keep
up with her as she leant the motor cycle and
accelerated round corners and bends with a skill
that surprised him.

She drove down a winding road which opened
suddenly on to a sandy beach. She was off
the Virago, had slung her saddle-bags over her
shoulder and was running down to the water's
edge as Phillip drew up alongside the bike.

He locked the car and jogged across the sand
to join her. She had pulled off her heavy leather
boots and was wriggling out of her tight leather
trousers.

'Get your kit off,' she said. 'No need to be shy.
We've got the whole beach to ourselves.' She
pulled off her T-shirt, slipped off her white
panties and stood up to look around.

There was a floating platform two hundred
yards from the beach, bobbing lazily to the swell
of the sea. The moon was full and reflecting like
a trillion mirror-flashes on the gentle ripple of
waves across the bay.

'Race you to the platform,' she said, ran down
the water and dived in head first. 'Last one there's
a ninny,' she called over her shoulder, as she
thrashed in a racing crawl towards the platform.

Phillip kicked off his trainers, quickly stripped off his tracksuit and pants and ran down into the water. It was a while since he'd swum and he relished the feel of his powerful strokes propelling him through the water like a dolphin.

Debby glanced over her shoulder and saw that he was gaining fast. She gave a yelp of surprise and swam harder, but within seconds he was alongside her, grinning, the moonlight rippling and gleaming on his back muscles.

'Ninny, eh?' He laughed and surged ahead. As his hands touched the edge of the platform, he hauled himself easily out of the water and spun round to sit on the edge, his feet dangling into the water as he waited for Debby to catch up.

'Bastard,' she spluttered, laughing. 'You told me you couldn't swim very well.'

'I lied,' he said coolly, and held out a helping hand.

Debby grasped it, swung her legs up until her feet were firmly against the platform and heaved Phillip over her head into the water. He disappeared under the surface, then she felt him sliding up in front of her until his head bobbed up and he pulled her tightly against him and kissed her. She wrapped her legs round him and returned his kiss hungrily, her tongue exploring deep inside his mouth as she clung to him like a limpet. She could feel him respond at once, his cock swelling and rising against her.

Phillip pushed her away and heaved himself up on to the platform, then held out his arms. Debby breaststroked to him and allowed him to lift her out of the water and on to his lap. She wrapped her legs round him and wriggled into position over his erect cock. Then she sank down taking the full length of him inside her.

She cupped his face in her hands and stared into his eyes. 'I love you,' she whispered. 'I've dreamt of this and longed for it since you left me in Lloret.'

Phillip pushed up hard into her, at the same time pressing down on her shoulders.

'No, don't move,' she murmured. 'I want to sit like this for ever.' She closed her eyes and savoured the feeling of his hot, hard flesh inside her. She clasped her hands over his knees behind her and, locking her legs round him, bent back, flinging her wet hair clear as he leant forward and kissed her breasts. His tongue teased and flicked from one nipple to the other, the mingled tastes of sea salt and sweat filling his mouth. She sighed with pleasure, pressing against him and easing off in a slow, gentle grind of her hips.

Phillip lay back and stared at the stars twinkling in the night sky as Debby slid herself slowly up and down his cock. She swung her legs round, lay down on top of him, and held him tightly as she rubbed her breasts against his chest and ground her pelvis against his. He turned her on to her back, raised her legs to her shoulders and started to pump slowly in and out. She moaned deep in her throat, rolling her head from side to side as he lunged into her, then slowly withdrew, his thrusts getting harder and faster as they approached orgasm.

'I'm coming,' he gasped.

'Yes, yes!' She pressed harder against him to receive his seed as her own orgasm exploded deep within her and she felt a flood of wetness as his cock jerked and spent deep inside her. Then he relaxed and let his weight slump on to her and they lay together, their sweat-soaked, exhausted bodies gleaming in the moonlight as they rocked gently to the swell of the sea.

Fingers of light swept the bay and passed over the platform as a car drove on to the hard shoulder by the beach and swung round in a U-turn. It braked to a halt and the lights went out. Phillip lifted his head and watched a young man and woman get out and wander hand in hand along the beach.

'Come on,' he said. 'It looks like we've got company.'

Debby sat up and watched the couple. 'They've only come here for a screw,' she said. 'I hope she enjoys hers as much as I did.'

Phillip grinned and slid into the water. Debby slipped in beside him and they swam gently back to the beach.

They dried each other with Debby's towel, pulled on their clothes and sat side by side on the sand, looking out to sea.

'What are your plans?' he asked.

She leant her head on his shoulder and said, 'I'm going to stick to you, like shit to a blanket.'

Phillip took her hand. 'I'm not ready for anything like that yet, Debby.' He looked up at the sky. 'It's at this time, after making love, that I really feel guilty, as though I'm being unfaithful to my wife.'

'She's dead, Phillip. I know it's terrible and horrible, but she isn't coming back. You mustn't be unhappy for ever. I want to make you happy. I love you, and I'll do anything for you. I know I can make you happy if you'll only give me the chance.'

They sat in silence for a moment, then Phillip said quietly, 'You know I have to kill Jimmy and Mike.'

She nodded. 'Yes, I know. I've had plenty of time to think about it, and I understand. I don't like it, but I understand.'

'Will you try to stop me?'

She shook her head. 'No. But I can't help you either. I won't let them hurt you, but I can't help you kill them. It wouldn't be right. It'd go right against everything I've been brought up to believe in. I couldn't live with that.'

'I've got to kill Pacetti first. I have to cancel that contract, and the quickest way is to kill the paymaster.' His face hardened. 'Besides, he's a scumbag. He needs killing.'

Debby shivered as she saw his expression and heard the relentless hatred in his voice. She couldn't keep a quaver of fear out of her own voice as she asked softly, 'You won't kill me, will you, Phillip?'

His face softened into a smile as he turned to look at her. 'I thought about it, but if I were going to it would have been in Lloret.' His smile faded. 'Don't give me any reason to, and I'll never harm you,' he promised.

She leant her head against his shoulder. 'I've been frightened. I thought – because I was there, part of the gang . . .' Her voice trailed into silence.

'Maybe, if you had reacted differently. If you'd driven on without stopping, if you'd been happy to carry on robbing banks, I'd have had to give the matter some very serious thought.' He chuckled to lighten the atmosphere. 'No, you don't have anything to worry about, Debby. Pacetti, Morino, North and Lambert are the ones who have to be worried. I intend to kill those bastards.'

'Be very careful, Phillip. Jimmy and Mike are tough bastards, and they'll kill you first if they get the slightest chance. But Pacetti and Morino are much worse. They're evil. They'd kill you just for the fun of it.'

'That's why I want you to stay out of it. If they get so much as an inkling that you've seen me, let alone that you're in love with me and might be helping me, you're dead. Don't forget that.'

Debby shivered. 'I know. Even Jimmy would kill me if he found out that I'd seen you, been with you, and not told him. He'd kill me, I know it. He'd think I'd been disloyal.' She turned and looked imploringly into Phillip's eyes. 'But I haven't been disloyal. I didn't tell you where they went, did I?'

'No, you didn't have to. I've got friends in high places. There's nowhere they can hide that I can't find them.' He jumped up. 'Come on, we'd better

get some sleep, I've got a heavy day tomorrow.'
He pulled Debby up to her feet.

She shook her long wet hair back from her
face and smiled up at him. But the smile quickly
changed to a look of horrified surprise as he
ran a strand of her hair through his fingers and
said, 'Maybe you should cut this off and dye
it. There are too many people round here who
might recognize you. You need to change your
appearance.'

'Not bloody likely! It's taken me years to get
it this length. Dye indeed!' She sniffed disgust-
edly. 'Hair with roots doesn't appeal to me in
the least.'

Phillip laughed softly. 'Well, all right, but you
must keep out of sight, and keep your hair tucked
in your crash helmet when you're out and about.'

'OK, I promise.' She reached up and put her
arms round him. 'Come back to my *pension*. Let's
spend tonight together.'

Phillip hesitated for a moment. Then, conclud-
ing it was best to keep her on his side – and
anyway he wanted to know where she was staying
– he agreed. 'Yes, let's go.'

They walked hand in hand up the beach,
unaware of the eyes that had watched their every
move. As the red lights of their vehicles disappeared down the lane, a swarthy Italian stepped
from the shadows. A match flared in the darkness
and he lit a cigarette.

Chapter Eleven

'Don't be fucking stupid, Vic,' said North irritably. 'Debby's miles away. If she was here, she'd have come straight to see me.'

Vic Morelli was adamant. 'It was her, I swear it was. Unless she's got a double who rides a black Virago registered in Gerona.'

'Who was the geezer she was with?' asked Lambert.

'A tall blond bloke. I've seen him hanging around the port recently. Looks like another tourist,' said Vic.

'Spell it out again,' commanded Pacetti.

Morelli said, 'Sal dropped me off outside the *puerto* to collect my car from the car park, so we could leave the truck with the drugs at the warehouse. The blond guy was walking to his car, and someone on a bike, a Virago, rode right up to him and got off the bike. I thought it was a bloke till she took her helmet off and I saw her face. I recognized her right away from when you brought her here last year. I was going to give her a shout, but she rushed up to the blond geezer and kissed him.'

'Well, what happened next?' asked North.

'She sat the car with him for a while, then she jumped out and hopped on her bike and belted off. The geezer in the car followed her and I followed him. They drove to one of the beaches along the coast, stripped off and swam out to one of those platforms the paragliders launch off, and he gave her a good seeing to. Lucky bastard,' he added. 'I quite fancied her myself.'

'It don't make sense,' said North. 'If it is her, she don't know anyone who lives down here.'

'What about Ted – or Ross, I mean?' said Lambert. 'She was screwing him. Perhaps she liked it. Perhaps she fell for him, and told him we're down here.'

'No, not Debby. That's the last thing she'd do.'

'Well, he's a good-looking bastard. If he's been giving her a good shafting, and she *has* fallen for him – who knows?'

'I spoke to her only a few days ago,' said North. 'She said she was pissed off being in the villa alone, and was going away for a few days.'

'Looks like she came straight here,' said Lambert.

North scratched the back of his head thoughtfully. 'She said she'd phone me. When she does I'll test her out, and if I don't get the right answers she's in fucking trouble.'

'What if this blond geezer *is* Ross? He could have bleached his hair for all we know,' said Lambert. 'I wish you'd told us last night, Vic. We could've gone looking for the pair of them. If it is Ross he could've knocked us off by now.'

Morelli shrugged. 'I didn't get back from the warehouse till seven this morning, and then I went straight to bed. I didn't know it was that important.'

Pacetti looked at his watch. 'Our guests'll start arriving for the party in about an hour, so we'll have to leave this on hold until tomorrow. Then we'll go looking for them. If it is Debby and this Ross' – he slashed his forefinger across his throat – 'we feed them to the fishes.' He turned to Morino. 'Phone London and get some more boys down here to help with the search. We'll comb this coastline from Gibraltar to Torremolinos. If they're here, we'll find them.'

At eight thirty the guests started to arrive. Pacetti welcomed them on the after deck, and two stewardesses, under Captain Miller's watchful eye, poured champagne into cut-glass flutes.

As the Mercedes, Porsches and Rolls-Royces purred along the quay and parked opposite the big yacht, a crowd gathered to watch the guests arrive. The men wore white tuxedos, the women, who included a number of startlingly beautiful, unaccompanied girls, wore expensive designer gowns and were draped in jewellery. Deck hands in crisply pressed whites helped them aboard. Morino, Giovanni and Morelli, dressed in black tuxedos and red bow ties and wearing mirrored sunglasses, stood at strategic positions to make sure that no uninvited guests tried to board. Pacetti was in his element as he played to the gallery of onlookers on the quay: he was the wealthy host, the big man.

With a burbling roar, *Charlene*'s twin engines burst into life, sending great gushes of cooling water and smoke from the exhaust pipes. Deck hands rushed to their positions, ready to cast off, as Captain Miller prepared to manoeuvre out of the berth. Two blasts on her air-horns, and the yacht was under way, heading for the harbour mouth.

Phillip watched from the sea wall as Captain Miller cleared the harbour and opened up the throttles to a cruising speed of fifteen knots. He walked quickly to his car and drove slowly along the coast, stopping here and there to monitor the yacht's course and to check that she did in fact anchor offshore, as Pacetti had said she would.

By the time *Charlene* got to her position off Victor's beach, Phillip was ensconced there, looking every inch the fisherman, with a beach rod propped up in the sand and two large tackle boxes beside him. He sat alone at the water's edge and watched her drop anchor a mile offshore and swing round in line with the southerly breeze.

The yacht was ablaze with lights, and the slight onshore breeze carried the faint beat of music across the calm water. Phillip studied her through powerful binoculars. Captain Miller, Vic Morelli and Giovanni Vicci were on the flying bridge. On the rear deck and through the lounge windows, he could see the revellers, some chatting in groups, some dancing.

He took out his flask and poured strong black coffee into a beaker. It was going to be a long night. He planned to wait until Pacetti and his guests were drunk and drugged out of their minds, then swim out to the yacht and kill Pacetti. He'd kill North and Lambert at the same time, if he got the chance.

He put on his earphones and switched on the receiver. Loud music, laughter and chatter filled his ears from the bug in the lounge. He switched to the bug in Pacetti's bedroom. Silence. He switched back to the lounge, turned down the volume and settled down to wait.

Morino set a large silver dish on the bar and removed the lid to reveal a huge pile of cocaine. Next to it he put a large silver cigar box full of marijuana joints. 'Help yourself to charlie and spliffs,' Pacetti called out. 'The captain and crew are confined to their quarters, so we can do as we like – no need to mind our Ps and Qs.' As the guests crowded to the bar he moved aside, beckoning Morino to follow. 'Leave Giovanni on watch. You and Luciano come and have some fun.'

'Sure thing, Tony,' said Morino. Carrying a small polythene packet and two spliffs, he went back to the flying bridge. He handed Vicci the drugs. 'You're on watch, so keep your eyes peeled. If any suspicious-looking boats head in our direction, call me on the intercom. I'll be in the lounge or in my cabin.'

'No problem, Sal.' Vicci tucked the drugs into his pocket and swigged from a can of lager. 'Send one of the brasses up to keep me company for a while, and I'll be as happy as a pig in shit.'

'OK, but keep your fucking eyes open. We don't
want to get busted.'

A few minutes later a giggling blonde climbed
the spiral staircase to the flying bridge. 'I'm
Olivia. Salvatore sent me up to keep you company.'

Vicci spun round in the captain's swivel chair,
looked her slowly up and down and smiled
approvingly. She had big breasts, which wobbled
as she giggled and threatened to pop out of her
tight red silk evening dress at any moment. He
produced the packet of cocaine, opened it and
sniffed a pinch into each nostril. He handed it
to Olivia. 'Help yourself.' He unzipped his fly.
'Then get to work on this.'

Olivia snorted the white powder and purred with
pleasure. She knelt down between his open legs,
groped inside his trousers and pulled his cock out.
Her eyes widened. 'Wow! We are a big boy, aren't
we?' she said happily, and took him in her mouth.

He leant back and clasped his hands behind
his neck, smiling up at the stars. 'This is the life,'
he said.

The curtains in the lounge had been drawn, the
lights turned low. A blonde and a brunette were
doing a striptease routine to catcalls and shouts
of encouragement from Pacetti and his guests.
When the two girls were naked, they began to
kiss and caress each other, pouring baby oil on
to each other's sun-bronzed flesh. They swayed
down on to the carpet and writhed together, their
limbs and hair intertwined.

Pacetti withdrew his attention for a moment

from the beautiful black girl sitting on his lap, and tossed the two strippers a vibrator. The brunette grabbed it with a whoop of joy and flicked the switch. Pushing the blonde's legs wide open, she inserted it and worked it slowly in and out.

Lambert, high on cocaine, looked at North and grinned wetly. 'I'm having some of that.'

He climbed unsteadily out of his chair, knelt behind the brunette and dropped his trousers. She turned her head to look back at him, grinned and lifted her butt in the air to take him, then turned back and in time to Lambert's thrusts worked the vibrator in the blonde. The guests roared their approval.

North shouted, 'If three's good, four's better!' He knelt beside the blonde's head, undid his fly and pushed his erection towards her mouth. 'Have some Brighton rock, darling.'

She began to lick his cock, her small pink tongue running up and down the shaft, teasing him and arousing him still further. Then she took him deep into her mouth, sucking him, squeezing him with her lips.

The other guests began to join in, stripping off their clothes and choosing the first partner who took their fancy. And all the time they shot lines of coke and smoked spliffs, the pungent fumes filling the air. It was a scene Caligula would have approved of: oiled, naked bodies of every kind and colour writhed and plunged to the slow beat of the music. The smells of perfume, sex and sweat almost overcame the fumes of the drugs.

*   *   *

Debby paced up and down the small room, constantly checking her watch. Before he left that morning, Phillip had made her promise not to leave the *pension*, under any circumstances, until he contacted her. But she was ravenous. At supper in the restaurant downstairs three hours ago, strain and pressure and anxiety about Phillip had taken away her appetite, and she'd done no more than pick at her food. Now her stomach was rumbling like the engine of a double-decker bus, and the thought of a pizza or a bowl of paella brought saliva flooding into her mouth.

Oh sod it, she thought, no one knows I'm here, and anyway who'd recognize me on my bike? Besides, if Phillip thought things were dodgy he'd have been in touch by now to warn me. She hastily pulled on her leathers, picked up her helmet and ran downstairs.

There was no one anywhere near the bike, and no one had paid any attention as she left the *pension*. Her confidence growing, she fired the engine and spun the rear wheel in the gravel as she accelerated down the drive and turned towards Gibraltar.

She felt as wild and free as a bird as she sped along the N340, swooping past cars and leaning steeply into the bends, the wind billowing her leather jacket and cooling her body. She could have ridden for hours, but all too soon the sign for Puerto Duquesa loomed ahead. She slowed to a more sedate speed, signalled, and turned left.

She tucked the bike into the corner of a car

park near the *puerto*. She debated keeping her
crash helmet on, but decided she'd be more
conspicuous than if she was bare-headed. Her
stomach rumbled again, making her giggle. It was
definitely time to eat. She wandered through the
complex, stopping occasionally to look in shop
windows and make sure no one she knew was
in sight, and went up the stairs to the first level.
A pizzeria was still open, several of its tables
occupied by groups of young people, eating,
drinking wine, laughing and talking loudly.

Debby sat at a small table near the back of
the restaurant and studied the menu: she felt as
though she could eat everything on it and then
come back for more. When she looked round for
the waiter, she found herself looking directly into
the eyes of a man standing at the bar. He hastily
looked away and turned his back to her. She
smiled to herself. She was used to men looking
at her, especially when she was dressed in her
leather biker's gear. Some men couldn't handle
it, others found it a real turn-on.

The waiter was evidently one of the turn-ons,
staring appreciatively at her breasts while he
wrote down her order. He brought over her
pepperoni pizza and glass of red Rioja in double-
quick time, then dawdled over setting them down,
fiddling with the cutlery, offering her pepper,
another paper napkin, some garlic bread, all
the time running his eyes surreptitiously up and
down her body.

Finally Debby got rid of him. She tucked into
her pizza with gusto, and the first few mouthfuls

went down a treat. But then anxiety surfaced again, and her appetite died. She had to force herself to eat. She hoped the wine would calm her nerves and took a big swallow, but it didn't seem to help. What if Phillip had met trouble? What if Jimmy or Sal Morino or someone had seen him? What if he'd been trying to ring her and there was no answer from her room? He might think there was something wrong, and God alone knew what he'd do then. How long had she been out? An hour? More? She must get back – fast. She decided to pay the bill quickly and get back down to her bike.

Earlier that evening on the flying bridge Giovanni Vicci had Olivia bent forward over the rail, her red silk dress pulled up over her back, her blonde hair flying in the breeze and her breasts jouncing as he shafted her from behind for the third time.

The telephone on the console bleeped. 'Who the fuck's that?' he growled, and reluctantly withdrew.

Trousers round his ankles, he staggered to the telephone. '*Charlene*,' he snapped.

'Hi, this is Kieran. I want to speak to Salvatore.'

'He's busy.'

'Look, I delivered some gear to Salvatore just before you left port. He asked me to keep an eye open for this bird on a motorbike, said it was important. Well, I've found her.'

'Are you fucking sure?'

'Well, I met her last year on Tony's boat, when she was there with Jimmy North. She's a right good-looking bird, so I remember her. She's riding a black Virago.'

Vicci tried to think clearly. 'Where is she now?'

'I'm sitting looking at her. She's in a restaurant in Puerto Duquesa. I came here to make a delivery, and while I was waiting she just rode up, large as life.'

'Are you on your mobile? Have we got your number?'

'Yeah, I'm on it now. Salvatore's got the number.'

'Well, stay with her. If she leaves, follow her. I'll get Sal to phone you right back.'

'He said there'd be a nice drink in it if I found her.'

'Yeah, you'll get your drink. But don't lose her, or you're in fucking trouble.' Vicci dropped the receiver back into its cradle.

Olivia, still bent over the rail, looked over her shoulder at him. 'Aren't you going to finish what you started?' she said, and wriggled invitingly.

He ran his hand down between her buttocks, penetrating her front and back. 'Keep it warm, kid. I've got a couple of calls to make.' He wiped his hand on her skirt, picked up the phone and dialled the lounge.

Pacetti spat the black girl's breast out of his mouth and reached for the phone. 'What the fuck is it?' he demanded.

'Is Sal there, Tony? Kieran just phoned. He's found Debby.'

Pacetti pushed the girl aside and sat up. 'Fuck me, that was quick! Where is she?'

'Puerto Duquesa. She's in a restaurant.'

'Is she alone, or is the blond guy with her?'

'He didn't say. But by the way he spoke, she's on her own.'

'Sal went down to his cabin about five minutes ago. Tell him that, and tell him to meet me on the after deck straight away. I'll get Jimmy and Mike out there now.'

The girl tried to pull him back to her breast, but Pacetti slapped her hands away. 'Wait here, Zoe. I've got some important business to deal with but I'll be back soon, so don't fuck with anyone else while I'm gone. Understand?'

She pouted. 'I don't want anyone except you, Tony.'

'Yeah, I know,' he said. 'When I get back, we go to my cabin and I fuck your brains out. Understand?'

She giggled and squeezed both hands over her pussy. 'Yes please, Tony. And don't be too long. I'm getting real horny watching everyone enjoying themselves.'

Pacetti stood up. He was still wearing his underpants. He never had sex in public because he was embarrassed about his small penis. But he got a kick out of watching others perform, and then going off to do his stuff in private.

He stepped across writhing bodies, calling out, 'Jimmy, Mike, where the fuck are you?'

North's head popped up between the bodies of two naked women spreadeagled over him. 'What's up, Tony?'

Pacetti cocked his thumb towards the after

deck. 'Find Mike and meet me on deck. It's important.'

North shoved the women off and hauled himself to his feet. He reached for his clothes, which were strewn on the floor nearby. Pulling on his pants, he began to search the darkened room, tripping over bodies and shouting Lambert's name.

At last there was an answer from a corner by the rear doors. 'What? What's up, Jimmy?'

'I dunno,' said North, 'but Tony wants us outside now. Said it's important.'

When the two men stepped on to the after deck, Pacetti and Morino were waiting. Morino was speaking into a mobile phone.

'We've found your Debby,' said Pacetti. 'She's in a restaurant in Puerto Duquesa.'

Morino switched the phone off. 'She's having a pizza. I've got a man keeping an eye on her. If she leaves before we get there, he's going to bell us and let us know where she goes.'

'She'll be well gone before we get to Duquesa,' said North.

'Not if we go in one of the tenders.' Morino pointed to the two sixteen-foot speedboats hanging from davits, one on each side of the yacht. 'We could be there in less than half an hour.'

Lambert said, 'Let's go then.' He took a couple of steps towards the nearer tender, staggered and almost fell.

North looked at him, then at Pacetti. 'Mike's too far gone to be any use. He's as high as a kite and spaced out.'

'Are you OK, Jimmy?' asked Pacetti.

'Yeah. I've had a snort and a couple of drinks, but I'm OK.'

'Go with Jimmy,' Pacetti ordered Morino. 'Grab that bitch and take her to the villa. Find out what the fuck she's up to, and who this blond guy is.'

Morino was already untying the launch and swinging it clear of *Charlene*'s side. He pressed a green button on the side of the davit and the launch descended to the level of the guard rail. He pulled it in close to the rail and said to North, 'Climb in. Release the cables when you're in the water and I'll pull you round and board off the bathing platform.'

North stepped over the rail and clambered into the launch. Morino pushed it clear and pressed the green button again, paying out the belaying guyrope as the launch dropped slowly into the sea. Then he ran aft and climbed down to the bathing platform. As soon as he was aboard, he pushed the starter button and the launch's big Mercury engine coughed into life.

Over the roar of the engine. Morino shouted to Pacetti, 'I'll phone you and let you know when we've got her.' Then he gunned the throttle and the launch's nose lifted high in the air as she powered away in a tight arc, leaving a swirling white wake in the calm water.

Pacetti turned to Lambert, who was leaning on *Charlene*'s guard rail for support, and took him by the arm. 'Come on, buddy, let's get you back inside. Have another line of coke, and some more pussy.'

'I feel bad. I should've gone with him,' said Lambert, staring after the launch.

'Don't worry about it. Nobody knew she was going to turn up so soon. Anyway, Jimmy and Sal will take care of everything, so let's go and have a good time. That's what we planned, so let's get on with it.' He started to lead Lambert back into the lounge, but Lambert pulled away.

'You're right, Tony, but it still don't feel right. I'm going to get my head down for an hour or so and sober up.' He staggered to the spiral staircase and half climbed, half fell down it.

Back in the lounge, Pacetti grabbed Zoe by the arm and shook her awake. 'Come on, kid, let's go to my cabin. I've got a little job for you.'

Zoe opened her eyes and smiled lazily as she climbed out of the chair. 'About time too. I was nearly asleep.' She held Pacetti's hand tightly as he guided her through the entangled bodies and led her down to his cabin.

Phillip turned the volume up to full again and listened intently. The music was now a low throb, but still only the occasional murmur of voices reached his ears. Frustrated, he opened one of his fishing-tackle boxes, took out a black neoprene wetsuit and balaclava, a snorkel mask and breathing tube, flippers and a wide rubber belt, from which hung a diver's sheath knife and several stainless-steel clips. He tugged on the wetsuit and balaclava, and strapped the belt round his waist.

He dropped receiver, headphones, pistol, silencer

and gloves into waterproof bags and clipped them to his belt. He studied the yacht one last time through his binoculars. Giovanni Vicci was on the bridge, still occupied with the blonde. The lounge was in darkness. Lights shone from the portholes of the crew's quarters and several guest cabins. It was time to go.

From the other tackle box he took a sleeping bag. He unrolled it, stuffed his clothes inside and fluffed it up so that it looked occupied. After a final check to make sure he was unobserved, he walked into the sea, donning the snorkel as he went.

The water was cool and calm. He swam a leisurely breaststroke, careful to make no sound and to leave no wake. Halfway to *Charlene*, he paused to survey her again. There was activity on the after deck. Silhouetted against the night sky, men were lowering one of the tenders into the water. Soon, the launch sped away to the south-west, with two men aboard.

Phillip waited until she was well clear, then began swimming again. Twenty yards from the yacht he stopped, trod water and panned the guard rails. *Charlene* towered above him. Shafts of light from the portholes cast golden twinkling reflections in the water alongside her. He strained his senses for any sign or sound of danger, but there was only the slow beat of soul music and the slap of the sea against the yacht's hull.

He swam to the bathing platform, hauled himself up and spun into a crouch close against the yacht's side, where he couldn't easily be seen from above. He removed the mask, snorkel and flippers, and clipped them to his belt. He unzipped the bag containing the Browning and fitted the silencer before tucking it into his belt at the small of his back. He put on the headphones and turned on the receiver. Music and the odd groan reached his ears. He switched to Pacetti's cabin. Bingo! he thought, as he heard background music and the high-pitched giggle of a girl.

He cautiously climbed the ladder to the after deck and peered up at the flying bridge. He couldn't see them, but he could hear the low murmur of conversation from Vicci and his tart. Vicci stood up and leant over the side. He looked idly around, flicked the butt of a spliff into the sea and sat back down out of view.

Phillip slipped silently over the rail. He crossed to the port gangway and peered into the lounge through a gap in the curtains. In the darkened room he could make out naked bodies sprawled across the settees, chairs and floor. Keeping an eye on the flying bridge, he went forward to the door to the crew's quarters and stepped inside. All was quiet.

He drifted silently down the passage, pausing to listen at each cabin door, until he came to the door leading to the guest quarters. He opened it a crack and looked down the dimly lit corridor to the door of Pacetti's master cabin. A door on the right was ajar, light spilling into the corridor. Phillip crept to the door jamb and peered in.

Mike Lambert lay on his back snoring loudly.

Phillip found the light switch by the door and flipped it, plunging the cabin into darkness. He drew his knife, stepped into the cabin and closed the door.

Chapter Twelve

Deep in thoughts of Phillip, Debby straddled the Virago and slid the key into the ignition. Rough hands grabbed her arms and she was dragged off the bike, her crash helmet torn from her head. She opened her mouth to scream, but was silenced by a violent open-handed blow that snapped her head to the side. Her eyes wide with shock and fear, she looked up at the rage-reddened face of her attacker.

'Jimmy!'

'You fucking treacherous little bitch!' he snarled. 'I didn't believe it when they told me. I didn't fucking believe it.' He hit her again, splitting her lip, and dragged her towards a car parked nearby, its lights on and its engine idling. The car door was flung open. She recognized the driver as the man who had stared at her in the pizzeria. Then she saw the face of the man who reached out to drag her into the car, and her fear became terror.

Salvatore Morino was grinning evilly. He grabbed her wrists, pulled her into the back of the car and flung her brutally to the floor. As she landed,

he slammed a foot on to her head, pinning her
down. North leapt in after her and slammed the
door shut, and the car lurched forward and raced
out of the car park.

Debby was shaking with fear. Where were they
going? What would they do to her? Phillip, oh
God, Phillip, where are you? Help me! Help!

It was difficult to breathe, cramped down on
the floor as she was, but she took the deepest
breath she could and summoned all her reserves
of courage. 'Where are you taking me?' For all her
efforts, her voice was high and unsteady.

The men ignored her.

'Jimmy, I didn't tell him where you where. I
swear I didn't!'

Still in silence, North turned his head and
looked out of the side window.

'Jimmy, I wouldn't grass on you, you know I
wouldn't. I swear I didn't tell him anything.'

North snorted disbelievingly.

Morino lifted the foot that pinned her down,
grabbed her hair and yanked her face up close
to his. She could smell whisky and dope on his
breath. His smile was full of sadistic anticipation.
'I don't think he trusts you any more, Debby. But
you're going to tell us the truth, aren't you?'

She managed to nod slightly. 'Yes, I promise to
tell you the truth.'

Morino smiled again and patted her head.
'Good. It will be better for you, I assure you.'
He shoved her back down to the floor and again
pinned her down with his foot. They travelled on
in silence.

After a while Debby felt the car turn left off the main road. They were now on a much windier road, but the driver hardly slowed at all and only the heavy pressure of Morino's foot prevented her from being thrown about. They turned again, to the right this time, on to a rough track which made the car's suspension judder and groan. Morino's foot was bounced off her head, and he laughed and let her be. She straightened up as much as she could and dragged air deep into her lungs, turning her head a little so that her face was in the draught from the open window.

The car stopped at a pair of heavy wooden gates. The driver leant out and pushed a button. A babble of Spanish crackled out of a speaker. The driver babbled back. All Debby could make out were the names of Salvatore Morino and Jimmy North. The gates jerked, then slowly ground open to allow the car in. Dread mingled with her fear as she looked back to see the gates closing behind them.

The headlights picked out an old Spanish villa with vine-strung arches and tiled terraces. As the car drove through an arch into a courtyard and slowed to a halt, floodlights were switched on, the iron-studded villa door opened and a dark, swarthy man wearing a sweat-stained white vest came out. He held a machine pistol trained on the car, but lowered it and smiled as Morino stepped out of the car into the light.

North opened his door and climbed out, dragging Debby by the hair. She stumbled and was yanked back up. He pulled her face close to his and snarled, 'Ross is here in Puerto Banús, ain't he? You brought him here, didn't you, you cunt?'

Debby fought to control her panic. 'I didn't, Jimmy. He was already here when I arrived.'

He twisted her arm high up behind her back and shoved her towards the open door. 'Get inside, bitch. We've got a lot of questions for you.' He gave her arm a painful wrench. 'And you're going to tell us everything we want to know.'

They went down a creaky staircase to the cellar, which smelt of damp and was strung with cobwebs. They marched through arches, past dusty old wine racks full of bottles. There was a squeal and a rustle, and a rat scurried out of sight into a pile of rubbish. Debby shuddered.

Morino unlocked a steel door and switched on a dim light. He led them into a dank, windowless room and slammed the door.

North flung Debby to the floor. 'Stay down there, slut,' he said, his voice full of menace, 'and start talking.'

'I don't know where he is. I've only seen him that once. I swear it, Jimmy.'

'You'll have to do better than that,' said Morino flatly. He crossed his arms and leant back against the wall.

'OK, tell us about the once,' said North.

'I was worried about all of you. Frightened that you'd all kill each other.'

North gave a twisted smile. 'So you went to Ross to protect us,' he sneered. 'Is that it?'

'Yes,' she said desperately. 'I don't want to see any of you hurt.'

North took a threatening step towards her. 'Then why didn't I know you were here? I'm your fucking friend and partner, remember? We rob fucking banks together. And you don't just work for me, you're family. You live in my fucking house.'

Debby shook her head. 'I don't know how to explain Jimmy,' she said hopelessly. 'I love him. I love Phillip.'

North let out a yell of rage. 'Fuck me hooray! He's killed Billy, Roger and Harry and he wants to kill me and Mike, and you're in love with the cunt!' He swung round to Morino. 'Christ, Sal, I don't fucking well believe what I'm hearing. She's been helping Ross. The only way he could have found us is through her. She's fucking grassed us, that's what she's done.'

Morino stepped forward. 'Start talking, bitch. Where is this Phillip fucking Ross? Where's he staying? What's he doing? And what does he plan to do?' He seized her leather jacket, hauled her to her feet and slammed her against the wall. Her head crashed against the plaster.

Debby doubled up with a yelp of pain as Morino's fist crunched into her ribs in a vicious upper cut. He grabbed her by the hair, yanked her head back and hammered his knee into the side of her head. The force of the blow lifted her off her feet and she collapsed on to the stone floor, dazed and bleeding. She lay there retching, her head spinning, as she waited helplessly for the next blow.

Morino drew his foot back to kick her, but North

caught him by the arm. 'Hold on, Sal. We don't want to kill her yet. She's got to tell us where Ross is.'

'Sure,' said Morino calmly. 'I can wait. I just want her to know that I don't fuck around.' He gave her a sharp kick in the ribs and stepped back. 'If she don't talk, I'm going to kick her to death. I've got my special kicking boots on, bitch, see?' He held one close to Debby's face and turned it so that she could see the metal toecap and the heavily studded sole. She shut her eyes, nausea rising in her throat.

North yanked her up into a sitting position, took a fistful of her hair and forced her head round so that she faced him. 'Where is he?' he demanded.

'I don't know.' She licked her split and swollen lips. Blood trickled down her chin and stained her white T-shirt. She wiped the blood from her chin with her hand and inspected it. Her hand dropped limply into her lap and she looked back up at North. Somehow she was no longer afraid. All she felt now was defiance.

She lifted her chin. 'I don't know, and if I did I wouldn't tell you, you bastard.'

'Do you know what you just did, bitch? You just signed your own death warrant.' North let go of her hair. 'You stabbed me in the back, Debby,' he said quietly. 'You was family, but you brought him here to kill me.'

'I know you're going to kill me. There's nothing I can do to stop you. So I'll tell you this. I didn't tell him you were down here. I said you'd gone to London, to the funerals, like you said I should. He said he'd find you wherever you went. He's got friends, Jimmy. He told me he's got friends in high places, and he can track you down anywhere in the world. He's too good for you,' she said with certainty. 'He's going to kill you. All of you.'

Morino stepped forward. 'What the fuck are you on about?'

Debby faced him defiantly. 'He knows about the contract Tony put out, so he's going to kill him first.'

'Who does this wanker think he is?' Morino was scornfully amused.

'Jimmy ain't told you, has he?' she jeered.

Morino looked sharply at North. 'What ain't you told me?'

Debby cut in before North could speak. 'He's an ex-SAS man. He's trained to kill and' – she laughed in Morino's face – 'he's proved he's bloody good at it. That's why Jimmy and Mike came running down here, to hide behind Tony's skirts.'

Morino rounded on North. 'SAS, and you never told us? What the fuck were you playing at?'

'I didn't think he'd find us down here, so it didn't seem important.'

Morino said furiously, 'You let Tony put out a twenty-grand contract on a fucking SAS man? You stood by and let him put his name to it, and you didn't think it was fucking important?'

'I never gave it a thought, Sal.' North shrugged uneasily. 'I just thought that would be the end of it. Someone pro would take the contract and kill him. No sweat.'

'These guys don't kill easy,' Morino growled. 'They run a hundred miles in ten minutes with a fucking bulldozer on their back. They jump out of aeroplanes at ten thousand feet without a parachute. They attack camps full of armed soldiers on their fucking jack, kill several hundred men, and piss off without a scratch. Tony'll fucking love this. He'll be right pleased to know you dumped him deep in a pile of the SAS's shit.'

'Well, I . . . Look, we'll worry about Ross when the time comes.' He jerked his chin towards Debby. 'What are we going to do with her?'

'She don't know fuck all,' said Morino impatiently. 'This bloke's a pro. He won't have told her anything that would put him on the line.' He pulled a lock-knife out of his pocket and snapped it open. 'But she tells us everything she knows or she dies now.' He reached down, hauled Debby to her feet and held the point of the curved blade three inches in front of her right eye. 'Answer every question truthfully, or you go blind,' he said silkily.

Debby swallowed and whispered, 'Yes.'

'Some of the questions I'm going to ask, I already know the answer to, so I'll know if you're lying.' He paused to let the threat sink in. 'When did you arrive in Marbella?'

Debby glanced nervously at North, then back at Morino. 'The day before yesterday.'

'When and where did you meet Ross?'

'Last night, in the car park at Banús.'

Morino looked at North and nodded. 'Where did you go?'

'To the beach.'

'What did you do?'

'We talked, and made love.'

'What then?'

'We went back to my *pension*. Phillip stayed the night.'

'What time did he leave?'

'Ten o'clock this morning.'

'Where did he go?'

'I don't know. He didn't tell me.'

'What did he tell you?'

'He told me to stay in the *pension*. He said I mustn't go out and that he'd contact me.'

'But you went out.'

'I was hungry, and bored.'

'What else did he tell you?'

'That he was going to kill Pacetti.'

Morino released her and looked at North. 'We'd better get back to the yacht. Tony might be in trouble.'

'What about her?'

'We keep her alive. She may come in useful later. We can use her as bait if we have to.' He shoved her roughly away from him and went to the door. 'Come on, Jimmy. Let her rot here for a while.'

They went out and Debby heard the key turn in the lock. For a moment she stood motionless, half expecting them to come back and start beating her again. Then she sank to the floor and started to cry.

Morino ran up the wooden staircase, yelling for Paco. North was right behind him. The Spaniard in the grubby vest ran to meet them at the top of the stairs, still clutched the Uzi machine pistol. 'Sí, boss?' he asked.

'I've gotta get back to the yacht. We're leaving the girl. She's locked in the back cellar. Don't go anywhere near her. I'll be back tomorrow with more men.'

Paco looked worried. 'Is there gonna be trouble, boss? Shall I wake my boys?'

Morino shook his head as he rushed to the door. 'No. Nobody knows she's here.' He stopped at the door and looked back as he pressed the button to open the wooden gates at the end of the drive. 'Keep the door locked and your gun handy, just in case.'

Kieran was standing by the car in the courtyard as Morino and North hurried out of the villa. He leapt into the driving seat as Morino shouted, 'Back to Duquesa. Fast!'

The three men travelled in silence. Kieran pushed the car for every ounce of speed. At the end of the track, he dropped into third and flung the car into a screeching left-hand turn on to the narrow tarmac road. The rear end slid as the tyres slipped on the shiny surface, the headlights cutting a swathe of light through the darkness. Kieran kept his foot hard down on the accelerator, yanked at the steering wheel and straightened the car, which surged forward, gathering speed.

Morino reached into his hip pocket and pulled out a thick wad of fifty-pound notes. He flicked through the notes as expertly as a bank teller and peeled off a wedge. He stuffed the wad back into his pocket and held up the wedge for Kieran to see. 'That's for you, my son.' He opened the glove compartment and tossed the money inside. 'You keep your mouth shut about the girl. You ain't seen or heard nothing, right?'

Kieran nodded. 'You can rely on me, Sal. Tonight didn't even happen as far as I'm concerned.'

Morino stared at the road ahead and said quietly, 'I don't need to tell you what happens if you open your mouth. Do I?'

Kieran swallowed nervously. 'I don't even want to think about it, Sal. Like I said, you can rely on me.'

North leant forward from the back of the car. 'Do you think we should phone the yacht and warn Tony?'

Morino shook his head. 'No, I don't want to panic everyone until we're back on board. If Ross's already been there, we're already too late. If he ain't acted yet, I want to return normally as if nothing's happened to alarm us.' He turned and smiled at North. 'Then we sit like spiders and wait for him to step into our web.'

Mike Lambert thought he was having a nightmare or a bad trip. He was pinned to his bed by a man in black who sat astride him, pinning his legs against his sides. He tried to make out his attacker's face, but all he could see was a silhouette against the dim light that showed through the porthole curtains. The man's left hand gripped him tightly by the throat, steel fingers clamping his larynx so tightly that he couldn't breathe or call out. Lambert lay rigid, every muscle taut with fear and tension.

Steel flashed as a wicked-looking blade with a jagged back edge was held up in front of his eyes. 'Say your prayers, Lambert. I'm about to cut your throat.' The calm whisper made the threat all the more horrific.

He tried to raise his arms, but they were pinned to his side by the man's knees. His attacker leant over and switched on the bedside lamp. With a sick lurch of horror, Lambert recognized the pitiless face and knew he was going to die.

The fingers round Lambert's throat slackened their grip. He drew a shuddering breath and forced words through his bruised throat. 'No, please, Ross, don't do it. I didn't mean to kill her. It was an accident. We were trying to get away. She was just there suddenly in front of me – I couldn't avoid her.'

As he looked down at the man who'd killed Julie, Phillip relived in an instant the moment of her death. He saw again her staring, half-open eyes, felt again the desolate grief of the moment when he knew she was dead. He was overwhelmed by an ice-cold, bitter hatred. It was all he could do to prevent himself using his knife to torture Lambert, to make him die slowly and in unbearable physical and mental agony. He forced the urge away, and said, 'You used to be a racing driver, didn't you? I don't believe you couldn't have avoided her. But that would have meant slowing down, wouldn't it? Risking being caught by the police and tried and sentenced for the shooting of the security guard. So you smashed into my wife and killed her. And it was purely by good fortune that my son wasn't killed as well.'

'Christ, Ross, I didn't mean to hit her. I aimed at a gap and she just ran into it. I did everything I could to avoid her. If I'd done any more and risked us getting caught, Jimmy would have fried my brains for breakfast.'

'Where is Jimmy? Which cabin is he in?'

'He ain't here. He's gone.'

Phillip remembered the speedboat leaving with two men aboard. 'Where did he go?'

'To get Debby.' Lambert registered a faint flicker of hope: perhaps he could use her safety as a bargaining counter.

Phillip pressed the point of the blade against Lambert's throat and cut him a little. Blood began to flow. Lambert could feel it run round the back of his neck. It dripped on to the sheet, bright red against the white.

'Duquesa,' said Lambert hastily. 'They went in a launch to Puerto Duquesa. Someone spotted her in a restaurant there.'

'Who went?'

'Jimmy and Sal Morino.'

Phillip felt a chill of anxiety. He knew from George Hill's file on the Pacetti gang that Morino was a cold-blooded sadist, who enjoyed killing slowly, savouring his victim's pain and terror.

'Where are they taking her?'

'If you kill me, you'll never save her,' Lambert said hopefully.

'I can torture you until you tell me. You won't like it, I promise you.' Phillip pressed the tip of the knife into the wound. Lambert began to howl with fear but was choked into silence as the grip on his larynx tightened like red-hot pincers.

Phillip waited until Lambert's eye's began to bulge in his head before slackening his grip again and letting his prisoner take another lungful of air.

'To a villa. I only heard Pacetti say, "Take her to the villa." I've never been there. I don't know where it is.'

Phillip withdrew the knife slightly. Lambert sighed with relief and visibly relaxed.

Phillip said, 'It's time to die, you murdering scum.' He stabbed the blade up under Lambert's chin into the back of his mouth, skewering his tongue. 'That's for my wife,' he said in Lambert's ear. 'And this is from me.' He withdrew the blade, sliced once across the man's throat, and released his grip. He climbed off the stricken man, stood back and waited.

Blood spewed from Lambert's jugular and bubbled in his mouth, choking him. He made a feeble attempt to stem the flow, then jerked twice and became very still.

Phillip paid him no further heed. He used the end of a sheet to wipe the blood off his wetsuit, then switched on his receiver and held the head-phones to one ear. He could hear rustles, groans and whispers of encouragement from Pacetti's cabin. He switched off the lamp, went to the door and opened it a crack. The corridor was deserted. A high-pitched squeal of protest, followed by laughter, came from one of the starboard cabins. Phillip ignored it and made his way soundlessly along to the master cabin. He eased the door open and, drawing the Browning from his belt, slipped inside.

The big cabin was in darkness, except for the king-sized bed, which was bathed in red light from an overhead spotlight. Pacetti was on his back gazing up at the mirrored ceiling as Zoe worked on him with her mouth. She knelt between his legs, her butt high in the air, her body gleaming in the light, and sucked and licked him, to hoarse whispers of encouragement.

Phillip stepped forward and clipped her behind the ear with the butt of the Browning, then stepped back into the deep shadows and was instantly invisible.

The shock of the blow made Zoe bite down and the full weight of her body lunged into Pacetti's groin. He screeched in agony as her teeth bit into the bulb of his cock, her chin crushing his balls as she collapsed on to him, unconscious.

'What the fuck! You silly fucking cunt,' he yelled, frantically pushing and kicking her away from him. He grasped his bleeding cock tenderly in one hand, trying vainly to stem the blood that spurted on to the black satin sheets. He rained furious kicks at the unconscious girl's head as she slipped off the bed into a heap on the carpet.

In panic he stabbed with a bloodied hand at the intercom button on his bedside phone. 'Sal, Sal!' Then he remembered Morino was not aboard and stabbed at the flying bridge button. 'Giovanni! Get the fuck down here. I'm bleeding to fucking death.'

Giovanni Vicci's voice crackled back. 'What's that, boss? What did you say?'

'Get the fuck down here. I need a doctor, I'm bleeding to death. The fucking bitch has bitten my cock off.' He stared horror-stricken at his penis. The bulbous tip was half severed, bruised, bleeding and hugely swollen. Pacetti rocked backwards and forwards, whimpering with pain.

Phillip heard the thump of feet running along the corridor and the cabin door crashed open. Vicci, pistol in hand, ran into the cabin. He took one look at his boss and stopped dead in his tracks, his jaw dropping open.

'Don't just stand there,' screamed Pacetti. 'Get a fucking doctor, and sling that fucking whore over the side.'

Vicci tossed his pistol on to the bed and hurried round to pick Zoe up.

'Get a fucking doctor first, you stupid fucking wop,' Pacetti bellowed. '*Then* throw her over the side.'

Vicci ran round the bed to the telephone. He picked up the receiver, then froze as a voice from the shadows asked, 'Can I help?'

Both men swung their heads in the direction of the voice and peered into the gloom.

'Who the fuck's that?' demanded Pacetti.

Phillip took a few steps forward out of the shadows, the blue steel of the silenced Browning in his hand gleaming ominously in the red light.

Pacetti and Vicci stared at it. It was the weapon of a professional killer, and they both knew the implications.

'I am Antonio Pacetti.' His voice cracked as he spoke. 'Do you know what that means?'

'It means you're dead, scumbag,' said Phillip calmly.

'Who's paying you? I'll double it – no, treble it. Don't pull that trigger. I'm a rich man. I can pay you anything. Name your price.'

Vicci inched closer to the bed. His eyes flicked to the pistol lying where he had thrown it.

The muzzle of the Browning lined up on his chest. 'Like the man said, "Go on, punk, make my day,"' murmured Phillip.

Vicci relaxed ostentatiously and said, 'Mr Pacetti is a very powerful and important man. Kill him, and you dig your own grave.'

Phillip smiled unpleasantly. 'That is exactly what he did when he put out a contract on me.'

'You're Ross?' Pacetti gaped at him.

Phillip nodded and allowed his eyes to drift towards the speaker. Vicci fell for it. He leapt for his pistol. He got his hand to it and was raising it to fire when the Browning coughed and spat a steel-jacketed bullet straight between his eyes, blowing off the back of his skull in an explosion of hair, blood and brains. He collapsed on to the bed, a sticky mess of blood, brain fluid and tissue slowly spilling out as his body heaved once and then was still.

Phillip turned the pistol on Pacetti, who cringed away, backing up against the headboard. One hand gripped his bleeding penis, the other was held up before his face, as if to ward off a bullet.

'I'll pay you anything. A million pounds. Cash!' he whined.

Phillip said unemotionally, 'No, sir, the contract is cancelled.' He squeezed the trigger. The Browning coughed once. Pacetti was slammed back against the headboard, his face a picture of disbelief as he looked down at the hole in his chest.

He jerked convulsively as a second bullet struck him in the chest, then slumped sideways, staring at Phillip Ross. The Browning was raised until it was level with his eyes. It coughed again.

'Two in the chest and one in the head. You're dead,' Phillip said quietly.

Zoe moaned and stirred. She was coming to. Phillip went to the door, listened for a second, then ghosted out into the corridor. He made his way silently up to the door that led on deck and peered out. The deck was deserted, and he stepped out into the hot night air. He unhooked his snorkel and flippers from his belt, put them on, leapt on to the rail and dived into the sea. Using a power crawl, he struck out hard for the shore. He had to find Debby before they killed her.

ary kept up to the end, and lifted Burnham up
Once a power, now he shook and hard his
... there. He had ... and really ... him
...him less

Chapter Thirteen

A scream of terror echoed through the yacht. Vic Morelli stumbled out of his cabin into the corridor. Zoe, naked, was running towards him from Pacetti's cabin, crying hysterically. She hurled herself into his arms and clung to him like a limpet.

As she sobbed in his arms he felt warm slime on his bare chest and arm. He wiped a sticky lump from his arm and examined it in the light from his cabin doorway. It looked disgustingly like congealing blood. He flicked it off with a shudder of revulsion.

'What the fuck you been doing?' he asked the distraught girl. She was beyond speech. She pointed to the open door of Pacetti's cabin and wailed in anguish.

Morelli pushed her aside and ran into the cabin. The sight of the two dead men stopped him in his tracks. Pacetti stared sightlessly back at him. Vicci's broken body lolled across the bed, his blood and brains smeared over the sheets. Morelli thought of the sticky feeling on his own hands and chest. Bile rose in his gullet and made him retch. He dropped to his knees and vomited the entire contents of his stomach on to the deep-pile carpet.

When he could vomit no more, he dragged himself to his feet, sobbing with rage and grief over the deaths of his boss and his friend. He forced himself to move close to them, snatched up the blood-stained receiver of the bedside phone and stabbed at the buttons.

The captain answered immediately. 'Miller here. What the hell's going on? It sounds like someone's being murdered.'

'This is Morelli. Get your arse down to Mr Pacetti's cabin – now.' He slammed the phone down and searched for a clean bit of sheet to wipe his hand on. Bile rose again, but he choked it back. He crossed to the door and looked down the corridor. It was crowded with naked and half-naked, spaced-out guests, who were listening with wide eyes and open mouths to Zoe's almost incoherent tale of horror.

'Get back to your cabins and the lounge,' shouted Morelli. 'There's been a murder. Get dressed and sober up. The police'll be arriving soon, so dump all the gear over the side. And I mean *all* of it – no keeping any little treats for later. And for Chrissakes keep your fucking mouths shut.'

Miller came hurrying through the door from the crew's quarters and worked his way through the throng of guests who were jostling past each other to get to their cabins or back to the lounge to find their clothes.

'What on earth's going on, Mr Morelli? Where's
Mr Pacetti?' asked Miller in astonishment.

'He's in his cabin.' Morelli jerked his thumb at
the door. 'Go see for yourself.'

Miller rushed in to the master cabin. A few seconds later, he emerged shocked and white-faced.
'We must call the police immediately.'

'Yeah, but give everyone a chance to get dressed
and sober up a bit. There ain't no rush. Nobody's
going anywhere.'

'Where's Mr Morino?' asked Miller. 'He should
be in charge now Mr Pacetti's dead.'

'He went off in one of the tenders with Jimmy
North. Christ, Sal ain't going to believe this.'
A sudden thought struck him. 'Mike Lambert's
still on board. He may know where they went.
Come on.'

He hurried down the corridor to Lambert's
cabin door, threw it open and stared incredulously at the ugly scene inside. He pulled the
door closed and leant against the frame.

'Jimmy's in for a shock.'

Miller said from behind him, 'What do you
mean?'

Morelli nodded at the cabin door. 'Mike Lambert's in there with his throat cut.'

Miller turned and ran for the bridge. He shouted
over his shoulder, 'I'm reporting this right now.
The killer may still be aboard.'

On a fucking bike, thought Morelli wearily.
He's long gone.

Morino swung the launch out of the harbour

entrance at Puerto Duquesa and opened the throttle to full. The launch lifted her bows high, then settled down into a plane as the big engine propelled her across the water at sixty knots, hurling sheets of spray into the air as she roared and slapped across the waves. Jimmy North gripped the handrail and clung on for dear life as the launch hit a swell and took off, nose high, propeller screaming until she crashed back into the water and sped on. Morino, grim-faced, paid no heed. He forced the throttle against the stop, to gain every ounce of speed from the launch.

As they rounded a headland, the blaze of *Charlene*'s lights came into view in the distance. Morino aimed the launch at the yacht and held course for several minutes. Then, abruptly, he shut off the engine and let the launch drift to a halt. He stared ahead.

'What's up?' demanded North.

Morino pointed at the yacht. 'That's a fucking helicopter circling *Charlene*.'

He strained to see more. 'And that looks like a police launch alongside.' He started the engine again and inched the throttle open. The boat moved slowly forward. '*Charlene*'s being raided. Or something serious has happened.'

He whipped his mobile phone from his pocket and stabbed at the buttons. Captain Miller answered.

'This is Morino. What the fuck is going on?'

He listened in numbed silence, as Miller told him what had happened and that the police were aboard. Then he said, 'I'm going back to

Banús, see if I can stir things up from there.'
He switched off the mobile and slammed it
down.

He looked accusingly at North. 'Tony, Giovanni,
and your mate Mike are all dead. That fucking SAS
man has done them all.'

'Christ almighty,' breathed North. 'I thought
Tony would be the safest man in the world, with
all his guys around him. Where's it all going
to end?'

'When we kill Ross,' Morino grunted. 'Or he
kills us.' He opened the throttle and turned the
launch towards Puerto Banús. Above the roar
of the engine, he shouted, 'The yacht's been
impounded and everyone's under arrest. Fuck
knows when they'll be released. We'll have to
go back to the villa and sort it out from there.'
He looked grimly at North. 'Thank fuck Tony told
me to send for some help to search for Debby. At
least we'll have some muscle here in the morning
to back us up.'

North nodded morosely, then, as anger built up
inside him, shouted back, 'I'll kill that bitch when
we get back to the villa. Christ, just wait till I get
my hands on her!'

'Not yet. She may still be useful. Ross won't
stand by while we hurt a bird he's been shafting.
We can use her to draw him on.'

'How?'

'We need more men to back us up. He may not
be on his own. Once we've got reinforcements,
we'll set a trap for him at the villa and wait for
him to turn up. Maybe we'll let him follow one

of us or something, just to make sure he gets there when we want him to.'

'What if he don't give a fuck what happens to Debby and don't come?' asked North.

'He'll come.' Morino smiled grimly. 'You're bait as well, you see, Jimmy. You're the one he wants most of all. Oh yes, he'll come. For you, if not for her.'

North hunched his shoulders as if cold. 'I feel like pissing off out of it.'

Morino put his face very close to North's. Even through the din of the engine and the spray, the ice-cold menace in his voice was clear as he said, 'You, mister, ain't going nowhere until we get Ross. You brought all this trouble to us, and now Tony and two of my boys are dead. So if you so much as think of fucking off, never mind take one step towards the exit, I'm going to kill you. And I'll enjoy doing it.'

North turned his face sullenly away and retreated into his own thoughts. He didn't give a toss for Morino or even for the fact that Tony Pacetti had been killed. He felt bad about Lambert, but it was too late to do anything about it, and after all it was Mike who'd killed fucking Ross's wife, so in a way it was fair enough that Ross should top Mike. Besides, he had his own neck to worry about, and that came before anything else. He was glad and relieved that Morino was angry with Ross and was taking it personally. Morino was a dangerous man. Now that Pacetti was dead, he would automatically take over as top dog and would, as a matter of honour, have to kill the man who had killed his friends and his boss or he'd lose the respect of all his men and everyone else in his world. Yes, Morino would have to kill Ross. And in doing so, he'd save North's life.

He came out of his reverie to find the lights of Puerto Banús alongside. Morino dropped the launch's speed right down to enter the harbour. He steered her over to *Charlene*'s mooring and tied up to the quay.

'He could be hiding anywhere,' said North, his eyes nervously scanning the quay and the yachts tied up along it.

Morino sneered. 'Come on, Jimmy, get yourself some guts and let's front it out,' he said as he marched off towards the car park.

North hurriedly caught him up and fell into step beside him. 'He could shoot us now, while we're walking to the car.'

'No, too many armed guards and police about.' He nodded towards the darkened entrance of a shop, where two uniformed figures stood in the shadows, light reflecting off the shiny leather of their belts and holsters. 'This place is always crawling with police. Lots of money down here, so they have to show a presence. Rich people like to feel safe, well protected from the poor people who might steal their goodies.'

They reached the car park. Morino stopped at a Mercedes saloon and fished under the nearside rear wing for the keys. He unlocked the car and they both climbed in.

'If he's here,' said Morino, straining to see

into the shadows, 'he'll follow us and try to
get us where it's quiet.' He opened the glove
compartment and took out a Beretta pistol. He
drew the slide back and watched a shell nose
its way into the chamber, then let the slide
slam forward. He put the safety catch on and
shoved the pistol in his belt. 'Reach under your
seat and you'll find another gun,' he told North
as he started the engine.

North groped under the seat and produced
another Beretta. He checked it was loaded and
held it with two hands between his knees. 'I feel
better now,' he said, grinning.

Morino let off the handbrake and the big car
nosed its way out of the car park to the entrance
barrier. A guard saluted and raised the barrier.
Once outside the *puerto*, Morino put his foot
down hard and the Merc leapt forward.

North pulled the sun visor down and pos-
itioned the vanity mirror so that he could watch
their rear.

'We're on our own now, Jimmy,' said Morino.
'If he just follows us, take no notice unless he
looks like he's going to attack.'

'Do you think he will just follow us?'

'If he does, we'll try to lose him. I don't want to
have to face him until the boys arrive tomorrow
and we've set up a trap at the villa.' Morino
checked the rear-view mirror. 'There are still
police and Guardia Civil about, and like I said
he'll want to do the business somewhere quiet.
When we least expect him . . .' He shrugged.
'Besides, he may know we've got Debby.'

'How could he know that? We've only just found her ourselves.'

Morino looked contemptuously at him. 'Start using your brain. He just cut Mike's throat and shot Tony. He meant to kill you as well.'

'So?'

'He must have watched us leave the harbour, or he might even have been on board, for all we know. Either way, he probably saw the launch leave. When he couldn't find you aboard *Charlene*, he'd have twigged that you were in the launch. And don't you think he just might have asked Mike where you were going and what you were up to, before he topped him? Mike would have talked if he thought it'd save his life.'

'I never thought of that.'

'We've got to start thinking about everything, if we're going to stay alive, Jimmy. This guy was in the SAS. I've read about them. He's a trained killer, one of the world's best and most highly trained soldiers. From now on we sleep with one eye open.'

'What about the contract Tony put out on Ross?'

Morino shrugged. 'No one's going to take that up now, not with Tony brown bread. We won't be able to keep his death quiet. It'll be in all the papers tomorrow, and then there'll be hell to pay. Besides, Tony put that out when he thought Ross would be in England looking for you. We don't need it now, because he's down here, looking for us.'

North checked the traffic behind them: several cars and a motorbike.

'Watch the cars in front, as well,' said Morino. 'Those fuckers follow from the front sometimes.'

North studied the cars ahead of them, but saw nothing suspicious. He turned back to Morino. 'How do you feel about Tony's death, and how will it affect you?'

Morino shrugged. 'I feel bad about it, sure, but it's an ill wind that blows nobody any good. And Tony being dead puts me in the driving seat.'

'What about his money and his assets? I mean, there's the yacht, the casinos, all the property he owned.'

'On paper, he owned fuck all. It's all tied up in trusts and offshore companies, behind front men, nominees. The cash is all tucked away in deposit accounts in every tax haven you could name, from Monaco to the Cayman Islands.' Morino smiled broadly. 'Now Tony's dead, I'm the sole signatory. It's all mine.'

North whistled and turned to look out of the rear windscreen as Morino flicked the indicator switch.

They turned right, off the main road. A car and the motorbike followed them. North nervously checked his gun again, but when they turned on to the unmade road leading to the villa both car and motor bike carried on past.

North let out a sigh of relief. 'They've gone past.'

Morino braked to a halt and switched off the lights. 'Let's wait and see if one of them turns back.' He drew the pistol from his belt and turned to study the lane behind them. After five minutes he said, 'Better safe than sorry,' and restarted the engine. Leaving the lights off, he slowly picked his way in the moonlight to the heavy wooden doors leading to the villa.

In the darkness, Phillip Ross trotted along the track behind them.

Phillip had swum only two hundred yards when he heard Zoe's long, high-pitched scream of terror. He stopped swimming and trod water as he looked back at *Charlene*. Lights came on in the crew's quarters and guest cabins, and there was movement on deck as people went to investigate. He turned towards the shore and struck out again.

Ashore, he slung all his gear into the tackle boxes, pulled on his trainers, grabbed his rod and jogged to his car. He drove at high speed to Puerto Duquesa. As he swept into the car park he saw the Virago. He pulled up beside it and saw Debby's crash helmet lying several feet away from it. He picked the helmet up and looked round. The car park was deserted, save for several cars parked for the night.

He inspected the Virago. The keys were still in the ignition where Debby had left them. He looked down at his wetsuit. It could be taken for biker's leathers in the dark. He tried the helmet. It was tight but it would have to do. He dipped into one of the fishing boxes and took out the Browning, a spare magazine and the diver's knife, tucked them inside the wetsuit and zipped it up.

He straddled the Virago, fired the engine, kicked it into gear and roared out of the car park. He turned right towards Puerto Banús and opened up the throttle.

As he sped along the coast road he glanced out to sea and saw *Charlene*. Lights showed now from bow to stern. A helicopter circled above her, and a police launch was tied up alongside. He pulled up and watched the activity for a moment. He had kicked the gear into first and was about to accelerate away when he saw a launch heading, at high speed, for *Charlene*. The launch suddenly slowed to a halt, then started up again and crept forwards for a few minutes. Abruptly, her bows lifted high as she altered course and headed at full speed for Puerto Banús. Two men were silhouetted against the horizon, backlit by the moon.

Phillip let out the clutch and roared off down the road. He parked in the approach road to the *puerto*, and waited astride the bike, its motor idling quietly. Several cars emerged before he spotted the Mercedes being waved past the barrier by the security guard. He bent over to conceal his face, and watched out of the corner of one eye as North and Morino drove past.

Phillip could see that Morino kept checking his rear-view mirror, while North was half turned, looking through the back window of the car as it passed. He waited until they had turned on to the main road and were out of sight, then gunned the Virago's motor and slotted into the traffic. He stayed several cars behind as they travelled south.

When they turned off the highway, he followed, keeping another car between himself and them and hanging well back.

The Mercedes turned right on to an unmade track. Phillip passed by without looking. A hundred yards further on, he slowed, looking for a suitable place for stop. A thick clump of bushes loomed up on his left. He turned off the road, forcing the bike between the bushes, and switched off the lights and ignition. He ran back to the track and peered cautiously into the darkness. The moonlight glinted on the polished paint and chrome of a big car parked, all its lights out, fifty yards along the track. Phillip crouched down and waited.

Five minutes passed, then the car started up and moved off down the track. Keeping well to one side of the track, Phillip trotted after it.

After a hundred yards the car's lights were switched on and it speeded up. Phillip increased his pace. He was sweating heavily, so pulled down the zip of the wetsuit to let the air cool his chest. Just as he was beginning to think that following on foot had been a bad idea, the car swung to the right and drew up in front of heavy wooden gates. He stopped and listened intently.

He could hear a man speaking Spanish. A metallic voice from a speaker answered and the gates swung open. The car drove through and the gates closed behind it. Phillip sprinted to the gates and watched through a crack in the wood as the car swept along the drive and disappeared into a courtyard which flooded with light as it entered.

Dogs began to bark. A man shouted in Spanish and they fell silent. A door banged and the floodlights went out.

Phillip squatted in the darkness and considered. It was odds-on that Morino and North knew Pacetti and Lambert were dead, or they would have returned to *Charlene*. They had Debby – the thought thudded in his mind. The likelihood was that she was being held in the old building they had just entered. But to go rushing in blindly was not the way he had been trained to operate. Any number of armed men could be inside. She could be anywhere in the building, or in an outbuilding, for all he knew. The dogs would sniff him out if he tried to get closer to the villa. He'd need something to silence them.

He turned and jogged back down the track. He needed more supplies. He'd come back in the morning to reconnoitre, and, if the opportunity presented itself, to set Debby free.

North unlocked the steel door and flung it open. Debby was sitting on the stone floor in the far corner of the room. She looked up in alarm as the door crashed back against the wall, then her alarm turned to fear North strode towards her, bitter anger and loathing on his face.

'Mike's dead, you cunt, Tony's dead and so is Giovanni, thanks to you and your lover boy.' He bent over her and drew back his fist. 'I could punch the fucking life out of you.'

Debby shrank away and held up her hands defensively. 'I never told him you were here, Jimmy. I swear it.'

North straightened and let his fist fall to his side. 'You're going to die anyway, bitch. But not yet. Oh no, not yet. You're going to suffer first. Then I'm going to burn you like Roger, cut your throat like Mike, and chuck you in the sea like Billy. If I could hang you as well, I would.' He spat in her face, then turned on his heel and marched over to the door. 'Salvatore's coming down in a while to have a word with you about Tony and Giovanni's deaths. You'll wish you were dead before he's finished with you. Think on that while you wait for him.' He slammed the door behind him and locked it, leaving Debby to her thoughts.

North stomped into the lounge, flung himself into a chair and scowled at Morino. 'She's all yours. Do what you like with her, but don't kill her. I want to do that.'

Morino grinned and sipped at a large brandy. 'I'll save her for later. I've got to pick up the boys from the airport in the morning. She'll have to wait till I get back. I need some sleep.' He topped up his brandy, stood up and yawned hugely. 'I'm off to bed. I'm knackered.'

'Give me a shout in the morning,' North said. 'I'll come with you, and you can drop me off at Banús to pick up the Porsche.'

'I'll get one of the boys to bring that back. You

and I are sticking together until we kill Ross. Two guns are better than one.' He smiled. 'You'd better get some sleep. This may be the last time we get a night's sleep without Ross knowing where we are.'

Chapter Fourteen

On his way back to the villa, Phillip bought a bottle of sleeping pills and two pounds of frying steak, which he stowed in his rucksack along with his other gear. He parked the Virago in the clump of bushes where he'd hidden it before, made his way stealthily along the inside of the hedgerow that lined the track to the villa.

He passed by the wooden entrance gates and crossed the track a hundred yards further on. He snaked through the bushes until he came to a six-foot-high chain-link fence. He cut the metal links close to the ground to form an opening and crawled through. Fifty yards of dense woodland and tangled bushes lay between him and an open pasture, on the other side of which, atop a rise in the land, sat the villa.

He made his way cautiously to the edge of the woodland and studied the villa and outbuildings through his binoculars. It was a massive old building with stone arches and a clay tile roof, built in a horseshoe round a courtyard. Phillip had a clear view of the drive leading from the

gates to the villa. A large barn and several smaller
buildings, including a stable block, were built
on the east side of the villa. On the left of the
courtyard was a large swimming pool, to one
side of which were a stand of fig trees and an
orange grove.

Two men were working in the yard outside the
stables. One was hosing down the yard while the
other, an older man, cleaned a saddle and tack.
An Andalusian stallion was tied to a steel ring
fixed to the stone wall of the stable block.

Phillip studied the farm machinery that stood
beside the buildings. It was rusty, with grass and
weeds growing round it from lack of use. This
was not a working farm but a front, or perhaps
a rich man's self-indulgence.

He took the steak from his rucksack and cut it
into large cubes. In each cube he made a deep slit
into which he inserted two sleeping pills, pushing
them in firmly with his finger and then squeezing
the slit closed. He scattered the doctored meat
on the ground at the edge of the woods and
retreated several feet to a knurled oak tree which
towered over the surrounding woodland. He hid
his rucksack in bushes at the foot of the tree,
then climbed to the highest fork, from where
he could see the villa over the bushes. After
checking the wind direction to make sure that
he was downwind, he took a deep breath and
whistled piercingly.

An Alsatian came bounding into view from
the courtyard. Two mixed-breed hounds quickly
followed. The dogs stopped, their ears cocked as

they sniffed the air and barked, unsure of the direction of the whistle.

Phillip studied the villa through his binoculars. No one took any notice of the dogs. He whistled again, briefly and shrilly. The Alsatian's ears cocked in his direction and the dog raced towards him, followed by the hounds.

Twenty yards from the woods the three dogs stopped running and sniffed first the air and then the ground as they circled and crossed trails, searching for a spoor. One of the hounds picked up a scent. It tracked forward to where Phillip had planted the doped meat and started to gulp it down. The two other dogs rushed up and joined in the feast, gobbling the meat as though they hadn't eaten for a week. Then, after a good sniff round to make sure they hadn't missed any, all three trotted back to the villa and disappeared from sight.

Thirty minutes later, the Mercedes purred out of the courtyard and drove down to the gates, which swung open. Phillip trained the binoculars on the car, but the sun was reflecting on the rear screen, so he could not make out who was inside, only the form of two men. The gates closed behind the car, and it rumbled off down the track: North and Morino, he guessed, on their way to the airport to collect the four heavies who'd been summoned to help search for Debby.

Phillip waited a further fifteen minutes, then whistled again. The dogs didn't appear. He climbed down from the tree and worked his way through to the edge of the woods. An expanse of open

land lay between him and the villa. To avoid
the risk of being seen in the open, he stalked
his way through the trees and dense bushes that
surrounded the meadow. The going was tough
and tedious, and it took him over an hour to
circle round. At last he reached the rear wall of
the villa. He stopped beside a door leading into
the courtyard and peered through. The three dogs
were curled up asleep under an atap awning. Also
under the awning were two parked cars, a white
Renault and a blue Citroën.

Phillip ducked under a windowsill, cat-footed
along the wall to the heavy iron-studded door
and tried the handle. The door was locked. He
checked the windows. Several were open, but
stout iron grilles covered them. He crossed to the
Renault and pressed the boot button. It clicked
open. In the boot he found a bottle jack and
handle. He returned to the open window nearest
the door and jacked the iron grille out of the wall,
the tongues of iron slipping quietly out of the soft
old mortar. One final yank with his hands and it
came clean away. He rested it against the wall
under the window and climbed inside. He leant
back out, lifted the grille up and pulled it back
into position. It crunched into place and held.

Phillip peered into the shadowed interior of
the villa. He was in a large flagstoned hallway,
off which several oak doors opened. One of the
doors was ajar, and from it came the sound of
a television soap opera. He drew his pistol and
screwed on the silencer, then crept to the doorway
and slanted an eye round. In a chair facing the TV

set a man was dozing, snoring softly. On a table beside his chair were an open bottle of beer and an Uzi machine pistol.

Phillip catfooted across the room and bent over the sleeping man. He inserted the muzzle of the silencer in the man's open mouth, grabbed his hair and wrenched his head back against the chair.

The startled Spaniard looked as though he was going to have a seizure: his eyes bulged and his face turned an unbeautiful purple. He tried to call out, but Phillip rammed the silencer hard against his tongue, forcing it back into his throat, half choking him. The man gagged as Phillip released the pressure and said in a fierce whisper, 'Where is the girl? Where is Debby?'

The frightened man shook his head in confusion. Phillip repeated it in Spanish: '*Donde está la chica?*'

The Spaniard pointed at the floor. '*Abajo, sótano,*' he said hoarsely.

Phillip yanked him by the hair out of the chair and stood back. He picked up the Uzi and jerked his thumb at the door. 'Show me,' he ordered, and pointed the Browning at the man's head.

'*Sí, sí, señor, claro. Pero esté tranquilo, señor, le ruego.*' He raised his hands placatingly and beckoned Phillip to follow him. Philip caught up the Uzi, slung it over his shoulder, and did so. He crossed the hallway, opened a door and pointed down the stairs. Phillip motioned with the pistol for the man to go first.

He followed the man through the dank cellar to

the steel door. The Spaniard pointed to the door. 'Dentro,' he said, and stepped to one side.

Phillip tried the door. It was locked. He banged on the steel with the butt of his pistol. 'Debby, are you in there?' he called.

Debby rushed to the door and hammered on it with her fists. 'I'm here, Phillip, I'm in here.'

He turned to the Spaniard and aimed the pistol between his eyes. 'Open it, or die now.'

The man fumbled in his pocket for his keys, then with trembling hands unlocked the door and pushed it open. Phillip shoved him roughly inside, then staggered as Debby hurled herself into his arms, shaking from head to foot and sobbing with relief.

'Thank God,' she cried. 'I thought the next time that door opened it would be Morino.'

Phillip put an arm round her shoulders. 'We've got to stop meeting like this,' he said solemnly, and guided her to the open door. He told her, 'Wait outside a minute,' then turned to the Spaniard and motioned to him to turn away. As the man faced the wall, Phillip gave him a sharp tap behind the ear with the butt of the pistol. He grunted and crumpled into a heap, out cold. Phillip stepped out of the room and closed and locked the door.

'That should keep him quiet for a while,' he said as he led Debby through the cellar to the stairs. 'There are still two or three of them about, so stay behind me and keep close. North and Morino have been gone about two hours. They could be back at any moment.'

He led the way up the creaky wooden staircase. As they reached the top of the stairs, his fears were realized: he heard two cars pull up in the courtyard. Car doors slammed and there was the sound of men's voices. Someone banged hard on the front door and shouted, 'Paco, where the fuck are you? And where the fuck are the dogs? Why aren't they on guard?'

Phillip recognized Morino's voice. He ran to the door and slid home the bolts, top and bottom, just as Morino turned his key in the lock.

'It's bolted from the inside,' Morino said. 'Something's wrong – Christ! That bastard Ross must have been here.' He turned the key to double-lock the door from outside, and yelled, 'Get round the back. Cover the back of the house. He may still be inside.'

Phillip snatched a look into the courtyard. He saw the Mercedes, North's red Porsche and, running to cover the rear of the house, four men he didn't recognize – presumably reinforcements whom Morino had just collected. He heard Morino shout, 'Stay here and cover the front. He can't get out this way. I'm going in to get him.' There was the sound of running footsteps fading into the distance.

Pulling Debby close to the wall, he crouched down by the window with the loose grille. He held up the Browning. 'Can you use one of these?' he asked.

Debby nodded nervously. 'At paper targets,' she said.

Phillip glanced out of the window. One of the

men Morino had picked up from the airport was standing next to the Mercedes. He held a Skorpion machine pistol and was panning the open windows of the villa. Phillip ducked out of sight.

'There's a guard out there. I'm going to slot him. As soon as I've done that, I need you to do something. Get out there – don't worry, this grille's loose and I'll knock it out for you – and check the cars to see if they've left the keys in the ignition. If they have, turn the car round to face the gates. We may have to leave in a bit of a hurry.'

'And if there aren't any keys?'

'Make for the woods at the back of the villa. I'll meet you there. Ready?'

Debby swallowed and nodded.

Phillip popped up in front of the open window and fired the Browning. The gangster in the courtyard was lifted off his feet as the heavy steel-jacketed slug smashed into his chest and ripped its way out through his back. He hit the ground, twitched once, then lay still.

Phillip passed the Browning to Debby, shoved the grille out of the wall and lifted her on to the windowsill. 'Go,' he said. 'I'll be with you in two minutes.'

He turned and ran across the hallway, unslinging the Uzi from his shoulder and cocking it as he ran. He pulled open the door leading to the rear of the villa. Two of Morino's thugs were creeping along the passage, checking rooms as they advanced. They swung round as the door

opened and opened fire with their automatic
pistols. The passage filled with explosions and
muzzle-flashes as the thugs emptied their magazines. Phillip poked the Uzi round the door frame
and fired a quick burst. One of the gangsters
howled, 'I'm hit,' and slumped to the floor. His
companion dived headlong through the nearest
open door. Morino appeared at the end of the
passage, fired a burst through the open doorway
and ducked out of sight.

'Give it up, Ross,' he shouted. 'You can't get
out. You're surrounded.'

Phillip answered him with another burst of fire,
then ran to the lounge, where the television was
still flickering. He ripped down one of the long
curtains, grabbed a bottle of Jack Daniel's off
a nearby table and ran back into the hall. He
poured the whiskey on to the crumpled cloth
and flicked his lighter. The spirit ignited with a
whoomph. He wrenched open the passage door,
fired another quick burst in Morino's direction,
tossed the burning cloth into the passage and
slammed the door on it.

The engine of one of the cars started up and
there was the sound of its wheels spinning as
Debby skid-turned it. He ran to the window
whose grille he'd removed. She'd chosen the
Mercedes and was waiting with the engine rev-
ving and the passenger door open. As he leapt
through the window, he heard a yell from the passage: 'He's getting away. Get round the front.'

Phillip turned back and fired through the window at the lounge door. After a few seconds,

the hammer clicked on an empty chamber. He tossed the empty weapon to the ground, ran to the dead gangster in the courtyard and snatched the Skorpion from his hand. He ran to the open door of the Mercedes. One of Morino's thugs slid round the corner of the villa and fired at him. Bullets pinged round him as he ran. A searing pain like red-hot coals burnt through his shoulder as a bullet tugged at his left upper arm, ripping his jacket and tearing skin and muscle. He dived to the ground, rolled and returned fire. A five-shot burst ripped open the thug's chest and slammed him against the wall of the villa.

Debby hit the accelerator as Phillip leapt in beside her. The big car leapt forward, its rear wheels smoking as they fought for grip on the dusty surface. The rattle of machine-pistol fire echoed round the courtyard as she hammered the car through the entrance and down the drive, leaving a trail of billowing dust in their wake.

Phillip slid a finger into the tear in his jacket and probed the wound. It was almost numb, but he could feel it beginning to burn and throb. The bullet had cut a groove in his muscle. It was going to hurt like hell later. He took out a handkerchief and twisted it round his arm, dragging the knot tight with his right hand and his teeth.

'Are you hurt?' asked Debby anxiously.

'It's nothing,' he lied, 'just a scratch.'

Bullets smacked into the bodywork and the rear windscreen disintegrated. Debby, kept her foot hard down on the accelerator, and aimed the car at the heavy wooden gates. Phillip clicked on his safety belt and grinned when he saw the wild determination on her face as she fought the bucking steering wheel, her knuckles white from the force of her grip.

Two tons of steel hit the gates at eighty miles an hour. The gates disintegrated into a thousand flying splinters of wood, and the Merc rocketed through them as if they were matchwood. Steam hissed from the twisted and ruptured radiator grille as Debby swung the car on to the dusty, rutted track.

The Renault, with Morino at the wheel, North beside him and two more thugs in the back, tore after them.

Phillip looked back at them through the billowing dust. 'Here they come,' he said, and he released his safety belt and pressed the button of the electric window. The Merc's engine coughed and missed, as water from the cooling system sprayed the electrical system. The car lost speed.

'Keep her going for as long as possible. Then broadside her across the track, to block it,' he shouted as he leant out the window and triggered off a short burst at the pursuing Renault.

'It's dying on us,' Debby screamed, and she pumped at the throttle. The car slowed even more, picked up speed briefly, then the engine cut out completely. Debby knocked the gear-select lever to neutral and let the car coast on. The Renault was closing rapidly.

'It's gone. I've lost it,' she said bitterly.

Phillip glanced forward. They were still several hundred yards from the road.

'Your Virago's a hundred yards to the right down that road,' he said urgently. 'When you stop the car, broadside it to the right and run like hell. I'll cover you.'

Debby nodded. 'Right, here we go,' she yelled. She slammed her foot on the brake and swung the steering wheel to the right. The car skidded broadside along the track and ground to a halt. Phillip took careful aim with the Skorpion and squeezed the trigger. The Renault's windscreen burst into a shower of flashing shards and imploded into the interior of the car.

He shot a glance down the track. Debby was running for all she was worth, the Browning gripped tightly in her right hand.

He looked back to the Renault in time to see it swerve off the track and crunch into the ditch. The doors opened and the four men scrambled out. They were all firing at the Mercedes. Phillip ducked down behind the door, crawled to the front of the car and returned fire. One of the thugs went down, the other three dived into the bushes for cover.

Phillip turned and ran after Debby. He stopped and turned back after thirty yards, to fire a burst into the boot area of the Mercedes. The car erupted in smoke and fire as the petrol in the tank ignited. Phillip turned and ran on.

He saw Debby running for her life. She stumbled, picked herself up and ran on. Bullets ricocheted round his feet, kicking up dust and splinters of stone. He spun and fired back. Two men dived for cover. He fired another burst, then ran on. Debby was out of sight. She was on the tarmac road and running for the Virago.

Phillip reached the road and turned back. He fired a long burst, then ducked out of sight. He heard North shout something and Morino answer. He heard men running along the track. He stepped into the open and fired from the hip.

The man in the lead took the full burst in the chest. He was flung backwards and sprawled in the dirt, his fingers gripped tightly on the machine pistol. He emptied the magazine in a long burst of fire, then died. Morino and North hurled themselves into the bushes and ducked into the ditch.

Phillip sprinted after Debby. She was riding the Virago towards him, the front end in the air in a wheelie. She dropped the front wheel to the tarmac and, braking hard, swung the bike round in a skid. Phillip leapt on the back and held on as she opened the throttle and dropped the clutch. The Virago fled towards safety, every second putting distance between them and the gangsters.

Phillip heard the crackle of fire behind. He looked back. North and Morino stood in the middle of the road firing after them, but Phillip and Debby were out of range of the machine pistols' short barrels. Phillip grinned and gave them the finger as the motorbike raced on.

'We made it, kid,' he shouted in Debby's ear.

She threw him a smile over her shoulder. 'Where are we going?' she called back.

'Anywhere we can get a drink.' He laughed and put his arms round her, holding her waist.

It was wet and sticky. Phillip withdrew his hands and looked at them. They were smothered in blood.

'You've been hit,' he shouted in alarm.

Debby didn't look round, just nodded.

'Pull over!'

Debby shook her head. 'I'm OK, and we're not far enough away yet. We can stop in a minute,' she shouted. She leant the bike steeply round a sharp bend and opened the throttle still more.

'They can't follow us. It'll take ages to clear the track. Pull over,' he insisted.

Debby shook her head again, and pressed on. She knew she couldn't go on for much longer, but she had to gain them every possible yard towards safety. She felt dizzy and weak, and her vision was beginning to blur. With relief she saw a woodland track, leading off to the right. She slackened speed and turned up it.

The Virago bounced in a rut and kicked up dust. Debby hung on grimly as they juddered down the track, deeper into the woods, winding round trees and bushes, until at last they emerged into a clearing on high ground, close to an escarpment.

She pulled up and kicked down the side-stand. Phillip leapt off and helped her dismount. She leant heavily against him, then went suddenly limp in his arms. He lowered her gently to the ground and inspected her wound.

'Is it bad?' she asked.

'Yes, but you're going to be OK,' he lied and stroked her hair back from her face.

The bullet had entered her back, then exited

through her belly, leaving a gaping wound. From the colour and amount of blood she had lost, Phillip knew she was dying. He couldn't possibly get her to a hospital in time. From the angle of penetration and exit, he suspected the bullet had ruptured her stomach, spleen and liver. He wondered how she had kept going for so long.

Debby tried to smile, but her face twisted with in pain. 'It hurts like hell,' she whispered. 'But we gave them shit, didn't we?'

Phillip nodded. He stretched out beside her and very gently lifted her head on to his shoulder.

She saw that blood had seeped though the handkerchief round his arm. 'What about you? You're hurt too. Are you all right?'

Phillip smiled down at her. 'Like I told you, it's only a scratch. It's stopped bleeding already. Don't worry about me. Just lie still and rest for a minute or two.'

Debby gave a little sigh of relief, then her face screwed up as pain jolted through her. When it had eased a bit, she tried again for a smile and this time succeeded. 'Kiss me, Hardy,' she said faintly.

Phillip kissed her gently on her lips, her nose, then her forehead.

'I love you,' she whispered, staring into his eyes. 'Tell me you love me. I know it isn't true. I just want to hear it from you once.'

Phillip stroked her cheek, and wiped away a tear as it spilled from her eye. 'I love you, Debby,' he murmured, and kissed her again.

'Better to have loved and lost, and all that shit,'

she joked weakly. She hadn't the strength to finish the line, so Phillip said it for her: 'Than never to have loved at all.' He hoped she didn't know how the tag really went.

She fought for breath. Her words came slowly, as if her strength was leaking out of her with her blood. 'If Jimmy runs . . . he'll go back to Lloret . . . to the villa. Don't . . . let him . . . get away with it.'

'I won't.'

'The cash . . . from the bank jobs . . . in a strongroom . . . under the garage floor . . . He'll go back for it.'

'If he runs, I'll be hot on his heels. He can't and won't get away from me, Debby. That I promise you.'

Debby looked puzzled. Her eyes were focused on a point somewhere above his head. 'Where's . . . music . . . coming from . . . ? Beautiful.'

Phillip cocked an ear, but could hear only the breeze rustling the leaves of the trees and a bird singing in the valley below the escarpment. 'Yes, it's lovely,' he agreed.

'Cold . . . so dark.' She sounded frightened. He saw that her eyes had turned up in her head until only the whites showed.

Phillip held her close and kissed her. 'I love you, Debby,' he whispered in her ear.

She smiled, sighed deeply and closed her eyes.

A soft rattle in her throat told Phillip she was dead. He looked up to the sky and said aloud, 'Look after her, Julie. I know you'll understand.'

Chapter Fifteen

'Fuck, fuck, *fuck*!' screamed Morino. He threw the machine pistol after the motorbike. 'I'm going to kill that bastard if it's the last fucking thing I do.'

'I thought we had him.' North kicked furiously at a stone in the road. 'I thought we fucking had him.'

Morino ignored him and went to retrieve the machine pistol. 'I told you the sodding SAS were good, didn't I?' he said over his shoulder.

'Yeah, yeah,' said North sullenly.

They started trudging back towards the villa.

'What do we do now?' asked North. 'Run for it?'

Morino grabbed North's arm and spun him round to face him. 'I don't fucking run from anything. You got that?' he snarled. 'He knows where we are. He'll be back, and we'll be waiting.' He turned and strode on. 'We've got to get this fucking mess cleared up, and get some more muscle down here.'

'Yeah, right.' North fell into step. Right? he

thought. *Right*? You must be bleeding joking. I ain't waiting for Ross to come back. First chance I get, I'm off. He glanced at the Italian out of the corner of his eye. You're so fucking tough, mate, you fucking deal with him.

Morino must have read his thoughts, because he turned, gave North a hard, shrewd stare, and said, 'Don't get any ideas about pissing off, Jimmy. You brought the cunt here. This is all down to you, old son.'

'Wouldn't even think of it, Sal. I want him dead as much as you do.'

They skirted the burnt-out shell of the Mercedes.

'Look what the bastard did to my fucking car,' said Morino angrily.

North pointed to the dead man lying in the road. 'What about him?'

'Fuck him,' said Morino impatiently. 'That Merc cost seventy grand. I can replace him' — he spat on the dead man's face — 'for peanuts.'

They walked into the courtyard. The two stablemen were looking at the two dead thugs. Flies were buzzing round the dead men's wounds and gorging on the blood.

Morino shouted to the stablemen in Spanish, 'There's another one in the villa, and one down the lane. Bury the stupid bastards. Then clear the two wrecked cars from the track.'

'Can they be trusted?' asked North.

'You bet. They're both junkies. They won't do anything to risk losing their supply.'

Morino went over to the sleeping dogs and kicked one of them hard in the ribs. No reaction.

'He drugged the fucking dogs,' he said sourly. He walked to the villa wall and examined the holes where the iron window grille had been forced out. 'These poxy grilles give you a false sense of security. I thought we had the bastard trapped.'

He stamped into the lounge, where he made and received several phone calls, to which North listened intently.

'Right,' Morino said at last, 'we've got more men coming. Two are on their way now and should be here' – he glanced at his watch – 'in an hour or so. Four more are flying out of Heathrow this evening. They'll be here late tonight.' He crossed to the door. 'Follow me. Got something to show you.'

He led North through the cellar to one of the wine racks and pulled a concealed lever. The whole section of racking slid to one side, revealing a steel door. He unlocked the door and flicked on the light.

The room was lined with racks of small arms, everything the aspiring killer could dream of. Piled high at one end of the floor were boxes of ammunition.

North whistled in amazement. 'Fuck me,' he said. 'You've got enough guns in here to start a fair-sized war.' He picked up an M16-A2 and examined it.

Morino hefted an ammunition box on to a workbench. 'We do the occasional bit of arms dealing,' he explained. 'This is our personal armoury, but if someone wants to buy some of it, and has got the money, we sell it to them.' He

pointed to a rack of Uzi machine pistols. 'Bring
two of them and two Berettas. I'll take this up.'
He stacked spare magazines for the Uzis on top
of the ammunition crate, and carried it up to the
lounge. He set the crate on the table and started
feeding rounds into the magazines.

North came in, with Paco following unsteadily
behind him, holding his head and looking decid-
edly sorry for himself.

North jerked his thumb over his shoulder. 'I
found Paco locked in the room we left Debby in.
He's had a nasty bang on the head.'

'What the hell happened?' Morino demanded
in rapid Spanish.

Paco shrugged blankly. 'I dunno. I was watching
TV. Then suddenly I got this fucking great pistol
stuck in my mouth.'

Morino looked at him measuringly for a moment,
then snapped, 'Go help Jordi and Manuel clear the
drive and dig some graves. I'll be out later.'

Paco nodded and went out.

Morino handed North three loaded magazines
and said, 'You'd better get outside and keep an
eye out. Ross could be back any time now.'

'He's only just run away,' protested North.

Morino shook his head. 'He didn't run away,
Jimmy. He came in here intending to take Debby
out, and that's exactly what he did.' He smiled
sardonically. 'If he hadn't had her to worry about,
he'd have done the lot of us out there in the open.
But he didn't, even though there were a couple of
times he could've put both of us down.'

'What do you mean?'

'Didn't you see the way the fucking man moved, rolled, fired? He was like Rambo. He took out all of our men. But he left you and me alive.'

'He missed,' said North.

'He missed deliberately, you arsehole,' said Morino scornfully. 'He's saving you for something special, Jimmy, and it looks like he's saving me as well. Dunno about you, but I don't much want to find out what it is.'

'How do you make that out?' asked North.

'Christ, Jimmy, use your fucking brain, will you? Think about it. Every time he fired at one of the boys, he zapped them full in the chest. When he fired at us, he aimed low and just sprayed us with dirt and stones. And we was so busy ducking for cover, and grateful he'd missed, we didn't catch on at the time. But I've had time to think about it now, and I know what he was doing. The bastard wasn't even trying to hit us.'

North fiddled nervously with a couple of rounds of ammunition. 'He's that good, you reckon?'

'He never wasted a round when he had a clear shot. Three-round bursts take a bit of practice with these fucking Uzis, and he's obviously had plenty of that.'

North fell silent and gave the matter earnest consideration. Brazil! he thought. That's where I'll go. First opportunity. Pop in and see Biggs.

'You'd better get out there,' said Morino, 'and for fuck's sake keep your eyes skinned and your head down. He's had time to drop the bird off. If he's got enough ammo, he'll be straight back.'

North peered round the hallway before stepping out of the lounge. He made his way down the smoke-blackened passage to the rear of the house and settled down by a window to watch the open fields and woodland beyond. He could hear the chunter of a diesel tractor engine, as Paco drove down the front drive to the lane.

It would take a good hour, he reckoned, to drag the wrecked cars out of the lane. He felt his trouser pocket for the keys to the Porsche, and breathed a sigh of relief when he found them. He checked his watch. Two of the reinforcements would be arriving in half an hour, well before Paco and his men had cleared the lane.

It would have given North no comfort to know that Phillip Ross was watching him through binoculars from the woods.

Phillip removed the Browning from Debby's belt and checked the magazine. There were still twelve rounds in it and he had a spare magazine loaded with thirteen rounds in his belt.

He quickly thought through the options open to Morino and North. They could stay where they were and wait for reinforcements, or get the hell out of it. There was only one way to find out. Get back to the villa now. If they didn't intend to stay and fight, they'd already be gone. If they were still there, it was because they were waiting for more men and intended to take him on. He decided that if they were still there he would attack immediately, rather than wait for them to get organized and surround themselves with more armed men.

He lifted Debby's body, and, holding her in front of him, straddled the Virago and kicked it into life. He drove back through the woods to the road and laid her gently on the grass verge, where she would be found and taken care of. He hated leaving her like this, but he had no choice: he couldn't compromise himself with the authorities. He repeated, silently, the promise he'd made her: Jimmy North won't get away with it, Debby, I swear it. Then, reluctantly, he left her, jumped on the Virago and headed back towards the villa.

He hid the bike in woodland a mile from the villa, and made his way back to where he had drugged the dogs. His rucksack was still at the base of the oak tree where he had hidden it, and he offered up silent thanks for the training the had taught him always to carry a medical kit. He peeled off his jacket and shirt, wincing as his bloodied shirtsleeve tore the wound open again; it started to bleed sluggishly. A good slosh of antiseptic and a Melolin dressing pad took care of that, and he hastily tugged his jacket on again. Then he slung the binoculars round his neck and climbed the tree, cursing under his breath as his injured arm took his weight, just in time to see Jimmy North take up his position at one of the rear windows.

He smiled with grim satisfaction. So that's the way you want it, he thought. He panned the house and grounds. He could see no other movement, but could hear the drone of a diesel engine in the distance. It was getting louder.

He swept the drive to the shattered entrance gates. A tractor, driven by the man he'd left locked in the cellar, the one they'd called Paco, was towing the smashed Renault out of the lane.

Paco pulled off the road and unhitched the tow chain, then went back down the lane for the Mercedes. The Citroën and North's Porsche must still be in the courtyard, and that the lane would soon be clear for them.

Phillip climbed back down to the ground and worked his way cautiously through the woods until he came to the open land between him and the villa. He could see North quite clearly, watching the woods and occasionally leaning forward to check left and right.

Phillip backed into the woods. No way could he cross the open ground without North spotting him. He'd have to go the long way round and approach through the orange grove and fig trees by the swimming pool. Thirty minutes later, he was in the stand of fig trees, overlooking the swimming pool.

The tractor trundled up the drive, towing the burnt-out wreck of the Mercedes. The two stablemen walked behind it, and a dark-green Range Rover, containing two men, crawled along behind them. The tractor pulled the Mercedes clear of the drive and the Range Rover accelerated up the drive and swept into the courtyard.

Interesting, thought Phillip, as the vehicle disappeared from view. Some of the hired help has arrived.

Paco and the two Spanish workers unhitched

the Mercedes and went on into the courtyard. Four toughs, and three workers. Phillip knew, because he'd taken one from him, that Paco normally carried an Uzi. He wondered if the other two were accustomed to firearms.

Soon find out, he thought. He ducked low, ran to the wall of the villa and peered into the courtyard just in time to see the heavy front door slam shut. He crossed the courtyard and crouched down behind the Citroën and waited for the door to open.

Morino was in the courtyard, talking to the two heavies, when Paco and his men arrived. He beckoned and called out. 'Paco, come with us.' The five men entered the villa and slammed the door. They trooped into the lounge, where an array of weapons was set out on the floor.

Morino pointed to two Minimi light machine guns. He said to Paco, 'Tell them to take those machine guns and cover the front drive and grounds. No one comes or goes without my say-so.'

Paco picked up an Uzi and three spare magazines, and gave the necessary instructions to his men. They collected boxes of belted ammunition and followed him out to the front door, the Minimis cradled in their arms.

Morino watched them go, then turned to the two heavies who had turned up in the Range Rover. Both men wore flowery shirts and light slacks. They were both heavily built and over six foot tall. They had the same swarthy look as Morino, and thick black wiry hair swept back from tanned faces.

'Jimmy North is covering the back of the villa. Paolo, you go and keep him company. I don't trust him. If he looks like he's going to fuck off, shoot him, understand?'

Paolo nodded. He picked up a Beretta pistol, checked it was loaded, stuffed two spare magazines in his pocket and left the room without a word.

Morino said to the second man, 'Modesto, you stay with me and cover my back at all times. Where I go, you follow.'

'OK, boss,' said Modesto. He asked, curiously, 'You don't really think this bloke Ross will come back, do you?'

A burst of fire from the courtyard made both men swing round in alarm.

'He's back!' Morino screamed, and grabbed for an Uzi.

Chapter Sixteen

Phillip watched, crouched down behind the bonnet of the Citroën, as the front door of the villa opened and Paco stepped warily into the courtyard, followed by two other men carrying Minimi machine guns.

Phillip straightened up. The Browning, held in a two-handed combat grip, was pointed at Paco's chest. Paco saw him immediately and spun round, bringing the Uzi up to bear and squeezing the trigger in panic.

One shot hit Paco in the chest and threw him backwards into one of the Spaniards, who stumbled and almost fell, then flung him aside. The other man swung his machine gun up, fumbling with the safety catch. Phillip fired two quick shots into him, then turned the Browning on to the man who'd been tripped by Paco. The Spaniard was too slow. A nine-millimetre slug ripped into his chest. He staggered backwards as Phillip fired again. A hole appeared in the Spaniard's forehead, the bullet snapping his head back and throwing him to the ground. Blood fountained into the air from his head wound.

Phillip ran forward. Paco was clutching his chest with one hand and reaching out for the Uzi with the other. Phillip fired another shot into Paco's head as he ran past and ducked inside the front door. He stepped to one side into the shadow and crouched down.

The heavy footsteps of a running man echoed through the villa. Paolo burst into the hallway. He stopped, framed in the doorway, not sure where to run. He shouted, 'Salvatore! Modesto! Where are you?' They didn't answer for fear of giving away their position.

Phillip tossed a glass vase into the corner of the hallway to draw fire. As it smashed on the floor, Paolo swung in the direction of the noise and fired six rapid shots into the shadows. Phillip popped up, fired and screamed as he put two more bullets into Paolo, killing him instantly.

Modesto called out to Morino, 'I think Paolo got him. He's hit – you hear that scream?'

'Go take a look, then.' Morino was not convinced.

'Fuck that,' said Modesto, covering the open doorway with his Uzi. 'He might only be wounded.'

There was the unmistakable sound of a Porsche engine firing up and being revved hard. North gunned the car out of the courtyard in a cloud of dust and hammered off down the drive.

'That fucking coward,' spat Morino. 'He's pissed off.'

'Who, Ross?'

'No, Jimmy fucking North. That was his car,

and I know he's been thinking doing a runner.'
But, Morino thought, it might not be such a bad
thing. What if . . . ? He called out, 'Ross, can you
hear me?'

No response. He tried again: 'Ross, it's North
you want. We've got no beef together. We can call
a truce, and both of us go after the bastard.' Still
only silence from the hallway.

'I think he's been hit,' said Modesto. 'I heard
him scream like he was in pain, then a thud as
he hit the floor.'

Morino looked at the grilled windows of the
lounge, then back at the doorway. 'There's only
one way out of here, and one way to find out.' He
motioned with the butt of his Uzi. 'Go and take a
look. I'll cover you.'

Modesto inched towards the doorway, picking
up another Uzi from the pile of weapons. He
checked that both guns were fully loaded and
cocked. With an Uzi in each hand he edged up to
the doorframe and braced himself. He looked at
Morino, nodded, took a deep breath and stepped
into the doorway, both Uzis spitting flame and
bullets and roaring like thunder in the enclosed
space. He sprayed the hallway until the hammers
dropped on empty chambers, then turned and
walked slowly back into the lounge.

He stood for a moment looking at Morino, his
face screwed up in pain and disbelief. He looked
down at his chest. His flowered shirt was turning
red as the blood pumped out and spread. Morino
dived behind an armchair for cover.

'He's still here,' Modesto whispered. His knees

buckled and he fell heavily to the floor, his eyes wide with shock. The guns slipped from his hands. 'He's still here,' he whispered again. Then he died.

Morino called out, 'OK, Ross, you can cut the crap. I know you're out there.' He waited. No answer. 'We can do a deal. I can use a man like you. I can make you rich.'

Phillip called back, 'What do you want me to do? Sell drugs to kids?'

'No, nothing like that. You can be my right-hand man. Two guys like us can rule the world.'

'I don't want to rule the world, Morino. Especially not by fear.'

'How much? How much do you want, to walk out of that door?' No answer. 'A hundred grand,' he shouted. 'I'll pay you a hundred big ones to drop this thing and just walk away.'

'No sale.'

'Why the fuck are you doing this?'

'Because it needs doing.'

'What did I ever do to you?'

'Nothing. It's for the others, for the kids you've killed and the lives you've destroyed with your drugs.'

'I didn't make them take them. They wanted to. It's their choice – nobody forced them.'

'And now it's my choice, and I want to kill you.'

'Shit,' Morino cursed. He looked round. He was trapped. His other men wouldn't be arriving for several hours yet, and he knew Ross wouldn't wait that long.

'Let's get it done then,' he shouted and stood up. 'I'm waiting, Ross. Are you coming in, or are you going to sit out there like a fucking pansy?'

'I'm coming.' Phillip sang it as if taunting a frightened child.

'Damn you, Ross! Fuck you to hell and back,' screamed Morino.

Phillip picked up a rug from the floor and hung it over a high-backed wooden chair, which he shoved into the open doorway. Morino squeezed the trigger of the Uzi and sprayed the rug with bullets. Splinters of wood and plaster flew in the air. Morino fired until the magazine was empty, flung the gun away and picked up another loaded one. Again he fired until the hammer dropped on an empty chamber. He threw the Uzi down and stooped to pick up another.

There was a low chuckle behind him.

Phillip had the Browning trained on him through the iron grille of the window. He said drily, 'There are two kinds of people, Salvatore, those who shoot through the door and those who shoot through the window.'

Morino swung the Uzi up but before he could fire, a bullet from the Browning hit him in the right shoulder, swinging him round. The Uzi spun from his grasp. He clutched at his shoulder, trying to stem the flow of blood. 'You bastard,' he snarled.

'Try again, Morino.' Phillip gestured with the Browning at the stack of weapons.

Morino's eyes darted from Phillip to the fire-arms as he weighed his chances. He didn't have any, and he knew it. He straightened up and stared defiantly across the room. 'I'm wounded and I'm not armed. You can't shoot me.'

Phillip lowered the Browning until it rested on the stone windowsill. 'Yes, that's just the sort of thing a rat like you would try, but it isn't going to work.' He aimed the big pistol at Morino's kneecap and fired.

Morino's leg was swept from under him as the steel-jacketed slug smashed through flesh and bone. He collapsed into the pile of Uzis and Berettas, his face contorted as he whimpered in pain.

'I'd say you were armed now,' said Phillip. He fired again, shattering Morino's other kneecap. 'I'm going to keep shooting little bits off you, until you pick up one of those guns.' He took careful aim and fired into Morino's belly.

Morino howled with pain and anger. He snatched up a Beretta, his bloodied hand slipping on the blued steel. Phillip calmly watched as he pulled the slide to the cocked position and let it slam back.

Morino lifted his head. He said viciously, 'Fuck you,' and raised the pistol.

Phillip shot him twice in the chest, then, as Morino's head slumped on to his chest, fired a third round into the top of his skull.

He looked down at the tangled, mangled mess that had once been Morino. 'Good riddance to bad rubbish,' he said softly and turned away.

He recovered the Virago from its hiding place and rode back towards where he'd left Debby. As he drew near, he saw a group of vehicles parked beside the road. He pulled up and watched for a moment. The flashing blue lights on top of the vehicles reassured him that she would be looked after and eventually given a decent burial. He spun the bike round and set off in the opposite direction.

He drove directly to Puerto Duquesa, parked the bike in a corner of the car park and moved his gear into his hired car. He checked out of his hotel, and drove to Málaga Airport, stopping at a rubbish skip on the way to dump his pistols and ammunition: he couldn't risk their being picked up by the airport X-ray machines. He returned the hire car and booked a seat on the first flight to Barcelona. He had a two-hour wait. He decided some of that time could usefully be spent reporting to George Hill.

He settled himself in one of the small phone booths at the airport and dialled Hill's office number. He was informed that Hill was off duty. He dialled his home number and Hill answered.

'Glad to hear from you, Phillip. I've been getting worried. We've been getting reports of gang war in Spain, and Pacetti's death has hit the headlines.'

'I've almost cleaned up,' said Phillip. 'But North's given me the slip. I think he's heading back to Lloret. I'm booked on a flight. I'm going after him.'

'What on earth makes you think he'll go back there?' asked Hill.

'He keeps his cash in a hidden strongroom at the villa.' Phillip checked the adjacent phone booths to make sure he wasn't being overheard. 'He's got a couple of hours' start on me, but he's afraid of flying, so it's a cert that he'll drive. I should get there well before him.'

'It's fourteen or fifteen hours' drive from Málaga to Gerona, even if he drives like hell,' said Hill.

'He's in his Porsche, so he won't exactly be hanging about. But he won't be as fast as a Boeing 757, and he'll be knackered by the time he gets there.'

Hill laughed. 'Good luck. Be careful, Phillip, and ring to me as soon as you get back to England.'

'I will. Bye, George.' He hung up and made his way to the cafeteria. He needed a strong coffee and some food in his belly.

As he tucked into steak and chips, he thought about North hurtling along in his Porsche. He'd certainly be armed. North didn't know Debby had told him about the strongroom, so he'd feel reasonably safe going back to the villa for a quick visit to collect a suitcase or two of cash.

Phillip smiled as he thought about North's fear of flying and how it would be the death of him.

It was time for him to check in for his flight. He reckoned that by now North should just about have passed Granada.

When his flight touched down at Barcelona, he reckoned North should be well on his way to Alicante. He collected his case and hired a Ford Escort for the hour's drive to Lloret.

Jimmy North drove slowly up to the gates of his

villa and had a good look round. He felt safe
here: Phillip Ross wouldn't have a clue where
he'd run to. He allowed himself a chuckle as he
thought, It's the last fucking place I'd come if I
didn't have to. He grabbed a Beretta pistol from
the passenger seat, checked its load and shoved
it into his belt.

He inserted his key and opened the electric
gates, then drove up to the front door and parked.
All the shutters were closed and the villa was
deserted. He climbed wearily out of the Porsche
and stretched. It had been a long, hard drive.

He opened the front door. The alarm bleeped.
He gave a sigh of relief. The villa was so well
alarmed that a mouse would set off the heat
sensors scattered round. He knew the place was
empty. He punched the buttons of the alarm and
set it to stand-by. The bleeping stopped. The villa
felt eerily silent as North stood in the hallway,
alone, and looked around.

He turned back to the front door to close it. The
sight of a smiling Phillip Ross, standing, arms
folded, in the doorway made him leap back in
alarm. He grabbed for the Beretta in his belt.

As he whipped it out, Phillip lunged forward
and snap-kicked it from his hand. The heavy
pistol smashed a gilt-framed mirror and skittered
across the marble floor. North was fast: he threw
a heavy punch that caught Phillip on the side of
the head, knocking him off balance, and dived for
the pistol. He slid across the marble floor and got
his hand on the butt.

Phillip leapt on top of him and grasped his wrist

as his fingers closed round the gun. He smashed North's fingers against the white marble floor tiles until he let go, then turned him and smashed his fist into the man's face. North fought back like a crazy animal. He was a street-fighter from way back, and as strong as he was dirty. They scrambled to their feet and swapped punches like two heavyweight boxers, sizing each other up as they circled the hall, breathing deeply and exchanging glares of hatred.

North grabbed a chair and swung it at Phillip, turned and ran through the passage to the kitchen as Phillip ducked to avoid the chair, temporarily off balance. North unlocked the kitchen door and sprinted round the swimming pool and across the terrace to the gardener's shed. He grabbed a long-pronged fork and, crouching, turned to face Phillip. He grinned as he advanced, jabbing the sharp prongs towards Phillip's stomach.

'I'm going to stick you like a pig,' he panted triumphantly.

'It's been tried before,' jeered Phillip, as he leapt to one side to avoid a vicious thrust.

North thrust again. Phillip sidestepped, swept the prongs to one side with an open-hand block and grabbed the wooden handle, pulling North towards him and head-butting him in the face. North's nose crumpled under the impact and blood spurted down his chin and chest. The sacs under his eyes swelled as they filled with blood.

The two men clung to the shaft of the fork and wrestled for control of it. Phillip suddenly dropped to the ground, shooting his feet up into

North's stomach and throwing him back over his head. North, still holding the fork shaft, was flipped through the air on to his back. He landed with a thud on the concrete tiles, breaking his coccyx, and the breath was knocked from his lungs. He lay there winded and unable to move as Phillip picked up the fork and threw it into the swimming pool.

North's bloodied face was contorted in pain. 'My back's broke,' he groaned.

'So what?' Phillip grabbed North's arm and hauled him to his feet. North couldn't stand. Ignoring his screams of agony, Phillip slung him roughly over his shoulder and carried him to the wrought-iron balustrade of the terrace.

Phillip turned and leant over the balustrade to give North a good view of the jagged rocks below. The blue water swirled round them into a white frothy foam. Several seagulls floated in circles a hundred feet below them.

North screamed hysterically, 'Nooo!' as Phillip slowly let him slide from his shoulder into the void. He grabbed the iron balustrade and clung on for dear life as Phillip slipped him over the rail. His knuckles were white from the force of his grip, his face screwed up in terror and from the agony of his broken back.

'Don't let me fall,' he pleaded.

Phillip eased his wounded arm and studied the man with utter contempt. Then he chuckled derisively. 'You asking me to save you now? You were the leader. The gang boss. You and your gang killed my wife.'

'I'm sorry, Ross. We couldn't help it, we didn't mean to kill her. She sort of ran in front of us.' North took a swift, terrified glance at the rocks below. 'Help me up, Ross. I can't hold on much longer.'

'What was my wife's name?' asked Phillip.

'I don't know her fucking name.' North's voice rose an octave as his grip slipped.

'Try to remember her name, Jimmy. You're going to die because of what you did to her. I think you should know her name.'

'Jean, June – I don't fucking know,' he screamed.

Phillip looked down at him implacably, hooked his fingers under North's and slowly prised them open.

'My wife's name was Julie Ross. Take a hike.'

He flipped North's fingers free from their grip and leant on the balustrade to watch North, his arms flailing, legs kicking, as he fell. He screamed all the way down to the rocks. The white foam turned suddenly red as he landed.

The sky was filled with squawking seagulls disturbed from their nests. They swooped down, circled and cried out in alarm and puzzled interest at the titbit thrown to them from above.

Dinner is served, Phillip said to himself. And he turned and walked away.

Epilogue

'So North's lookout was a woman,' said George Hill. 'Richards from robbery squad was always on about the gang having a lookout, but couldn't put the finger on anyone.' Someone knocked at the door. 'That'll be John Thorpe. Come on in, John.'

Thorpe was carrying a tray with coffee and sandwiches for the three men.

'Good man,' said Hill. 'I reckon we can all use something to eat. You two know each other, so no need for introductions.'

Thorpe put the tray down on the desk and held out his hand. 'Good to see you, Phillip. Well done. How's your arm?'

Phillip shook his hand and looked questioningly at Hill.

'It's OK. John knows all about your operation, and you have my word that he can be trusted completely. In fact, if I'm ever not available and you need help or information, speak to him.'

The three men sat round the desk eating their sandwiches and drinking their coffee as Phillip described the events of the past couple of weeks and answered questions.

When he had finished his story, Hill said, 'Well, that's all in the past. What about the future? Are you still game?'

Phillip said simply, 'Yes.'

Hill opened the middle drawer of his desk and pulled out a stack of folders. 'While you've been away, John and I have been doing a little bit of homework, choosing some deserving cases.' He patted the files. 'You won't ever run short of work, I can assure you.'

Thorpe picked up the top folder. 'For example, this man makes North and Pacetti look like a couple of saints.'

Phillip took the offered folder and opened it. The pictures inside made him feel physically sick. He flicked through them, shaking his head in disbelief at what he saw. He shut the folder and handed it back to the inspector. 'If ever a man deserved to be brought to justice that man does. And I shall see that he is. That I promise you.'